IT COULD HAVE BEEN ME
THE COPS WANTED.
MAYBE NEXT TIME IT WOULD BE.

My imagination took off running hog wild, obsessed, one crazy out-of-control thought after the other. I envisioned myself serving hard time for the bra heist. How long did first-time offenders get sent up for? Would the prison have a vegetarian option on the menu? Was it really up the river? If so, which river? East? Hudson? Mississippi? What if I didn't get along with my cellmate? Or, in a system crowded with hardcore offenders, would it be cellmates?

And what about Jackhammer? I'd sure miss the little guy. I simply could not imagine life without him. I scratched the special spot between his ears. He licked my face, then jumped out of my lap and scrambled down the stairs, straining against the leash.

Oh right. Reality . . .

"MS. WILSON WRITES WITH HUMOR,
AFFECTION, AND GOOD TASTE.
READ ONE OF HER BOOKS
AND YOU'LL WANT THEM ALL."
The S...

Other Brenda Midnight Mysteries by
Barbara Jaye Wilson
from Avon Books

DEATH BRIMS OVER
ACCESSORY TO MURDER
DEATH FLIPS ITS LID
CAPPED OFF
HATFUL OF HOMICIDE

ATTENTION: ORGANIZATIONS AND CORPORATIONS
Most Avon Books paperbacks are available at special quantity discounts for bulk purchases for sales promotions, premiums, or fund-raising. For information, please call or write:

Special Markets Department, HarperCollins Publishers, Inc., 10 East 53rd Street, New York, N.Y. 10022–5299.
Telephone: (212) 207–7528. Fax: (212) 207-7222.

BARBARA JAYE WILSON

MURDER AND THE MAD HATTER

A BRENDA MIDNIGHT MYSTERY

AVON BOOKS
An Imprint of HarperCollinsPublishers

AVON BOOKS
An Imprint of HarperCollins*Publishers*
10 East 53rd Street
New York, New York 10022-5299

Copyright © 2001 by Barbara Jaye Wilson
ISBN: 0-380-80357-7
www.avonbooks.com

First Avon Books paperback printing: January 2001

Avon Trademark Reg. U.S. Pat. Off. and in Other Countries, Marca Registrada, Hecho en U.S.A.
HarperCollins ® is a trademark of HarperCollins Publishers Inc.

Printed in the U.S.A.

10 9 8 7 6 5 4 3 2 1

Dedicated to my father,
Jay B. Wilson, Jr.

ACKNOWLEDGMENTS

Thanks to Brocolli Prune Pit and X-Dot Potato, who still make me smile, and Tanker G. Bean, who keeps up the good work, and the hot dog vendor whose claim to be a time traveler got me thinking and who so vividly demonstrated how drastically things can change at the drop of a hat.

"I do."

2

You didn't!

I sure as hell did.

I might as well get it over with, come right out with the brutal truth, and fess up to the fact that I, Brenda Midnight, being of relatively sound mind, really did get married to Lemon (Lemmy) B. Crenshaw.

And yeah, I figure I know exactly how you're going to react to this bit of news. You'll shake your head in disbelief. Too polite to question my sanity while I'm in the room, you'll come up with a diplomatic question like "How could you go and do a damn fool thing like that?"

Don't worry. The marriage won't last. It was never meant to.

So how come I came to do the old I-do with my ex-boyfriend's slimeball agent?

My ex, as you probably know, is Johnny Verlane, star of the formerly top-rated recently canceled *Tod Trueman, Urban Detective* television series. Although I often refer to Johnny as my ex, that's somewhat misleading. Our on-and-off relationship has been oning and offing so long it has achieved a hard-as-rock solid base. It is the most long-term, most stable relationship—or whatever—either of us has ever had. It's just that Johnny and I aren't much for talking about this kind of stuff. Or acting on it.

Despite our best efforts at sabotage, whatever it is between us refuses to curl up and die. It hovers in the background like a dark cloud or a silver lining or a wasp poised to sting—the most apt metaphor depends on my mood. And my mood lately—thanks for asking—has been pretty great, that is, until goddamned Lemmy Crenshaw came along and screwed it all up.

I'm a milliner. I make gravity-defying, mostly one of a kind, couture hats. Last year, for the first time ever, my Greenwich Village shop, Midnight Millinery, actually ended up a few beans into the black. That's not to say I'm rolling in dough, but I was able to sock away some cash, enough to get me through a lousy season, an artistic crisis, a fashion misforecast, and still make the rent and feed myself and my five-pound Yorkshire terrier, Jackhammer.

The best part is that I didn't have to sell my soul and crank out inferior product to succeed. It's so rare that artistic integrity leads to profits. I consider myself extremely lucky in that regard.

I know I've veered off the explanation of how I managed to end up married to Lemmy. Unlike millinery, Lemmy is one mighty tough subject. The thought of that man and what he did to me makes me so mad I can barely speak.

When Johnny's *TTUD* show got canceled, his acting career took an immediate nosedive. He was typecast, with a colossal, high-profile, prime-time failure under his belt. Nobody wanted him.

As Johnny's agent, Lemmy had as much to lose as Johnny. He swung into action in a desperate attempt to resurrect Johnny's career. You know those comedy clubs where anybody with guts can stand up and do their three minutes? Johnny did that. And got heckled. He appeared in quiz show audiences and even did the karaoke circuit, anything to keep his face in front of an audience.

The strategy this summer was to send Johnny to a small town in Massachusetts to do dinner theater. He failed to get the lead role, although he ended up with it anyway after the star, another of Lemmy's clients on the skids, surfaced with a fourteen-year-old girlfriend and a tragic drug habit. Johnny stepped into the lead and rescued the production. Audiences—women especially—loved him, and the performances sold out so fast the producers added more shows, which meant Johnny was constantly busy and I almost never heard from him.

This, in our relationship, was good.

It was during the time Johnny was away in Massachusetts that Lemmy dropped by Midnight Millinery unannounced.

The bells on the door jangled, and he burst in, a tight little bundle of energy in an ill-fitting shiny green sharkskin suit, reeking of too much citrusy cologne. The hot summer sun beamed in through the open door and gleamed off Lemmy's fresh-shaved head when he bent over to give Jackhammer a friendly scratch between the ears.

"Hiya, squirt," he said, "how's it going?"

Jackhammer wagged his tail stub in response. He had no problem with Lemmy.

I barely glanced up from my work, acknowledged Lemmy's presence with a grunt, and said, "Shut the door, will you?"

He kicked it shut, then sauntered over. He stood before me, hands clasped together prayerlike. "I'm inna jam, Brenda. You gotta help me out."

"Uh-huh." So what else was new? Lemmy, a hothead, often found himself in some kind of jam. He also had a tendency to catastrophize.

Racing the clock to finish a tiny pale-peach silk-satin pillbox for a very important client—one who always paid all cash up front—I was in the middle of handstitching the head-size band to the inside of the hat, tricky work because of the small diameter. I kept jabbing the number five needle into my thumb. So far, I'd managed to keep my blood drops off the fine silk.

"I'm kinda busy right now," I said.

"They're after me," said Lemmy.

Nobody ever said Lemmy Crenshaw wasn't paranoid.

The bells on the door jangled again, and Brewster Winfield, a lawyer acquaintance of mine and sometime partner of Lemmy's in several slightly sleazy money-making schemes, glided into the shop, elegantly outfitted in summer-weight cashmere. He was a big, round-faced black man, with shoulder-length medusalike dreadlocks and an amazingly warm smile, which he had turned on full force.

Jackhammer trotted over and gave Winfield a quick sniff, probably checking to see if the esteemed lawyer had brought along his pet snake, Myrtle—yet another of Lemmy's clients.

"Good afternoon, Jackhammer, Brenda, Lemmy," Winfield said, in his mellow, deep-as-the-ocean voice.

Weird. Popping by unannounced may have been just like Lemmy, but it certainly was not Brewster Winfield's style. It occurred to me that maybe something really was up.

With a sigh I put down the pillbox, stuck the number five needle into the pincushion, and leaned back, ready to listen to whatever Winfield had to say.

It turned out to be quite a lot.

"Brenda," said Winfield, "were you aware that our good friend Lemmy here is not a citizen of the United States?"

"He's not?"

"I'm not," said Lemmy.

I looked at Lemmy. "I thought you came from some dinky town in the midwest. At least that's what you told me."

Lemmy frowned and looked at Winfield.

"You have a very good memory, Brenda, and you are quite correct," said Winfield. "As a young adult Lemmy moved to New York. Much like you, he hailed from a small town in one of our flat central states. However, he was born in Canada. His parents were . . . oh, how do I say, how can I express . . . ?"

I'd rarely seen Winfield at a loss for words.

Lemmy took over. "Mom and Dad were a couple of low-life grifters on the run from the law."

"Whatever," said Winfield with a shrug. "Lemmy's parents, with infant Lemmy in tow, sneaked over the border, put their sordid past behind them, settled down, and became upstanding illegal aliens."

"I had no idea."

"Nobody knew," said Lemmy. "Except, of course, my trusted attorney."

"On my advice," said Winfield, "Lemmy kept this matter hush-hush."

That seemed reasonable enough. "So why are you telling me now?"

"Things, as they sometimes will," said Winfield, "have changed. Somehow the INS found out about my client's status."

"Busted," said Lemmy. He drew his forefinger across his neck. "In a heap of big trouble with the immigration dudes."

Winfield paced back and forth, gestured dramatically, and threw around a lot of big words, scary-sounding legalese, to describe Lemmy's immigration troubles. After fifteen minutes of glorious oratory and well-choreographed theatrics, Winfield kneeled down before me, gently took both of my hands into his, looked me straight in the eye, and said, "I shall give it to you straight. Brenda, my dear, Baby-cakes, unless you agree to marry our mutual good buddy Lemmy, I fear he will be deported, returned forcibly to the nation of his birth."

It was, I admit, a very impressive presentation.

"So sorry," I said, meeting Winfield's steady gaze. "Not my problem." I pulled my hands free from his.

With a sigh, Winfield struggled back to his feet.

Lemmy threw up his hands in frustration. "She freaking doesn't get it."

"Oh yes, I do," I said. "I get it quite well. You want me to make light of the holy state of matrimony to save your sorry ass."

"Gee, Brenda," said Lemmy, "you act like you've never been married before. Twice is it? Or if that rumor is true, maybe even—"

None of his business. I cut him off. "Right, Lemmy. However, you've missed an important point. Those times I married for love, perhaps unwisely, but it's the thought that counts. I will not marry you so you can stay in the country."

Lemmy, petulant, with his hands on hips, leaned in close to my face. "Fine, Brenda. Have it your own selfish way. And you be the one to explain to my client of the failed, faded career, Johnny Verlane, your sometime boyfriend, how your lack of cooperation with his hardworking agent— that's me—screwed up negotiations and killed *The All New Adventures of Tod Trueman, Urban Detective*."

"No kidding? You got them to bring back *Tod Trueman*?"

The answer, of course, was not yet and unless Lemmy could remain in the country long enough to complete the delicate negotiations, not ever.

"Tell me," I said, "how far along are the negotiations?"

Lemmy rubbed his chin. "Hmmm. Let me put it this way. It would be a done deal except for one little bitty problem."

"Which is?"

"Remember the *TTUD* series finale?"

I nodded. How could anybody forget? In that last episode one of the recurring characters, an evil drug kingpin, bored with being merely a high-level international drug trafficker, got involved in a heavy-duty armament deal. It turned out to be more than his burned-out drug-addled brain could handle, and in the final scene he accidentally blew up New York City, including the outer boroughs, and a good chunk of New Jersey. *TTUD* went out with a bang.

"One of the network honchos," said Lemmy, "is uptight about setting the new show in New York."

"Because fiction-wise New York City doesn't exist any-more?"

"Right. And then this other big honcho refuses to use any location other than New York. He says Tod and New York were made for each other."

"He's right."

"Perhaps, but it is the ultimate sticking point between the two of them. They're both being real jerks. I've got some ideas about how we might realistically bring back New York, but these kinds of things take time."

"And with the immigration people breathing down Lemmy's neck, threatening deportation any day," added Winfield ominously, "time is one luxury we do not have."

"If time is a factor," I said, "your scheme would never work anyway. It takes time to get married. You can't just haul off and do it at the drop of a hat."

"I wasn't exactly planning a reception at the Waldorf," said Lemmy. "We don't have to register flatware patterns or hire a band."

"That's not what I meant," I said. "There's a blood test and the license and after that a three-day—"

Winfield shook his head so violently his dreadlocks flapped. "No more blood test."

"No more blood test? Are you sure?"

"If you don't believe me, call the City Clerk yourself."

"They didn't get rid of the three-day waiting period, did they? And besides, how can we get a marriage license if Lemmy's not a citizen?" I turned to Lemmy. "I assume you're not a registered alien."

"You got that right. I'm one hundred percent illegal," boasted Lemmy. "But you see, Brenda, we've got our attor-ney on our side. Tell her, Brew."

"As you should know by now, Brenda," said Winfield, "New York functions on multiple layers of favors. You owe me, then I owe you, perhaps together we owe somebody else, and so on down the line. As an attorney I've done my share, fixed this, that, and the other for everybody and his brother, and I happen to be very well connected. To help Lemmy I cashed in a couple of favors to expedite the license procurement. I assure you, Brenda, the license is all taken care of. No problem with Lemmy's status. No waiting period."

"No questions asked?"

"Nope."

"Oh," I said. It seemed I'd painted myself into a corner.

"So you'll do it?" said Lemmy.

"I didn't say that," I said.

"Nine o'clock tomorrow morning," said Winfield. "City Hall. Be there or—"

"Watch Johnny's career go straight down the toilet," said Lemmy.

And so you see I really had no choice but to marry Lemmy. "All right, I'll do it."

"I knew you would," said Lemmy. He tried to hug me, but I pushed him away.

"That's our Brenda," said Winfield. "She always comes through for friends in need."

"Friends in deed," said Lemmy.

"Stop it, you two." I hated that aspect of myself. I wished I were the kind of person who could come right out and say no with enough force to make it believable.

Lemmy and Winfield were on their way out the door.

"Hang on a minute," I said. "We better call Johnny in Massachusetts and tell him the news." I reached for my phone.

Lemmy ran over and slammed his hand down on the receiver. "No! Don't call Johnny. That would be total disaster."

"What are you talking about? We're all friends and grown-ups. He'll understand."

"I'm talking Johnny doesn't know about the negotiations for the new *Tod* show."

"Why not? It's his career."

"Trust me, Brenda. I'm doing what's best for Johnny.

That man is like a brother to me. If you tell him we're getting married, he'll wonder why, and because you're such a lousy liar, you'll tell him the truth, and if he finds out I'm in the middle of tense negotiations, he'll get stressed out or depressed or both and he could blow his whole dinner theater gig, which will be a huge embarrassment and put us at a serious disadvantage in the negotiations. You wouldn't want that to happen, would you?"

3

At the peak of rush hour the very next morning, I found myself hurtling downtown in a crowded, ice-cold, super-air-conditioned subway car, squished up against grumpy commuters, in complete and total disbelief, and marveling how this could possibly be, that I really was on my way to City Hall to say "I do" to Lemon B. Crenshaw, a man who, to be honest, revolted me.

Always a bride, never a bridesmaid. I had to keep reminding myself that this had nothing to do with Lemmy. Or me. I was doing this for Johnny.

I did not wear a long white veil or any kind of headgear whatsoever. I may be a milliner, but I hate frou-frou. I don't do weddings, even my own, even if it were not a sham. Or a scam, whichever this would turn out to be.

I was dressed in black head to toe. Appropriate.

The only part of my ensemble not funereal was the bright orange canvas bag slung over my shoulder. Hidden deep inside was Jackhammer. His presence comforted me, but I wondered if dragging him along had been a good idea. He squirmed around like crazy, fighting to get out. As diversion, I stuck my hand into the bag and tickled his belly.

The room at City Hall was painted that startling bright blue the city used to use in all the subway stations—MTA blue I call it. Overhead fluorescent lights bathed the blue in a sickly death-glow.

I was, of course, experiencing attacks of serious second thoughts. I skulked in the doorway, computing the consequences of ducking out and heading back home when Lemmy spotted me.

"Photo op!" he shouted. He raced over, grabbed my hand, and yanked me over to the far corner of the room. He positioned me next to him beneath the branch of an artificial tree festooned with hot-pink plastic roses.

"This is a joke, right?"

It wasn't. Winfield popped up out of nowhere, aimed his little point-and-shoot. "Say cheese."

Limburger, I thought, and made a face.

The flash went off.

I blinked.

Then I pulled away from Lemmy.

"Not so fast," said Winfield. He moved in closer, stuck the camera right in my face. "I want to get a few more candid shots of the happy couple."

"What the hell for?"

By way of answering, he snapped several more pictures.

Elizabeth bustled into the room. A long, flowing skirt made out of bright, multicolored paisley scarves swirled around her moccasin-clad feet. Her frizzled silver and black hair was pulled back into a single thick braid that fell almost to her waist.

"Oh, there you are!" she said. "I hope I'm not too late. Did I miss it?"

"Nope," said Lemmy. "Great to see you, Elizabeth. Thanks for coming."

Winfield gave her an affectionate squeeze.

Dammit. I didn't want her here.

Elizabeth Franklin Perry, my across-the-hall neighbor, was a dear friend, and so last night I confided in her about me and Lemmy getting married. Big mistake. I should have kept my mouth shut. For some strange reason she wanted to attend this humiliating fiasco. I'd tried to discourage her. Failing that, I simply left this morning without her.

"Shame on you, Brenda Midnight," she said. "I could not believe it when Ralph told me you'd already split."

Ralph was one of the doormen in our building. When I headed out, he was busy taking in the UPS deliveries. I thought I'd slipped by without him noticing.

Elizabeth went on, "I ought to be insulted, but I'll chalk up your uncharacteristic rudeness to wedding day jitters." She glanced around the room. "Is Chuck here yet?"

"Chuck's gonna be here too?"

"The more the merrier," said Lemmy.

The preliminary proceedings went by in a blur. In a state of denial, I sort of remember standing in line, approaching a counter, and eventually signing my name in a large book alongside Lemmy's bold, illegible scrawl.

Elizabeth signed as witness. "See," she said. "It's good I'm here. At a time like this, everybody needs a friendly witness."

A shoulder to cry on was more like it.

Lemmy made a big show of digging deep in his pants pocket to extract a twenty-five-dollar money order and reluctantly handing it to a woman behind the counter, who logged it into another book.

"You know what this is?" squawked Lemmy.

The woman ignored his query.

"It's highway freaking robbery," he said in a nasal whine loud enough to be heard halfway down the hall.

Other couples, along with assorted friends, family, and witnesses, nervously milled around the room. Every last one of them stopped milling to stare at Lemmy.

The woman behind the counter stayed cool as a cucumber. Lemmy didn't get the slightest rise out of her. She'd no doubt seen all kinds in her job. "If you'll please take a seat, sir, Mr. Crenshaw," she said, "we'll call your name when we're ready."

Lemmy is the kind of guy who craves a reaction. He loves a conflict. Making waves is his passion. And so, frustrated, he ranted at the woman louder than before.

"What's the city do with all this moolah anyway? I already gave you guys thirty smackers for the marriage license—a crappy little piece of paper, for chrissakes. Anybody with a computer could forge this garbage. Now you take twenty-five more for the ceremony. Whaddya gonna do with the windfall, pave over a pothole?"

Winfield was in the dim part the room beneath a burnedout fluorescent tube, putting a new roll of film in his camera. He waved his arms to catch Lemmy's attention. When Lemmy finally looked, Winfield put his finger over his lips, signaling his maniac client to shut the hell up.

I rolled with the flow, thinking if Lemmy got thrown out, I'd be rather gracefully off the hook.

The man in line behind us, a solid-bodied two-hundredpounder, who smelled like a stubbed-out two-day-old cigar, wasn't so easygoing. "Hey, Bub," he said, muscling up to Lemmy, "your turn is done. It's not like we got all day here."

The woman with the bruiser was busy yapping into a cell phone. She seemed highly agitated and barely aware of her surroundings. I wondered if their marriage was also for reasons other than true love.

Lemmy sized up the guy, saw that he was way out of his league, and wisely chose to take the hint.

Lemmy, Elizabeth, and I quietly walked away and joined Brewster Winfield.

At the back of the room were several rows of drab, beige molded-plastic chairs. The four of us filed in and sat, no choice but to face forward. The arrangement was not conducive to conversation, which was fine with me.

Not long after we got situated, Chuck Riley showed up.

"Hey, Brew," he said.

"Hey, yourself." Winfield stood so Chuck could squeeze by.

"Chuck, my man," said Lemmy.

"Chrome Dome," said Chuck, slapping Lemmy on the shoulder. "Hi, Brenda." Chuck slid by me and settled at the end of the row next to Elizabeth. He patted his giant fuzzball of red hair, "Hiya, Elizabeth. Is this some glorious event, or what?"

"It most certainly is," said Elizabeth. She fiddled with her own hair, flinging the braid over her shoulder.

Chuck's unrequited crush on Elizabeth was starting to get really tiring. Ditto her gracious attempt not to notice it just because she was old enough to be his mother. Those two were almost as bad as Johnny and me.

"It is not," I said, in an attempt to set the record straight. "It is not glorious. It is not even an event. It is merely a short-term business arrangement."

"While not infrequent," said Chuck, as if I wasn't even present, "it's not every day our Brenda takes the plunge."

"Will you cut it out?" I was in no mood to be teased.

"Well, excuse me," said Chuck, "for my attempt to add a bit of levity to this oh-so-serious occasion."

"It's like a dress rehearsal for when you and Johnny finally tie the knot," said Elizabeth with a swoony sigh and a sickeningly sweet smile.

"Crenshaw and Midnight. You and your party may go in now."

"It's about freaking time," commented Lemmy under his breath.

My knees turned to rubber, my palms alternated between sweaty and ice cold. The moment I dreaded, the moment I didn't believe was really real, had arrived.

I quite literally dragged my feet, but with Lemmy and Winfield prodding I somehow managed to make it into a chamber off to the side of the main waiting area. All of us plus the nondenominational officiator pretty much filled up the space.

The air was stale. It was hotter than hell. I felt woozy.

In my whole life I've never fainted, but if it was ever going to happen, I willed that it be now.

Now! Right now! Anything to get out of this.

I remained steady on my feet.

I was blinded by another flash. Goddamned Winfield was at it again with the camera.

Before I knew it, the deed was done. I said my "I do." Lemmy said his. And that was that.

The entire ceremony was over in forty-five seconds, a real New York minute.

"Pucker up," said Lemmy.

I spurned my new husband's attempt to kiss the bride.

Flash. Winfield caught it all on film.

As soon as we got outdoors, I let Jackhammer out of the canvas bag and snapped on his leash. With him scrambling ahead, minesweeping the sidewalk, the whole bunch of us paraded west to the Chambers Street subway station. I had to put Jackhammer back in the bag. After a short wait we piled onto a Number One train and took it to Fourteenth Street.

When we surfaced, Lemmy invited everybody out for what he called a celebratory champagne brunch. The restaurant, a twenty-four-hour greasy spoon diner, called it Breakfast Special Served Till Eleven.

We made it in just under the wire.

Lemmy pulled a brown-bagged bottle of champagne out of his briefcase. Keeping it under wraps so nobody could see the label, he splashed a little in everybody's orange juice glass when the waiter had his back turned.

My friends seemed to be having a swell time.

Lemmy loved to play the generous host. "Order whatever you want," he said. "Don't even think about the price."

Winfield didn't even remark on Lemmy's choice of restaurant. He seemed content to brag incessantly about his snake Myrtle's latest accomplishment, rolling over on command.

Elizabeth, a formerly famous artist who for political reasons had given up art for decades, had recently returned to the easel. She talked about her new series of paintings, which she termed abstract with a tinge of feminist imagery, whatever the hell that meant.

Chuck didn't say much. He devoured a giant mound of french fries drowned in ketchup. When Lemmy asked him what he'd been up to, he muttered something about time travel.

Everybody got a good laugh out of that, even me.

If the circumstances had been anything but what they were, I would have enjoyed the rollicking gathering of good friends. But the circumstances absolutely sucked, and so I kept to myself. I didn't eat much. I sneaked Jackhammer most of my fluffy goat cheese and dill omelet.

What was that godawful noise?

Apparently our festive brunch had ended. Everybody scooted their chairs back; metal legs clanged and banged and scraped across the tile floor.

The waiter snatched egg-encrusted, ketchup-smeared dishes and flatware from the table and heaved them onto a metal cart, making a terrible clatter.

It was enough to give anybody a headache. In fact, it gave me a real rager.

Ugh.

"Brenda," said Lemmy, "love of my life, brand-new wife, whatsa matter? You're looking a little green around the edges."

"Too much champagne, I'd say," said Winfield.

"Brenda doesn't do so good with bubbles," said Elizabeth.

"Beer, champagne, soda pop—they all make her sick," said Chuck.

"You're not gonna puke, are you?"

I sure as hell better not. "It's all that fizz," I said, "must have got to me."

"What you need is some fresh air," said Lemmy. "Take my arm, my dear, and off we'll go."

"Wait a second," said Winfield. "You forgot the check." He picked up the slip of paper and waved it in the air.

"Ah, gee, Brew," said Lemmy, patting his pockets. "I'm a little short on cash today. Would you take care of it? Put it on my bill."

Jackhammer, once again thrilled to be out of his canvas bag, scrambled around my ankles, jumped up, and licked at my knee. I know he was trying to make me feel better, but it wasn't working.

"You gonna be okay?" asked Lemmy.

I took several deep breaths. "Yeah, I guess."

"That's good. It wouldn't do to have my brand-new wife—"

"Cut the crap already, Lemmy. Tell me, how soon do we get divorced? When's your hearing?"

"Hearing? What hearing?"

"You know, with the immigration people. The reason we got married."

"Oh, that. It's not like an official hearing or anything. Winfield is hard at work behind the scenes."

"You don't have to appear?"

"Nope."

What a relief. I'd been a little worried about how Lemmy might conduct himself, especially after I'd seen him in full obnoxious action back at City Hall.

"It pays to have a good attorney," he said. "With Winfield on the job, my immigration troubles will be over before you know it."

"That's great. When exactly?"

"Really really soon. Tomorrow, I think Winfield said."

"So by this time next week we'll be happily divorced?"

"Well . . . maybe."

"What do you mean, 'maybe'?"

"I mean maybe. Anything can happen, right?"

"I'm getting a bad feeling, Lemmy. Tell me it's my imagination."

"All right, Brenda, I'll be straight with you. About that divorce, it's gonna maybe take a little bit longer. It's not gonna be next week. There's like a six-month separation period before either of us can file. After that, we've gotta wait for an overburdened judge to rubber-stamp it."

"Goddamn it, Lemmy. Why didn't you mention this before?"

"I assumed you knew through experience. It's not your first marriage, so it can't be your first divorce."

"And I assumed Winfield was going to pull some strings, like he did with the marriage license."

"Yeah, well, it's like he was gonna, but then he springs on me how that would cost more—lots more—so I figure you and me, we'll wait it out."

"Wait it out!"

"Look at it this way, Brenda, as long as you're married to me, you're protected from making some stupid mistake you'll live to regret. If you get the crazy notion to marry somebody else, you can't."

4

Sure I was pissed at Lemmy. Winfield too. Mostly I was pissed at myself. I should have said no at the very first, made it stick, and then thrown goddamned Lemmy and Winfield out of the shop.

At the very least I should have asked more questions, considered all possible consequences, and insisted on some guarantees. In my weak moment, I hadn't even considered insisting on a prenup.

Lemmy refused to bend to Winfield's demands for additional money to speed up the divorce. Winfield refused to bend to my demands that he do it anyway because he knew damned well it was the right thing.

"Pro bono," he'd exclaimed. "No way."

I held out on principle and quashed the urge to squander my own savings. And so for the time being I was stuck married to Lemon B. Crenshaw.

Not that it changed my life in any way. Lemmy went about his business of agenting, and I went about mine running Midnight Millinery. With him on the Upper West Side and me in the West Village, our paths didn't cross.

Still, I hated the very thought of being married to Lemmy, and burbling in the background, a part of my brain constantly seethed.

Except for that, my life was going super-swell. I buckled down and designed some hats. Fall, always my best season, was just around the corner. I had no time for self-indulgent brooding. My challenge was to top last year's sales.

On a terribly hot and humid day in July, I was at Midnight Millinery releasing short bursts of steam to form a rich, blood-red, felt-brimmed hat. The worst part of the millinery biz is that fall hats get made in the summer, which means I end up steaming in the most disgustingly brutal hot weather. After an hour or so, I kind of got into it and let myself turn into one big ball of sweat.

The overworked air conditioner heaved and churned, making so much racket I didn't hear the bells on the door when they jangled. I did, however, hear the door slam. It slammed with such force the display window rattled and the whole building shuddered.

Johnny Verlane stormed into the shop.

Johnny's *Tod Trueman, Urban Detective* television series had been overly heavy on evil drug lords, fast cars, explosions, and big-breasted damsels in distress. In my opinion the only reason the show went anywhere at all was that women viewers couldn't get enough of Johnny's looks— high cheekbones, thick, dark hair that fell over deep-set smoky-gray eyes, great body. All in all, a good package. Beyond the physical, he had an indefinable edge. Johnny radiated the essence of cool.

At the moment, his cool did not show. His jaw was tense, his face all red and distorted with anger. In the years I'd known Johnny, I'd never seen him this mad.

I figured I should try to be cool myself. I put on my very best nonchalant act.

"Oh, hi, Johnny. I didn't expect you back from the dinner theater gig so soon."

Johnny, who almost never cursed, spat out a tirade worthy of a sea captain. I didn't take his words to heart. Somehow, through the string of invectives, he managed to convey the idea that he wanted to know what the holy hell I thought I was doing.

"Steaming," I answered. To prove my point I released a whoosh of steam from the iron. It hung heavy in the air.

Veins in Johnny's temples throbbed. With each word he came a step closer to me. "How. Could. You. Do. It?"

Obviously, steaming was not the answer he was after.

What could have possibly got him so riled? It wasn't his birthday. I hadn't forgotten the anniversary of the day we met.

Dinner theater in Massachusetts. That had to be it.

"Oh, Johnny. I'm so sorry. Did you get a bad review? You know how those reviewers—"

Johnny pounded his fist on my blocking table. "I'm not talking about reviewers."

"Then what *is* the matter?"

"Don't you know?"

"No."

"All right, I'll tell you. You went and married goddamned Lemmy—that's what."

"Is that all? Believe me, I'm plenty pissed about that myself."

"How can you be so blasé about the sacred institution of marriage? I guess your attitude explains why you've been married . . . hmmm . . . let's see, how many times now? Lemmy would make three, right?" One at a time he extended three fingers and waved them around in front of my face. Very aggressive. Had it been anybody else, I would have felt threatened.

I didn't answer his question. Post-Lemmy, the actual count was four, but one of them I don't think about much, and I couldn't remember if I'd ever mentioned it to Johnny.

"And to think," he yelled, "I was gonna . . ."

"You were gonna what, Johnny?"

"Nothing. Nothing at all. Goddammit." He stomped away from the blocking table, plopped his butt down on the bench in front of my vanity, and put his head in his hands.

I didn't understand.

At the first sign of Johnny, Jackhammer had scurried into

the storage closet. Now that things had quieted down a bit, the little dog pranced out and circled Johnny's feet, looking for a pat on the head. He adored Johnny.

Johnny didn't acknowledge Jackhammer.

Jackhammer stood on his back legs, pawed Johnny's leg, and squeaked.

"Shut up," said Johnny. He pushed Jackhammer away. When Jackhammer came back, thinking it was a game, Johnny pushed him away again.

That did it. Nobody gets away with mistreating Jackhammer, not even Johnny.

"Who the hell do you think you are?" I said.

Johnny stood up, stomped over to me, leaned over the table, brought his face within an inch of mine. "Who am I? Just the poor clod who thought I had a faithful girlfriend and then I go away for a couple of weeks of hard work and bullshit to try to save my stinko down-the-drain washed-up career and while I'm gone she runs off and marries my best friend."

"Strange," I said. "I never knew you considered Lemmy to be your best friend." Pride kept me from telling him how it gave me goose bumps to hear him actually come right out and admit that he considered me to be his girlfriend.

"Don't be a smart ass, Brenda."

"You ought to be thanking me. I did it all for you, Johnny."

"For me? You married Lemmy Crenshaw for me?"

"Why else? Of course for you."

"That's a good one, Brenda. Someday, that is, if I ever talk to you again, you can try to explain your convoluted logic."

"You can't possibly believe I married Lemmy to . . . well, marry Lemmy. I married Lemmy for you and that career you're so intent on saving, and now you come storming in here acting like a crazy man."

"If you didn't marry Lemmy to marry Lemmy, then why the hell did you marry Lemmy?"

"Haven't you talked to Lemmy?"

"No, I have not. My soon to be *former* agent left voice mail news of your nuptials at my motel in Massachusetts. The slimy, conniving little bastard didn't have the guts to wait until I got back to my room so we could have a real conversation. Such a wonderful tidbit of news to find waiting for me after two back-to-back shows and a bad meal at a mall."

"Didn't you return Lemmy's call?"

"I did not."

"In the voice mail, did Lemmy happen to mention why we had to get married?"

"*Had* to get married. Don't tell me you're pregnant!"

"Of course not. How could he even think such a thing?"

"Well, then, I guess I know why."

"If you know why, why do you keep asking me why?"

"Because I can't believe you did it, that's why."

Johnny and I were not communicating, which was not at all unusual. I knew why I married Lemmy. Johnny claimed also to know why I married Lemmy. I began to suspect that the problem was that the why that Johnny knew and the why that I knew were totally different whys.

"So why'd you do it?"

"All right," I said. "I thought you already knew, but I guess you don't. I married Lemmy to keep him in the country. If he gets deported, especially now, in the middle—"

"Deported?"

"Surely you know your agent's an alien."

"Oh yeah. Which planet?"

"Canada."

"Give me a break. Lemmy's not from Canada. He's like you, Brenda. Comes from some jerkwater whistle-stop in the midwest. I can't remember the name of the place."

"That's what I thought too. But Lemmy was born in Canada. His parents entered this country illegally when he was an infant. According to Winfield—"

"Brewster Winfield is in on this too? I should have known. Lemmy couldn't pull this off by himself."

"Lemmy wanted to finish negotiations for the *New Adventures of Tod Trueman.*"

"New *Tod!* That's what he told you?"

"He didn't want you to know. He was afraid you'd get nervous and mess up your dinner theater gig."

"What a crock! There's no new *Tod,* Brenda. How could there be? The genius writers blew up New York City."

"Lemmy said he had some ideas to fix that."

"Lemmy's full of shit."

Johnny squatted down and called Jackhammer's name. Jackhammer tentatively approached. Johnny reached out his hand. "Sorry about before."

Jackhammer forgave him.

I wasn't such a soft touch. I went back to steaming the hat, still upset, but working settled my nerves.

Every so often I heard Johnny mumble to himself. Then finally loud and clear, he said, "I figured it out."

"That's wonderful. Tell me."

"It's a long story, and I could sure use a drink."

Without a doubt Angie's is the best neighborhood bar in the world. Dark and cozy and perpetual midnight. An eclectic jukebox. Edible food.

Tommy, the owner, manned the bar. He flashed a grin. "Hey, Brenda, whatcha got in that bag?"

"Millinery materials," I lied.

He knew what was in the bag. Jackhammer. As far as Tommy was concerned, Jackhammer was always welcome as long as I pretended to sneak him in, because you never know when an undercover health inspector might be on the premises, looking to make a bust.

"Welcome back, Johnny," said Tommy. "How'd the Massachusetts gig go?"

"Good as could be expected," said Johnny. "Got my picture in the local paper."

He hadn't told me that.

Tommy did a thumbs-up. "Way to go."

Johnny and I elbowed our way through the dense-packed crowd of neighborhood regulars plus a smattering of outer borough bridge and tunnelers who'd probably seen that misguided article that named Angie's as one of the top ten pickup spots in the city.

What luck. When we got to the back room, our favorite booth was unoccupied. We slid in across from each other.

Ages ago, when Johnny and I first started to hang out together, he'd carved our initials inside a heart on this very tabletop. I can still see it sometimes, but only when the light is exactly right and I tilt my head just so. That night the light wasn't right and I didn't feel like tilting my head. I didn't want Johnny to know I remembered the heart. I wondered if he did.

Without asking, Raphael, the waiter, brought over a glass of red wine for me and a dark beer for Johnny. "The regular?"

"Sounds good," I said.

"Not for me," said Johnny. "Bring me another beer right away. No, make that two. And hold the food."

After Raphael left, Johnny and I had an exceedingly uncomfortable silence. It went on for quite some time, growing more and more uncomfortable with each passing minute. Idly, I rubbed the spot on the tabletop where I knew our heart was.

Johnny downed his first beer and immediately started in on his second. When it was half done, he pushed the mug away, frowned, and cleared his throat. "Remember the last time I asked you to marry me?"

Huh? Talk about surprised.

"No, Johnny, as a matter of fact, I don't remember anything like that."

"Seriously?"

"I told you, I don't remember."

"This is not a joke, Brenda."

"I never said it was," I said. "Exactly when and where did this marriage proposal occur?"

"Few months ago, I think. Yeah, it must have been in the early spring." Johnny jabbed the table with his forefinger. "Right here at this very table, our table."

"Let me get this straight. We were here. Eating. Drinking."

"Yes. And talking. We talked a lot."

"And during all this eating and drinking and talking, you asked me to marry you?"

"Not in so many words . . . but yes. I did. Ask you."

"To marry you."

"That's right."

You'd think I'd remember such an event. "Tell me, Johnny, how did you phrase this proposal?"

"I don't remember the actual words. I think I said something about how good we'd been getting along and how I was sorry about that goddamned rug."

Ah yes, that goddamned rug.

What Johnny referred to had to have been the absolute nadir of our relationship, the time we broke up over his hideous orange and yellow shag rug. You'd think a guy who looked and dressed as good as Johnny would have better taste in home decor. "You *should* be sorry about that rug."

"Don't you remember how I said I wished I'd given it the heave-ho sooner?"

"No, not really."

"Well, you should have paid closer attention. That was it."

"It? That was you asking me to marry you?"

"I thought you knew."

"Kind of subtle, don't you think?"

"You're sensitive, an artist. I didn't think I had to club you over the head. So anyway, not too long after you spurned my proposal—"

"I did not."

"Yes, you did. Anyway, Lemmy and I were sitting around shooting the breeze. I was feeling low—not only about you, it was not long after the *Tod* show got axed. Lemmy told me how lucky I was to have a girlfriend like Brenda, and I said what are you talking about, I asked Brenda to marry me and she turned me down flat, and Lemmy found that hard to believe, he said you were ripe for marriage, and I said you weren't, and one thing kind of led to another, and we got real drunk, and Lemmy bet me he could persuade you to marry him."

"How dare you put a monetary value on marrying me."

I stood up and made a move to go.

Johnny gently touched my hand. "Come on, Brenda, you know me better than that. I didn't bet money. I bet my bra."

Before anybody gets the wrong idea about Johnny, I should mention that my soon-to-be ex-husband, Lemon B. Crenshaw, is more than a mere hothead agent. He also happens to be one of the world's premiere brassiere collectors and an expert in the field. He has hundreds of rare specimens mounted on his living room wall. A memorabilia newsletter termed his collection of major significance.

One Sunday, while cruising the aisles of the Twenty-sixth Street flea market on a quest for wacky embroidered kitchen towels, Johnny stumbled on a bra that he thought was pretty. It only cost a couple of bucks, so he bought it, thinking I might like it. I didn't.

To avoid hurting his feelings, I examined it carefully for a size label, hoping it wouldn't fit. I was surprised to discover hand stitches.

"Nice work," I said. "Maybe you ought to show this to Lemmy."

Lemmy recognized the bra as the long-lost prototype of a bra that had later become very common. Priceless, he claimed. Naturally he wanted it for his collection.

Johnny wouldn't let him have it. Lemmy's birthday was not long off, and Johnny fully intended to give it to him then. But before he could, they had a big fight over a movie project Lemmy wanted Johnny to do. Depending on who you believe, either Johnny fired Lemmy or Lemmy dropped Johnny. That didn't last, and they were soon back together as agent and client, but Johnny never gave Lemmy the bra, which bugged the hell out of Lemmy.

It took a while for the absurdity of this to settle into my brain. At first I was insulted and a little huffy, but the more I thought about it, the more deeply hurt I became. When the full impact finally hit home, I tossed aside the hurt for anger. I was goddamned mad as the maddest hatter ever in the entire history of millinery. My Anger-O-Meter clanged.

"What was the rest of the bet? What were you gonna get if I didn't marry Lemmy?" I asked.

"It never went that far, Brenda. I didn't think Lemmy was serious."

There was only one thing to do. Without another word, I walked out.

5

From out of cool, dark Angie's, I stepped straight into hell.

The night was searing hot and steamy. New York City clutched the heat of the day to its bosom in a concrete death-grip. The temperature had continued to rise long after the sun had the good sense to call it quits and slip behind New Jersey.

The Empire State Building, shrouded in air dense with humidity, was barely visible from the avenue. Looking downtown, I saw no indication of the World Trade towers. It was as if they'd taken a deep dive into the harbor.

Hordes of people were out and about on this evil night, roaming zombielike through the seething streets, not interacting. New York's background buzz, that electrical charge we all plug into, was stifled by the white noise as millions of air conditioners battled the heat. From somewhere far off in the distance a fog horn sounded.

Half a block away from home Jackhammer zeroed in on his favorite fire hydrant. After a couple of quick sniffs around the base he lifted his leg.

As I waited for him to finish, a shiny silver sedan with dark-tinted windows careened around the corner, screeched to a stop, then backed up to where I stood, and idled ominously by the curb.

It would have scared the hell out of me, except that the

car had diplomat license plates. That could mean only one thing.

The passenger-side window whirred down far enough to allow a sliver of ice-cold air to escape.

"Dweena?" I said. It better be.

"Yo, Brenda. Jackhammer."

Definitely Dweena.

"Hop into my chariot," she said.

"No thanks. I'm not in the mood for a joyride."

"Oh, but this is no joyride. I am on yet another mission to right a grievous wrong."

That was a matter of opinion.

My good friend Dweena is a filthy-rich ex-stockbroker and sometime nightclub bouncer. Once, between gigs, she apprenticed herself to a master car thief. After a fight with a chop shop manager, she opted for more legit pursuits but retained a passion for boosting cars. Now she confines this activity to the relocation of illegally parked diplomat vehicles. She hates the concept of diplomatic immunity.

One other interesting little fact about Dweena: She hasn't always been a she.

I heard a lock pop.

"You gonna join me or not?"

"Yeah, I guess." I figured a diversion might not be such a bad idea. It would be good to get my mind off goddamned Lemmy and goddamned Johnny. Hard to say which one pissed me off more. I opened the door and climbed in. Like all of Dweena's target vehicles, this was a classy number, and ultra-chilled inside, so cool, the buttery-soft gunmetal-gray genuine leather upholstery didn't stick to my bare thighs.

Dweena punched the accelerator, and we peeled out.

Her wig for the evening, a platinum bouffant, glowed. She had it styled into an elaborate upswept French roll. One long tendril sprang loose and curled down the back of her neck.

I scoped out her getup, black and white short shorts and a

coordinated crop top. Surprisingly, what little there was of it appeared to be wrinkled, like it was made out of natural fibres. Not exactly Dweenalike.

"Cute outfit," I said. "Is it cotton?"

"Thank you," she said. "Actually, it's a cotton and linen blend. On a night like this even I wouldn't be caught dead in spandex. Or sequins. That stuff doesn't breathe, you know." She gave me a sidelong glance and frowned. "But what of you, Brenda? You look a mess. No offense."

"None taken," I said. "I've had a rough day."

"Steaming hats?"

"Steaming," I said, "in more ways than one."

"Then it must have something to do with you getting hitched to Lemmy Crenshaw. Whatever possessed you?"

"You know about that?"

"But naturally. Dweena makes it her business to know absolutely everything about absolutely everybody. I must say I was devastated that you didn't invite moi to the festivities. You broke my heart."

"I didn't invite anybody."

"Then how come Elizabeth went and Chuck Riley and Brew Winfield?"

"They attended, but I didn't invite them. They sort of showed up. It was way too early for you anyway. Before noon."

"Oh. In that case, I suppose it's just as well. You can make it up to me by inviting me to the gala divorce proceeding. How soon will it be?"

"Don't ask. Lemmy screwed up on that. I thought I was as mad as humanly possible, but after what I found out tonight, I'm even madder. If I were to see his bald head right now, I don't know what I'd do, but it wouldn't be pretty. Strangle him maybe till his beady little eyes popped out and he collapsed lifeless on the floor."

"Oooh, that it sounds like such fun. Plus it would save you the trauma of another divorce. Whatever did Lemmy do to get you thinking homicide?"

"I don't want to talk about it."

"Come on, Brenda. You'll feel much better if you unburden."

"No, I won't."

Dweena drove around the twisty streets of the West Village, up one block, down another, in no discernible pattern. It lulled me into relaxation. Eventually, despite my intention to keep the details of my humiliation under my hat, I spilled.

By the time I wound up my sorry tale she'd looped back and we were just around the corner from my apartment building. Dweena pulled into a vacant parking space and killed the engine.

"You're stopping?" I said.

"Yep. I had planned to drive around most of the night and eventually ditch the car in the Wall Street vicinity, but your horrific story has inspired me to cut short my vehicle relocation project. What say we go back to your apartment and plot what you're gonna do?"

"Do about what?"

"About Lemmy, of course. Don't you dare wimp out on me, Brenda Midnight. Oh my, how I love sweet revenge."

I'm not a vengeful person, but I thought more talk might help diffuse my anger, which hadn't yet played out. "Okay, sure. Come on home with me."

"I see light under Elizabeth's door," said Dweena. "Does that mean she's still up?"

"Probably."

"Then I'll ask her to join us. She's real good at thinking up stuff."

While I unlocked my door, Dweena rang Elizabeth's bell. "Yo, Liz, open up."

I went into the kitchen, put on a pot of coffee, and checked inside the cabinets for refreshments. Not a crumb of snack food. I thought for sure I had a box of graham crackers somewhere. While I poked around, I heard

Dweena tell Elizabeth that Lemmy wasn't really an alien.

"All that crap about poor Lemmy's troubles with immigration was a complete and total crock. He married her to win a bet with Johnny and score a coveted bra for his collection."

"Screw that," said Elizabeth.

I gave up the search for graham crackers and carried the coffeepot and mugs out to the room.

"Smells delicious, but no coffee for me, thanks," said Dweena. "Might I suggest you bring on the wine?"

"Now you're talking," said Elizabeth.

I had to agree.

I got out my fancy wineglasses and my house red. Dweena uncorked. Elizabeth poured. We all consumed.

Dweena sprawled out on the floor and tucked a throw pillow under her head. "This is so cool," she said, "just like a slumber party. I love getting smashed, hanging out with the girls and talking about the guys."

Actually the topic was mostly one guy, Lemmy. And I didn't say much. Three sheets to the wind, I flopped down on my couch, and let Elizabeth and Dweena dish. They were much better at it than me anyway.

"That Lemmy Crenshaw is pond scum," said Elizabeth. She'd settled into her favorite chair by the window with Jackhammer curled up in her lap.

"Nope, I disagree," said Dweena. "Pond scum floats to the top. Lemmy is definitely a bottom feeder."

"You are so right," said Elizabeth. "What are you gonna do, Brenda?"

I didn't answer. I hadn't yet made up my mind but was leaning toward nothing. I mean, what could I do?

"Earlier Brenda was talking murder," said Dweena.

At that point I had to put a stop to this foolishness. In Elizabeth's state she might believe Dweena. "It was a figure of speech," I said, trying to remember exactly what I'd said. "You can be sure, I'm not going to kill Lemmy."

"Me," said Elizabeth, "I'd be mighty tempted to choke the lousy bastard with a strap from one of his precious bras."

"Oooh, that's a fitting end," said Dweena.

"I repeat," I said, "I am not going to kill Lemmy. Or for that matter anybody else. Ever."

"Then," continued Dweena, "she could roll him up in a rug and drag him over to my neighborhood and dangle him from a meat hook."

I chose not to comment on that, although to tell the truth I kind of enjoyed the image of Lemmy strung up on a meat hook.

Dweena and Elizabeth must have liked it too. For a couple of minutes nobody spoke.

Finally Elizabeth broke the silence. "Well, there *is* a problem with murder."

"I can't possibly imagine what," said Dweena.

I certainly could. I don't even like to joke about the taking of a human life.

"Brenda might get caught," said Elizabeth.

At last somebody was talking sense, although maybe not from the highest moral ground.

"Good point," said Dweena.

"I don't think she'd do very well in prison."

"Well, then how about simple harassment? Brenda could write Lemmy's name and cell phone number on bathroom walls in the Port Authority."

"That's the spirit."

"Put glue in his locks."

"Put rocks in his socks."

"Post naked pictures of him on the Internet."

"Yuck! She'd have to see him naked."

"You're right. Scratch that idea."

They went on like that until the eastern sky turned red, signaling another hot day.

I'd heard enough. "Stop it," I said. "It's a brand-new day. I have a brand-new attitude. All this negativity is a waste of energy."

"That's our Brenda," said Elizabeth. "Too damned nice for her own good."

"All primed to forgive and forget," said Dweena.

"No, I'm not. About all I'm primed for is sleep. I'm gonna get some rest and then see how I feel."

6

I awakened to the ringing of the telephone. I didn't feel capable of handling much, so I let the machine take the call.

"Brenda, pick up. It's me, Lemmy. Your husband. Remember? Come on, Brenda, wife—"

I made a grab for the phone. "Cut the wife crap, Lemmy."

"I knew you were home. Sleeping late, dear?"

"What do you want?"

"My, my, aren't we cranky this morning."

Had Lemmy talked to Johnny? Did he know that I knew how thoroughly he'd deceived me? Was this call for damage control? I played it innocent. "Cranky? I don't think so." Cranky barely scraped the surface of my mood. "Have you talked to Johnny recently?"

"No, as a matter of fact, I haven't." It sounded like the truth, but then Lemmy was an accomplished liar. "Why do you ask?"

"Oh, just curious," I said.

"I know you're a busy woman, what with running Midnight Millinery and all, so I won't keep you long. I thought you should know that I've reconsidered the timing on the divorce. I'm willing to fork over the extra money for Winfield to put in the bribes to push it through pronto."

An alarm went off in my brain. It took a lot to get money out of Lemmy. The sudden turnabout must mean he had a new angle. Perhaps he *had* talked to Johnny. Or maybe it had dawned on Brewster Winfield that I could sue his slime-ball client Lemmy for breach of promise or fraud or something and that even the esteemed lawyer himself could get in a lot of trouble with the bar association for his role in the scheme. I was so involved in my attempt to analyze Lemmy's motive, I didn't bother to comment.

"Well," said Lemmy, "aren't you at least gonna thank me?"

No, I wasn't. "Why the big change of heart, Lemmy?"

"It's really very simple, Brenda. I feel your pain. I'm not the insensitive clod you think I am. I assume you're still game for a quickie divorce?"

"Absolutely."

Whatever Lemmy's motivation, I wasn't about to look this gift horse in the mouth.

"Great. Then it's all settled," he said. "Meet me at Winfield's loft at noon. All we've gotta do is sign on the dotted line."

Brewster Winfield lived and worked out of a vast two-thousand-square-foot loft on the top floor of a building on Broadway a few blocks below Canal Street. From the outside the place seemed ratty. The crumbling facade was covered with graffiti. It was a front to keep the burglars from knowing the riches within.

To get inside the locked building I usually had to ring the buzzer and wait for Winfield to drop a set of keys out of his arched front-facing window. But today, just as I arrived, Winfield's paralegal, Susan, was coming out of the building, carrying an elaborately tooled leather case.

She held the door open for me. "Hi, Brenda. I hear congratulations are in order. I wish you a long and fruitful divorce."

"Thanks." I nodded my head at the case. "Myrtle?"

"Yeah. Time for her midday outing."

I felt bad for Susan. She seemed an earnest sort, truly

dedicated to the law, but she spent an awful lot of her time taking care of Winfield's pet snake.

If possible, the foyer of the building was even more off-putting than the outside. There were real live cockroaches, real dead cockroaches, and a real bad smell, possibly indicative of real dead rodents somewhere behind the wall.

At least I didn't have to stay long. The elevator was on the ground floor, its door open. I stepped inside the tiny, creaky, slow claustrophobia special, pushed the button for the top floor, and hoped for the best.

Minutes later the elevator lurched to a stop, the door scraped open, and I was safely delivered to the rear of the loft. Thankful the harrowing experience had ended well, I got off and headed toward Winfield's office, all the way at the front of the hundred-foot-long loft.

Winfield always makes a big deal about being a hotshot criminal lawyer, a champion of the poor, downtrodden, and unjustly accused, some of which might actually be true. I had a hunch he also did some slip-and-fall stuff on the side. He had to pay for his lavish lifestyle somehow.

The loft was truly amazing in an understated kind of way. Scattered throughout the expanse were ridiculously expensive pieces of antique furniture, each spotlit and displayed like a work of art.

I walked slowly toward the office, soaking up the money-eyed atmosphere, thinking what I'd change if the place were mine. As I got closer, Lemmy's rat-a-tat whine and Winfield's deep-as-the-ocean smooth, mellow voice drifted my way. I heard my name mentioned.

I wasn't making an effort to be quiet or to eavesdrop, but I had on my red high-top sneakers, and they lived up to their name. I was privy to a conversation Lemmy and Winfield didn't want me to hear.

"May I remind you," said Winfield, "I advised you to draw up a prenup agreement with Brenda."

That low-down creep. I now felt like a complete fool for not insisting on a prenup myself. I hadn't even broached the subject. I crept a little closer so I could hear better.

"That may be true," said Lemmy, "but you also advised me a prenup would cost an arm and a leg."

"I am a professional, and as such I charge professional fees."

"Yeah, well, I thought we were supposed to be friends."

"We are. In addition to our friendship we maintain a professional relationship. As Myrtle's agent, you take your fifteen percent of all her earnings. As your lawyer, I charge you legal fees. I don't see how you can find fault with such an arrangement."

"It bugs me because my fifteen percent is just that—fifteen percent. Your fees skyrocket from one minute to the next. But hey, what the hell, I'll pay."

"I'm worth it."

"You better be. Do what you have to do to make sure I rake in my entire inheritance. None of this community property crap, right?"

"In law, as in life," said Winfield, "there are no guarantees. I doubt Brenda could make much of a case, but your position would be stronger if you two weren't married. The sooner you divorce, the better. Brenda is an unnecessary complication."

Unnecessary complication!

No words could possibly do justice to the degree of my anger or to the rate at which it was escalating. And believe me, I tried every expletive I knew, albeit silently. Oh, how I wanted to charge in and confront Lemmy and Winfield, blow off some steam, and give those two scumbuckets a piece of my mind. I knew it would be better for me if they didn't know how much I knew. And so from somewhere I summoned up the willpower to restrain myself.

I tiptoed all the way back to the entrance of the loft, then shouted out as if I'd just arrived, "Yoo-hoo. Anybody here?"

"Brenda, is that you?" called Winfield.

"I ran into Susan, and she let me in."

"We're up front. In my office. Please join us."

"Hello, Brenda," said Winfield. He halfway stood up to greet me, showing off the full effect of his baby-blue silk lounging pajamas, then sank back down into his maroon leather ergonomic executive chair.

Lemmy had on one of his signature shiny ill-fitting shark-skin suits.

"Brenda, my dear ex-wife to be, how lovely you look today." He patted the chair next to him. "Here, sit by your hubby of the moment."

I plastered a fake smile on my face and did as asked. My brain was in overdrive. I didn't know what to do, but I had to assert myself somehow. I couldn't let them get away with this.

Acting as Lemmy's mouthpiece, Winfield took the floor. "As you no doubt know, thanks to you, Brenda, and to me, our good friend Lemmy's immigration troubles are now behind him."

"That sure was quick," I said.

"Thank you," said Winfield.

I hadn't meant it as a compliment.

Winfield continued, "In gratitude Lemmy feels it would be entirely appropriate to do whatever he can to bring about a speedy dissolution of the marriage. To that end he has requested my services. I called in some favors to enable us to move forward on the divorce."

"That's terrific," I said, "but what about the six-month waiting period?"

"No prob. Once you sign these papers I've drawn up, a friend of a friend's friend will goose your case to the top of the pile. If all goes well, you and Lemmy will be blissfully divorced in a matter of days."

"Are you positive all threat of deportation is over? I mean, I wouldn't want to risk Lemmy's ability to negotiate for Johnny."

Winfield clammed up on that. Maybe he could only lie once per day per subject.

Lemmy said, "Like Brew already said, all that stuff worked out swell. I want to thank you, Brenda, from the bottom of my heart for coming through for me in my time of need. I will be forever grateful to you. If there's ever anything—"

"How are those *Tod Trueman* negotiations going?"

"Uh . . . swimmingly. Yes, I'd say that's an apt description."

Winfield squirmed in his chair. It was hard to tell what was happening in his head. Maybe he didn't like his client telling blatant lies in his presence, especially blatant lies so easily provable as such.

"So," he said, again taking command of the conversation, "shall we proceed with the divorce?"

"Yes, let's," said Lemmy. He glanced nervously at his watch. "I've got to be somewhere."

"Brenda?" said Winfield.

"Okay by me," I said.

"Good, then we're all in agreement."

Winfield centered a document on his desk, plucked his prized lucky antique silver fountain pen from its faceted crystal base, and inked an X at the bottom of the top sheet.

"Brenda, if you would sign right here." He slid the papers over to me. He reached into his desk drawer and took out a red-barreled plastic ballpoint pen and rolled that across the desk.

I picked up the pen, balanced it in my hand, and frowned. "Come on, Winfield. This is a momentous event. Let me use your lucky pen."

"No, I'm sorry. I could never."

A glimmer of an idea formed. "The problem is," I said, "I'm feeling a bit superstitious today."

"What do you mean?"

"No lucky pen, no signature."

Lemmy propelled himself across the room, banged his hand on Winfield's desk. "Will you give her the goddamned pen?"

A full minute of tense silence followed. I sat back and

pretended to be totally blasé, as if I couldn't care less how the two of them worked it out.

Lemmy glared at Winfield.

Winfield glared at Lemmy.

At last Winfield said, "Certainly you may use my pen. But please, Brenda, Babycakes, be exceedingly careful. The nib, you know, is quite sensitive."

He caressed the pen, then held it out to me.

I grabbed the damned thing, twirled it around in my hand, admired the intricate design etched into the barrel, and thoroughly enjoyed watching Winfield's attempt not to show how freaked out he was. The more I twirled, the more he freaked. As a pen, the thing was probably worth several hundred dollars. As Winfield's lucky pen, which he believed was endowed with magical qualities, it was priceless.

I leaned over the desk, poised to sign. No more than a sixteenth of an inch before the pen touched down on the paper, I stopped abruptly. "You know, Winfield, I'm having second thoughts about this divorce. I've grown rather fond of Lemmy. At times he can be quite endearing."

"Very funny, Brenda," said Winfield.

A high-pitched giggle erupted from Lemmy.

With an exaggerated sigh, I straightened up and strolled over to the magnificent arched window, thankful it was open. Then, before I could change my mind, with a quick flick of my wrist I chucked the pen out the window.

Time slowed. The sun gleamed off the silver as the pen fell, nib-first, to the sidewalk.

"My god," shrieked Winfield. He ran over to the window and leaned out in time to see a bicycle messenger who was zipping along the sidewalk jump off his bike, pounce on the pen, and slip it into his nylon messenger bag.

Winfield tilted so far out of the window I was afraid he'd fall. His dreadlocks whipped around his head. "Stop! Thief!" he yelled. "That fountain pen is mine."

The messenger looked up and shouted, "No way, man.

Haven't you heard, possession is nine-tenths of the law?"

"Bull freaking shit," screamed Winfield. "I'm an attorney."

"So, dude, sue me." With that, the messenger hopped back on his bike and merged into traffic surging down Broadway.

Winfield didn't say a word.

Lemmy's mouth flapped open and shut, but no sound came out.

I could think of no reason to stick around any longer.

"Don't worry about me. I can show myself out."

During the cab ride home I sat back, closed my eyes, and stewed. My anger intensified by leaps and bounds, exponentially, as Chuck would say. I was too preoccupied to pay attention to our uptown progress until the cab swerved.

The cab driver stuck his head out the window. "Asshole," he shouted. He said lots more but in a foreign tongue that I didn't understand.

What I did understand was the object of his attention. It was the very same bicycle messenger who'd taken Winfield's lucky silver fountain pen. He was about three cars ahead and twisted around, giving us the finger. Then he cut over to the curb, chained his bike to a post, and with a final wave of his middle finger, disappeared into a building.

In a snap decision I told the driver, "I changed my mind. I want to get out right here."

We were in the center lane, so right here wasn't realistic. The driver managed to get the cab to the curb about half a block later. I got out and ran back to where I'd last seen the messenger. His bicycle was still there.

While waiting for the messenger to return, I checked my wallet. I didn't have much cash on me. Unless the messenger was stupid, he'd never take the amount I had to offer.

The messenger was not stupid.

First he turned down my offer, then he said, "Besides, I don't even know what you're talking about."

"Oh, I think you do. I was a witness."

"Possession is nine-tenths of the law."

"Look," I said, "I don't know what the law is and I don't much care. I don't want to get you in trouble. All I want is the pen and all I've got is this much money." I thrust a wad of bills at him.

"Assuming I had in my possession the item in question, why should I sell it to you when I can put it up for auction on eBay."

I had no good answer for that. "Tell you what, here's my card. Find out what the pen is worth, and I'll make you an offer you can't refuse."

"Fair enough," he said.

I was happy he agreed. Not that I was the least bit sorry I'd heaved the pen. It had been a glorious moment, and one I was damned proud of. However, I did think it would be in my best interest to get it back in case someday I needed to bribe Winfield.

When I got back, five messages had already accumulated on my home answering machine—three from Lemmy, two from Winfield—and five more on the machine at Midnight Millinery—two from Lemmy, three from Winfield.

I'd intended to work, but mostly I played with Jackhammer, fumed, and wondered about Lemmy's inheritance. I couldn't remember him ever mentioning a rich relative, but then we didn't talk all that much.

Winfield and Lemmy kept the calls coming fast. I didn't answer, but I did listen to each message.

Lemmy asking why.

Winfield asking why and bemoaning his lost property.

Then Lemmy again.

Then Winfield again.

Lemmy. Winfield. Lemmy. Winfield.

I finally got annoyed enough to pick up. "You've got a lot of nerve, Winfield."

"You stole my antique fountain pen."

"I did not. I tripped, and it fell from my hand, a tragic accident, but as long as we're making accusations, you're a party to a fraud."

"I assure you, Brenda, the practice of greasing the wheels of justice to speed up the divorce process could not in any way be considered fraud."

"That's not what I'm talking about."

"Then what are you talking about?"

The time had come to reveal what I knew. "You and Lemmy tricked me. I know about the bra and the bet, and I know Lemmy is not an alien."

Winfield sighed. "How'd you find out?"

"Little milliners sure do have big ears. She musta heard us talking today." That was Lemmy piping up.

"What are you doing on the line?" I asked.

Winfield said, "Lemmy, perhaps you should hang up."

"No," said Lemmy. "This concerns me."

"Here's something else to be concerned about," I said. "You better give Johnny a call. I think he's gonna fire you."

That got rid of Lemmy.

Winfield tried to placate me. "Whatever you think might have happened in the past or whatever you think you might have overheard today was out of context."

"Yeah, right. Tell me about Lemmy's inheritance."

"It's really nothing. Lemmy's aunt—"

"Another illegal alien?"

Winfield started to answer, but I was sick of listening to his bullshit.

I cut him off midsentence. "Toodle-ooo, screw you and Lemmy too."

After that sign-off I unplugged the phone and spent the rest of the day making hats and doing some soul-searching. By late afternoon I concluded that Elizabeth and Dweena had a point.

Revenge could be very, very sweet.

7

I woke up the next morning determined to do something. What exactly I didn't know. Vengeful acts do not come naturally to me.

On Jackhammer's morning walk I focused intently on the sidewalk and steered the little dog away from all those yummy disgusting tidbits he loved to snarf up. I didn't think about Lemmy at all. Instead I wondered if the fact that very few plastic crack vials were crushed into the concrete signaled the end of that drug trend or the onset of dealer-accessible affordable biodegradable packaging.

It was garbage pickup day. Big black plastic bags were heaped at curbside, many ripped open by nighttime scroungers on the prowl for bottles and cans—at a nickel a return, viable commodities. Beside one deflated bag was a pile of old jeans. Denim is also a commodity but not that easy to trade in. A little farther up the street I spotted a bunch of faded ragged T-shirts and a lone polyester satin bra. I felt sorry for the castoffs, once loved, now rejected.

Then I thought of Johnny's bra, once rejected but now coveted by Lemmy and the source of my current mess. One thought led to another, and it hit me with tremendous force and total clarity: To get back at Lemmy I'd steal his goddamned bra collection.

Now, that idea had bite.

Could I pull it off?

I went to Midnight Millinery to hand-finish several hats. While stitching, I considered that question.

Getting into Lemmy's Upper West Side prewar building would be a snap. Sure, he had a doorman. Strange as it may seem, that might make access even easier. Entrances to attended buildings were usually unlocked. I wouldn't have to resort to the old food- or flower-delivery ruse.

Once inside I'd have to get past Lemmy's doorman and onto the elevator. No problem. With the right clothes and attitude and a little bit of luck I could sneak past almost any doorman in Manhattan.

Most likely I could make it up to Lemmy's floor. After that things would get a little trickier.

Challenge number one: Like almost everybody I knew, Lemmy worked out of his home. I had to figure out a way to get him the hell out of the apartment.

Challenge number two: I had to figure out a way to get me into the apartment.

I needed help on both counts.

First I called Johnny.

The other night, when I'd stormed out of Angie's, I intended to be forever done with Mr. Johnny Verlane, the man who'd wagered my hand in marriage. I didn't want to see him or talk to him or even think about him or his stupid orange and yellow shag rug ever again.

And so I fought the urge to call him. And failed. He fit so well into my plan, I had to at least ask.

He picked up on the first ring.

"It's me," I said, somewhat tentatively. I hated being the one who broke down and called first.

A moment of silence, then in a tense voice he said, "So, Brenda, I hear you've been spreading rumors about me."

"No way."

"Yeah, you did. You told Lemmy I planned to fire him. He called me yesterday to find out if it was true."

"Oh. I might have said something like that in a fit of anger. I truly am sorry."

"That's okay. Lemmy's asking made it much easier to do the deed. I knew damned well I had to fire him, but it was difficult. It's been a while since the last time I fired him. Guess I kinda forgot how."

"Want to help me get back at Lemmy?"

"What do you have in mind?"

"I'm gonna steal his precious brassiere collection."

"From his apartment?"

"That's where he keeps them."

"You're talking breaking and entering. Illegal acts. I don't think so, Brenda, but thanks so much for thinking of me."

That's Johnny for you. Straight as an arrow. Sometimes he acts more like a cop than a real cop.

"Come on, Johnny. You owe me."

"Why are you so hell-bent on revenge anyway? It's not at all like you."

"That's right, you haven't heard the latest insult." I filled him in on Lemmy's sudden turnaround and how I'd found out about the inheritance. "Brewster Winfield referred to me as an unnecessary complication. Can you believe that? First they trick me into marrying Lemmy, now they want to get rid of me."

"I can see why you're mad."

"Does that mean you'll help?"

"I don't know, Brenda."

"Please."

"Experience shows that helping you with your schemes can be dangerous."

"You won't be directly involved. All I need you to do is keep Lemmy amused for a couple of hours. Get him out of his apartment."

"How?"

"You could invite him to lunch."

"You want me to eat with Lemmy? For chrissakes, I just fired the man."

"It's a perfect setup. Tell him you want to discuss the possibility of rehiring him."

"But that would be a lie."

"Like Lemmy never lied to you."

Johnny didn't reply, but I picked up on a distinct change in his breathing that meant he was considering.

When I felt the moment was right, I prodded. "So, will you do it?"

"Yeah, I guess."

So much for getting Lemmy out of his apartment.

Now I had to get myself in. For that I needed Dweena.

It was too early to call, but I didn't let that deter me.

"Rrrro," she said.

"Oh, Dweena. Did I wake you?" As if I didn't know.

"Uh-mmmmm."

"Sorry, but this can't wait. I need you to help me break into Lemmy's apartment."

That woke her up. "No shit?"

"Absolutely for real."

"Fabulous. Give me a couple of minutes to finish waking up. I'll call you right back, okay?"

I waited a half-hour for Dweena to call back, but she didn't. Not even the thrill of breaking into Lemmy's could get that girl out of bed before noon. I should have fibbed and told her Jeffrey's was having a seventy-percent-off sale on shoes and handbags.

To call her again would be a big waste of time. I decided to go in person.

"Hey, Jackhammer, want to go smell some putrefying flesh?"

Dweena lived way over on Gansevoort Street at the westernmost edge of the far West Village—the meatpacking district. Jackhammer strained on the leash. His nostrils quivered as he sniffed the air.

In the past he didn't have to sniff so hard to catch the scent, but in recent years most of the neighborhood's meat-packers had shrink-wrapped their final animal parts and taken off for friendlier climes, squeezed out by real estate developers who smelled big money where Jackhammer and I smelled meat. The district had become hot, Manhattan's next last frontier.

The streets where complete cow spines once tumbled from offal trucks, where pools of blood coagulated in the gutter, where guys in blood-drenched white aprons coexisted with pioneering artists and writers and hookers were now jammed with professionals who crammed themselves into new rentals and millionaires who bought space in coops and condos built as high as allowable under the law, which pissed off everybody who already lived in the area. But then, everything pisses off Greenwich Villagers. For a community known the world over for its rampant liberalism, we turn pretty damned reactionary whenever anybody tries to mess with our neighborhood.

The outer door to Dweena's building was unlocked. I walked up a worn wooden stairway to the second floor and banged on her hot-pink door.

And waited.

No response, so I banged again and shouted, "Dweena, it's Brenda. Wake up."

Finally the door opened. Dweena stood there looking like hell but outfitted in very nice turquoise baby doll pajamas with a sheer, feather-trimmed matching robe.

"This is so weird," she said. "I was just this second dreaming you called and asked me to break into Lemmy's."

"That was no dream."

I told her what I had in mind, wrapping up with, "Johnny's getting Lemmy out of the apartment. For the locks I need your expertise."

Dweena, now fully awake and smiling, said, "Cool. Just when I was beginning to think my pal Brenda Midnight had turned into a total wimp, she goes and orchestrates a daring daylight robbery."

"Actually I think it is a burglary."

"Whatever."

"Will you help me?"

"Damn tootin'. I'm flattered you asked. I'll be there with bells on."

"You know what, I think it might be better if you leave the bells behind and tried to appear . . . well . . . you know, kind of normal. We have to make it past Lemmy's doorman."

"Gotcha. I'll keep that in mind as I choose my costume."

While Dweena rooted through her totally stuffed walk-in closet, I plopped down on her couch and thumbed through several investor magazines. They all had similar articles, cautionary tales of day traders gone berserk.

"So," said Dweena, "do I look like an Upper West Sider or what?"

Her ensemble—Day-Glo-orange cross trainers, a tight midriff-baring tee, and low-riding belly-button-revealing baggy striped capri pants—was a bit more "what" than she apparently thought, but at least she'd picked out a conservative wig in a shade of auburn that could pass for bona fide human hair. Besides, I knew better than to push. "You did good," I said.

"Thank you. In my own way, I do strive to fit in."

"I've been flipping through your magazines," I said, "and I'm curious. How come you haven't jumped on the day trade bandwagon? With your knowledge of the market, you could make a fortune."

She shrugged. "With what I know I already made two fortunes, three depending on who's counting. How much money can one person spend? Those day traders have to get up with the birds, and besides, all that keyboarding is murder on a manicure."

*   *   *

From Dweena's I called Johnny. "Did you talk to Lemmy?"

"Uh-huh. He seemed happy to hear from me. I told him I'd done some soul searching and concluded that I may have been too harsh to fire him without giving him an opportunity to defend himself. I asked if he had plans for lunch. He told me he was taking a meeting with some guy who was gonna be a big star. But when I mentioned it would be my treat, he backpedaled and said he could reschedule."

"Great."

"To give you as much time as possible, I told Lemmy to meet me at this little place I know in a remote part of Tribeca. It's famous for really good pasta and excruciatingly slow service. It's also located far from the subway. He'll probably take a cab down, and when we're done, he'll have a tough time finding another cab to take him home."

"Excellent work, Johnny. I always knew you were more than a pretty face."

Dweena and I stopped by my apartment to drop off Jackhammer.

As I unlocked my door, Dweena bounded across the hall to Elizabeth's. "Does Liz know yet?"

Before she had a chance to push Elizabeth's doorbell, I yanked her into my apartment and slammed the door. "I don't want Elizabeth to know what we're doing."

"How come?"

"Because she'll want to help."

"So?"

"Elizabeth's got a criminal record. I don't want to involve her in an illegal activity."

"What criminal record? You mean that antiwar stuff?"

I nodded.

"Don't be silly, Brenda. That happened decades ago. Liz's criminal record has probably turned to dust at the back of a long-forgotten file cabinet in the rat-infested subcellar of some city building. Nobody cares about those kinds of crimes anymore. Vietnam is like way over, or hadn't you noticed?"

"Look, Dweena, this is my gig, I get to pick the gang."

"All right. Whatever. You're the boss."

"Good. I'm glad you see it my way."

Dweena moped for a minute, then brightened. "What say I procure a majestic vehicle for our journey uptown? I'm thinking a big, brawny SUV would be appropriate."

"Thanks, but I want to cab it. I can't stomach breaking more than one law a day."

"The way I see it," said Dweena, "every time I stand up, I'm already breaking the law of gravity. Who the hell cares if I break a few more along the way?"

I chuckled at Dweena's special brand of flaky science. She bends rules this way and that to accommodate her immediate needs. While amused, I didn't cave in. Once again, I pulled rank. "I care, that's who."

"What a drag."

I succeeded in getting Dweena out of my building without running into Elizabeth, past several parked SUVs and other temptations, and into the backseat of a cab. She was grumpy at first. Then to make the best of what she called a sucky situation, she leaned forward and talked to the cab driver through the slot in the bulletproof divider. They became involved in a technical discussion about rapid lane-switching. To Dweena's delight and my horror, the driver demonstrated a few new techniques.

I fastened my seat belt.

8

"This is fine right here," I said to the cab driver.

He cut across two lanes of traffic and braked to a stop a couple of feet away from the curb.

Dweena peered out the window. "This isn't Lemmy's block."

"Yeah, I know." I paid the driver and hustled Dweena out of the cab. After the cab pulled away, I explained, "Savvy burglars cool enough to stay out of prison do not take cabs from their own personal residences to the scene of their crimes. I figured it would be a good idea if we hoofed it a couple of blocks."

"Subterfuge, huh?"

"Yep."

"You really thought this all out, didn't you?"

"I have a plan, if that's what you mean."

"I still say if you'd let me boost a car, there'd be no record or witnesses that we ever ventured above Fourteenth Street. It would have been easier. Cheaper too."

Dweena had a point, but I didn't give her the satisfaction of telling her so.

Up ahead on the sidewalk a woman pushing a cart loaded down with provisions barreled full speed toward us.

I jumped left. Dweena jumped right. We avoided collision.

The woman plowed straight ahead, oblivious to the near miss.

Dweena turned to me and said, "Ever notice how people on the Upper West Side always seem to be food shopping?"

I'd never thought of it before, but she was right. "It's probably because apartments in this part of town have more bedrooms, so you get more families. More families, more cooking. More cooking, more food shopping."

"In other words, like most New York phenomena, it boils down to real estate."

"Right." We passed by a luscious display of fruits and vegetables. "I've never seen asparagus so cheap."

"You should buy some."

"I don't want to lose focus."

"Wow," said Dweena. "It's hard to believe that slimy little Lemmy of the big mouth, shaved head, and shiny, puke-colored suits resides here. It's quite a spread." Dweena gazed up at the elaborate detail on the twenty-five-storey prewar yellow brick building. "I mean, dig the big blue awning. It's like from out of an old movie. And the entrance with all that carved stone and wood and beveled glass isn't bad either. Where does Lemmy get the money to pay for an apartment in such a fancy building? It's like Johnny's his biggest client, and we both know what happened to Johnny's career."

"Rent control. Lemmy's lived here forever. His rent is ridiculously low."

"Lucky Lemmy."

There have been events in my life that when I look back on them, I wonder whatever had possessed me to plunge ahead and do what I'd done even though I knew damned well I shouldn't. From a vantage point safe in the future it's easy to identify the very instant when if I'd turned left instead of right or hung up the phone instead of punched in the number or picked blue instead of pink, the outcome would have been very much different.

As I stepped into the revolving door to Lemmy's building and placed my hand on the brass push plate, I recognized such an instant at the time it actually occurred. This was the instant of no turning back, my last chance to turn sane, change my mind, and chicken out. I paused a moment to give that a fair chance to happen. It didn't. I was too damned mad. The bra heist was on.

I pushed.

The door revolved. I whooshed into Lemmy's lobby with Dweena right behind me.

I'm no expert on art deco furniture, but it seemed to me that somebody on the decorating committee must have known their stuff. Lemmy's lobby was appointed with shiny black tables, glass-doored cabinets, and blue mirrors. Streamlined chairs and couches upholstered in plush midnight-blue velvet were half hidden by potted palms.

"*Très* elegant," whispered Dweena.

Lovely, yes, but distracting as hell. "Try not to ogle too much," I whispered. "We've got to pretend like we're accustomed to the surroundings."

Taking my own advice, I forced my attention from the decor to the general layout. It was as I remembered from my last visit. The doorman's station, a high desk, modern but in keeping with the overall deco theme, was on the left toward the back. Past the doorman, off to the side in an alcove, were the elevators, my immediate goal.

"What's wrong with that dude?" said Dweena.

"Keep your voice down," I said. "Which dude?"

"The doorman dude. The fool has got on a Mets cap."

Dweena never ceased to surprise me. "Since when are you a sports fan?"

"You don't have to be a sports fan to know that the Mets suck and the Yankees rule."

I didn't know about that. What I did know was in buildings like this the doormen did not wear baseball caps of any team as part of their uniform. Yet the man at the doorman's desk definitely had a baseball cap plunked down on top of his head. He also wore a dark blue jumpsuit with the building address embroidered above the pocket, not exactly doorman issue either.

The obvious conclusion: This man at the doorman desk was not the doorman. In my building the handyman fills in for the doorman at lunchtime. It seemed the same was true here.

This was very, very good. I hadn't realized at the time, but my idea that Johnny take Lemmy to lunch turned out to be brilliant.

Not only was the doorman apparently at lunch, but also at this time the lobby was extra active with food deliveries in addition to the usual package and mail deliveries and random comings and goings, all of which made my task a whole lot easier.

I took it as a good sign, held my head up, and with Dweena by my side boldly proceeded through the remainder of the lobby, counting the brass-rimmed black and white terrazzo tiles between me and the guy in the Mets cap.

Three tiles, two tiles, ground zero.

Feeling quite brazen, I looked right at the guy. The sight of several security monitors sunk into the desk gave me a momentary jolt, but I covered up my panic with a big old friendly grin and a hello nod like I had every right to be in the building.

The guy nodded back.

So far, so good.

An elevator had just arrived. Several people filed out, Dweena and I hurried in.

"How posh," said Dweena. "Never before in my life have I seen a furnished elevator." She sat down on the small velvet-covered daybed and crossed her legs in a ladylike gesture.

I pushed the button for twenty-one, two floors above Lemmy's. I doubted anybody was paying the slightest bit of attention to where we were headed, but after seeing the array of security monitors in the desk, I wanted to be on the safe side. No reason to get sloppy now.

The elevator deposited us on the twenty-first floor. Shell-shaped wall sconces lit our way to the staircase, but once inside, the deco decor stopped. A fire exit, it was no nonsense totally twenty-first century. Dweena and I walked down to nineteen. Very slowly I pushed open the door and peeked out.

"The coast is clear."

Beckoning Dweena to follow me, I made a right turn and led her around to Lemmy's apartment. I then backtracked and positioned myself at the corner so I could see both the elevators and Dweena.

I stood guard while she worked.

I recognized this time as yet another of those crucial turning points. I could still call the whole deal off with no consequences other than Dweena calling me a wimp.

Should I? Or not?

Yes. No. Maybe so.

My thoughts were interrupted.

"Deed's done," said Dweena.

Oh well, what the hell.

With a sweep of her hand Dweena gestured me through the open door. She followed me in, and I shut the door behind us.

"It's freezing cold in here and dark as a grave on a moonless midnight," said Dweena.

"Lemmy keeps it this way for the sake of the brassiere collection. He claims the air conditioning system is museum quality, whatever that means. The draperies are extra thick. He almost never opens them before the sun goes down."

"How boring. I was thinking maybe he'd turned into a vampire."

"Lemmy is a lot of things but not that. He eats tons of garlic."

"Yeah, I've noticed. I guess it's for the best. The thought of Lemmy as a vampire . . . well, he doesn't cut it. Vampires are suave and sexy and tall and dark. Johnny, now, he'd make a fabulous vampire. Of course, he'd have to suck his cheeks in a little and . . ."

While Dweena babbled, I felt around for a light switch. I found one to the right of the door, but when I flipped it, nothing happened.

I remembered a lamp by the couch. Inch by inch I made my way through the dark room, over spongy carpet, and two steps down into the cozy conversation pit. The lamp was by the couch. I switched it on, and the whole room lit up bright.

Dweena shrieked.

You'd have thought she'd seen a dead body. Or maybe a blood-sucking vampire.

I turned around to tell her to cool it before the neighbors called the cops. Before I could get a word out, she collapsed.

My heart stopped.

I ran over and kneeled down beside her. She thrashed around, squealing like a pig, tearing at the plush wall-to-wall carpeting with her hands.

It must be some kind of seizure, I thought, and forcibly rolled her over. I had no idea how to help, but one look at her face, and I knew she didn't need any help. She was okay, laughing her ass off.

Dweena had never seen Lemmy's groovy bachelor pad. It was, I suppose, kind of shocking the first time.

"Like it?" I asked.

"Ahhhhh! This is too much!" She pushed herself up to a sitting position. Tears streamed down her face. She wiped them away with the back of her hand.

Being technically married to Lemon B. Crenshaw, I found the hideous surroundings ever so slightly less hysterical. "I should have warned you."

"And spoiled my fun? I thought I knew bizarre, but this"—she waved her arm around, taking in the entire tableau—"this takes the cake. I was prepared for the brassiere collection, but the rest of it! I mean, the zebra skin rug is to die for. And dig that crazy fuzzy couch. You sure know how to pick 'em. What's he got in the bedroom? A round vibrating bed spinning beneath a mirrored ceiling?"

"I don't think the bed vibrates, not that I know firsthand. I've never set foot in that room. Johnny advised me against it. He said . . ."

I was talking to Dweena's back. She'd taken off and was zipping across the carpet, headed straight for Lemmy's bedroom. "Oh boy," she said, "this is one room Dweena has got to see."

Lemmy didn't deserve it, none the less I felt compelled to protect his privacy. "Please, Dweena, stay out of the bedroom."

"Why?"

"I'm on kind of a tight deadline. I'm not sure how long Johnny can keep Lemmy occupied."

"Then we'd better roll up our sleeves and get cracking. There's a lot of bras strung up on yonder wall."

Oh boy. I took in a deep breath. This would not to be easy. "Uh, Dweena, before you get all excited, it's not actually going to be 'we.' I can finish up alone."

"That's okay, I don't mind helping."

"No. I want you to leave now."

"What, you're throwing me out?"

"More or less."

"That sucks, Brenda. I can't believe you'd do this to me. I thought we were equal partners. You used me. You needed me to break in, and now when the fun part begins, you dump me."

"I'm thinking of what's best for you."

"Yeah, sure."

"I didn't want Elizabeth to come along, and I don't want you to stay. Something could go wrong. I don't want anybody else involved."

"But I already am involved."

"And this is where your involvement ends. I mean it, Dweena."

"All right. Have it your own way. But if we're not equal partners, I demand payment for services rendered."

"Fair enough. How much?"

"Not money. You think I'd take money from you? I hate to squeeze blood out of a turnip. As compensation I will choose one of Lemmy's bras for my very own."

How strange. Here I thought I'd planned thoroughly, but until that moment I hadn't considered what to do with the bras once I had them. The driving force behind the heist was to make sure that Lemmy was deprived of his precious collection—at least for a while. I suppose I halfway planned to give them back some day.

So, big deal. I'd give them back minus one. "Okay, Dweena, but only one and make it snappy."

"Yessiree, Ms. Midnight. Snappy it is." Dweena saluted.

Dweena's idea of snappy was to pace back and forth and examine each and every bra over and over again while giving me the decision process that swirled through her complex brain as a running monologue. "Too pointy, too droopy, not enough lace. Too big, too little . . ."

I tuned her out and went into the kitchen in search of a stepladder. Many of the bras were mounted out of my reach. Lemmy's too, so I figured he had to have a ladder somewhere. I found one wedged into a narrow cabinet beside the stove. I struggled to pull it out.

Dweena pranced into the kitchen, dangled a pale pink satin push-up bra in my face. "What do you think?"

"For me, a definite no, but for you, Dweena, it's probably just the thing."

"Why, thank you. We're talking serious cleavage. Of course I will be needing a new frock. My current wardrobe won't do this exquisite undergarment justice. Does the bus that goes through Central Park come all the way over here?"

"It stops on the corner."

"Good. This girl is on her way to Madison Avenue. I'm gonna shop till I drop."

"Do me a favor. On your way out, take the stairs for a couple of floors, like we did coming up."

"Will do. Catch you later."

9

I wished Dweena the best of luck on her Madison Avenue shopping spree and watched her go into the stairwell. When she was gone, I chain-locked the door behind her.

Boy, was I ever excited. I couldn't wait to get to work and rip those goddamned bras down from Lemmy's living room wall.

Or so I thought. But as I stood, hands on hips, surveying the collection and wondering where to begin, a creepy feeling snuck up on me.

The apartment was dead silent and—I hate to admit it—with Dweena gone, a little lonely. Without her constant chatter as distraction, the full impact of my actions hit with a wallop. I'd broken and entered and was now poised to take what wasn't mine, thus depriving another of what was rightfully his.

I do not believe in stealing. It is illegal and morally wrong. Except this particular case had one hell of an extenuating circumstance. Namely, the deprived was none other than Lemon B. Crenshaw, a man who deserved whatever I could dish out.

Besides that, taking the bras was utterly appropriate karmically and maybe not really so terrible because someday I probably would return the collection—that is, minus the pale pink bra I'd let Dweena take.

Enough rationalizing. Either do it or get out.

I chose to do it.

The task couldn't have been simpler. I had to hand it to Lemmy, he'd devised an excellent method to install the collection. Each specimen was lovingly suspended from flesh-toned quarter-inch silk-satin ribbon, the ribbon then being draped over tiny, almost invisible tacks in a way that no metal ever came in contact with the delicate brassiere fabric.

All I had to do was lift the ribbons off the tacks, which I did ever so gently. No matter how mad I was at Lemmy or how much I wanted to get back at him, I had no desire to desecrate a valuable historical collection.

On the highest rung of the stepladder, I stretched to reach for a see-through black strapless peekaboo bra when a noise scared the hell out of me. My first thought, which arose irrationally out of my panic, was that Johnny and Lemmy had had a fight and Lemmy had returned earlier than expected from lunch and was one second away from catching me red-handed.

I froze in place, held my breath, and waited, counting out a full minute's worth of seconds. The only sound was of my own rapid breathing.

Thinking better, I realized it couldn't have been Lemmy at the door because the chain lock would have rattled. The sound had been more like a dull thump. It seemed to emanate from a vague somewhere above. Probably somebody moving furniture. Whatever, it was not my concern. However, I took it as a warning. Get out while the getting is good.

Only a few more bras to go.

I got them down quickly and carried them to Lemmy's couch. I'd brought my red nylon laundry bag to smuggle the goods out of the building. I packed the bras inside, carefully placing the heavier padded ones at the bottom and the gossamer little nothings on top. When they were all in, I pulled the drawstring tight and slung the bag over my shoulder. The load was bulky but not heavy.

I took a final look around for incriminating evidence of my visit, then prepared to make my exit. Still cautious, I put my ear to Lemmy's door and listened for signs of life in the hallway. Except for the general building hum, all was quiet.

The peephole gave me a wide view of the hallway outside. No one lurked, so I undid the chain lock, slipped out, and silently pulled the door shut. I gave the knob a turn to confirm that the safety lock had caught. Without a key I couldn't lock the deadbolt, but I figured it would be safe enough until Lemmy got back. This was a secure building. Besides, what was the probability that the same apartment would get broken into twice in the same day?

All in all a job well done. My only regret was that I couldn't stick around to see the expression on Lemmy's face when he got home and discovered that his precious brassiere collection had up and left.

Time for caution. It was a little too soon to feel so good. I still had to get the bras past the doorman and out of the building.

I didn't take the elevator directly from Lemmy's floor. I wound my way down two flights of stairs and planned to catch it on the seventeenth floor.

On seventeen I heard voices—two women talking about the best way to paper-train a puppy.

"No need to rub his nose in it," said one.

"You sure about that?"

"Positive. Take it from me, and I have a lot of experience, a firm scolding is quite enough. You're the leader of the pack. The puppy wants to please you."

"Well, I'll give it a try. At this point I'd try anything. I'm at my wits' end."

I thought they were done, but they switched to another subject. "He chews on furniture too."

Best for me to move on. This conversation could quite possibly go on for hours.

No big deal. I'd walk down one more flight and catch the elevator on the sixteenth floor.

I proceeded slowly and as quietly as possible, so the two women wouldn't hear me. I'd got halfway to the next landing when a door clanged shut on one of the floors above.

Footsteps clattered on the metal stairs.

Damn. Somebody was coming. And fast.

I couldn't go back up to the seventeenth floor. The women were still talking. I didn't know what was happening down on sixteen, and there wasn't time to find out. I decided to tough it out and stay in the stairwell.

Act natural, I reminded myself, like you have every right to be on these stairs at this time toting a red nylon laundry bag stuffed full of collectible brassieres that don't belong to you.

And here he came, all six feet of him, thundering down, wing tips pounding, the jacket of his three-piece suit flapping in his wake. He had dark blond hair combed straight back off his longish face, thick, arched eyebrows, and deep-set eyes, blue I thought, but he moved too fast for me to tell for sure.

He sped up when he saw me. As he passed by, he smacked me in the thigh with his hard-constructed scuffed black leather briefcase. It almost seemed intentional.

"Hey! Watch it!" I said.

The guy kept right on running down the staircase. No apology, no stopping to make sure I was okay. What a rude, arrogant . . .

Yeah, I knew better, but I lost my cool anyway.

"Asshole!" I screamed. "Why don't you watch where the hell you're going?"

Right away I regretted my outburst. For a booty-carrying burglar sneaking away from the scene of her crime, trying to keep a low profile, that was a really stupid thing to do. Fortunately, the rude arrogant asshole ignored me and continued his rapid descent. Nobody else seemed to have heard me, or if they had, they didn't stick their head into the stairwell to investigate.

I remained on the stairs long enough to regain my com-

posure, then descended to sixteen and crept out into the hall.
I scurried over to the elevator, pushed the call button, and
thanked my lucky stars when the elevator came right away
with nobody in it and transported me nonstop all the way to
the lobby.

Thirty more feet across the lobby's shiny floor, and I'd be
home free.

It was a tense thirty feet.

The man in the Mets cap was no longer at the doorman's
station. In his place was a mustachioed man with salt and
pepper hair, outfitted in full doorman regalia: a dark gray
suit trimmed with red braid and a matching hat.

I assumed he was the regular doorman now back from his
lunch break. His name tag read Stanley. I wondered if tenants called him Stan and if I should do likewise.

It seemed best if I kept my mouth shut.

So far he hadn't paid a speck of attention to me. He was
busy leafing through some papers on his desk.

I shifted the laundry bag so it partially obscured my face,
took a deep breath, kept my eyes forward, and walked
on by.

Only when I got a few feet past the desk did I resume my
regular breathing. It took a lot of willpower not to turn
around to see if the doorman was watching me.

I caught myself speeding up as I neared the door and
slowed down. I didn't want to risk attracting attention.

Just a little farther.

I made it.

I was through the revolving doors and out on the street.

Quickly, I merged into the everyday crowd of people on
their way somewhere.

After rounding the corner, with a quick glance to make
sure no one was looking, I broke into an all-out run. My
goal was to get far away from Lemmy's building in the
quickest way possible. I headed to the subway station at
Seventy-ninth Street.

10

A track fire way down the line caused system-wide subway delays. The station was jammed, and I had a hell of a time maneuvering through the crowd with the big bag of delicate stolen bras. Somehow I managed to dig out my MetroCard, swipe it, and get through the turnstile unscathed, but about halfway down to the subway platform I ran smack into a tide of pissed-off people surging up the stairs, fresh off a train that had been stuck between stations.

Keeping far to the right, holding the bag high out of the way with one hand, clutching the banister with the other, I pushed and twisted my way down and squeezed onto a Number One downtown train just as the doors slammed shut.

Whew.

What a relief I felt as the train pulled out of the station, assuring me a speedy escape from the Upper West Side. Until that moment I hadn't realized how nervous I'd been.

A foghorn voice cut through the subway racket.

"Hey, Brenda! Brenda Midnight! Midnight Millinery girl!"

That could only be my friend and fellow milliner Fuzzy. No one else on the entire planet sounds quite like her. She's not quite five feet tall, but it was easy to spot her bright red plume of hair and big-brimmed hat silhouetted against a poster ad for a hemorrhoid medication at the far end of the subway car.

I pushed through the crowd.

"Hiya, Fuzzy."

"Brenda, great to see you. It's been a long time."

"Sure has. Interesting hat you've got on."

That, of course, was a huge understatement. Fuzzy's hats are the absolute essence of extreme to the max. She'd fashioned this particular model out of roofing composite. A painted yellow stripe ran midway around the wide, flat brim so it resembled a two-lane highway. On that she'd glue-gunned tiny plastic toy cars and trucks, road signs, drive-in burger joints, and several bloody multivehicle pileups complete with strewn charred doll body parts.

"Why, thank you." With one hand lightly touching the brim and the other on her hip, she preened, cheesecake style. "Hot off the old hat block. I call it American Smashup, the Wreck of My Dreams."

"It flatters you," I said, amazed that it actually did.

"Thank you. I think so too." She nodded toward my laundry bag. "Whatcha got in there, your brand-new Midnight Millinery fall collection?"

"No. I have stolen goods acquired only moments ago during a daring daylight burglary."

"Oh sure, Brenda. You don't fool me for one minute. I know exactly what you're up to—trans-neighborhood transportation of top-secret millinery prototypes. Don't sweat it. I don't even want to see your new creations."

"Damn, you caught me. I ought to know better than to try to sneak anything past you, Fuzzy. You're too astute."

"I work at it. Tell me, Brenda, what's this totally insane rumor I hear that you married Lemmy Crenshaw?"

"Where'd you hear that?" I didn't want to admit that the totally insane rumor was the totally insane truth, even though I suspected she already knew and had only asked to get me to spill the whole totally stupid story.

"Oh, you know how it is. I probably picked it up on the

millinery grapevine. Weird how once these stories get started they snowball."

"It certainly is." I had a good hunch it was Chuck Riley who'd blabbed. He and Fuzzy were friends.

"One thing for sure," she continued, "if it was me wanting to start a rumor about somebody, I'd at least make it halfway believable. You and Lemmy? That's got to be somebody's idea of a bad joke. He once tried to hit on me at a bar. What a sleaze. If you care about your reputation, you better find out who's spreading that kind of stuff around. You could sue for defamation of character."

"That's a bit extreme." If I got my hands around Chuck's skinny, freckled neck . . .

"Here's an idea. Why don't you issue an official statement of denial of matrimony? I'll put it on my web page free of charge."

"Thanks, Fuzzy, I may take you up on that."

"So, what's shaking at Midnight Millinery? You selling gobs of hats?"

"Too soon in the season to tell."

"Well, I am doing gangbusters. You know what they say: Hats are back." She winked.

I laughed. It's what they say all right. And they say it and say it and say it. At least twice a year they say it. Usually in the spring and fall articles pop up in the fashion press trumpeting that hats are back. It's become an in-joke among milliners.

The train began its slowdown on the approach to Fourteenth Street.

"This is where I get off. It was real good to see you, Fuzzy."

"Yeah. You too, Brenda. Take care."

Crime is down; subway use up. The impact of the track fire was still being felt up and down the line. In other words, half the population of New York City wanted on this downtown Number One train. I wanted off.

This called for strategy.

It was a local train, which meant the doors would open on the side of the car closest to where I already stood. I shoved my way toward the door, careful not to bump the bagful of bras. Despite my efforts, just as the train stopped and the doors opened, the bag got hung up.

I gave it a hard yank; but it held fast. I yanked again. It didn't budge.

I turned around. The bag was stuck between a pole and a leather briefcase—a very familiar leather briefcase, in fact the very same goddamned leather briefcase that had smacked me in the thigh on the stairwell at Lemmy's. I found myself face to face with the goddamned rude arrogant asshole who owned the briefcase. He'd been in the subway car the whole time, only a foot or two away from me and Fuzzy, no doubt plotting to make it hard for me to get off the train to get back at me for calling him an asshole.

"Let go, asshole!"

He did, with a smirk. The bag and briefcase disengaged from each other, and I charged through the closing doors out onto the subway platform.

From inside the train, the asshole stared at me through the grimy window. As the train pulled out of the station, I silently mouthed a couple of choice words.

I ran into Elizabeth in the hallway outside our apartments.

"That's a mighty big load of laundry for one teeny little person," she said.

"It's not laundry. In this humble red nylon bag you will find the freshly burgled Lemon B. Crenshaw brassiere collection."

"Oh."

"Is that all you've got to say? I thought you'd be thrilled that I went for revenge like you and Dweena urged."

Elizabeth frowned.

I figured she needed more explanation of my action. "You won't believe what Lemmy went and pulled." I filled

Elizabeth in on Lemmy's latest, winding up with, "After that crap, I was a thousand times madder than before, and so I stole his goddamned bras."

Elizabeth didn't say a word.

"What's the matter? I thought you'd be proud of me."

"Hmpf. Pride in your action is overshadowed by the tremendous insult I feel that you didn't include me in your caper. Did you think I was too old, that I'd get in the way?"

So that's what was bugging her. "Of course not. I was looking out for you."

"Bullshit."

"I was too. You've got a criminal record. What if you'd been along and we'd been busted?"

"You should have at least invited me along. I'm old enough to make up my own mind."

"Sorry."

"I bet your good pal Dweena got to go."

I hesitated, considered a lie, but knew I'd be caught. Sooner or later, Dweena would be bragging about the heist. "Yes," I admitted, "Dweena went with me, but only to pick the locks. As soon as we got into Lemmy's apartment, I sent her away."

"Somehow I can't picture Dweena leaving the scene of a crime in progress."

"She didn't want to, but after she picked out her bra, she got all excited about going to Madison Avenue to find a dress to fit over her new contour."

Elizabeth shook her head in disgust. "You gave Dweena a bra."

When would I ever learn to keep my mouth shut? "It seemed fair, what with her doing the locks and all."

Dead silence.

Elizabeth glared at me.

"Elizabeth, how about I give you one of Lemmy's bras?"

"I thought you'd never ask."

She followed me into the apartment.

Jackhammer ran from me to Elizabeth then over to the bag of bras and back again.

With him scrambling around my ankles, I carried the bag into the room, opened it, and emptied out the bras onto my banana-shaped couch.

"That's a hell of a lot of bras," said Elizabeth. "What are you going to do with them?"

"Don't know. I've got to stash them somewhere. They're too delicate to cram into my closet. To his credit, Lemmy took extraordinary care of his collection. Now I feel responsible."

"Why not mount them on your wall?"

"Too blatant. They're evidence."

"Well, then, how about hiding them in your dishwasher? You never use it."

"That's because I've got two cases of wine inside."

"You clever girl. I'd offer my dishwasher, but that's where I store my cactus potting soil."

The realities of living in a studio apartment. It's not all glamour.

I looked around. The only empty space was in the middle of the room. I needed that at night for the mattress.

"I've got an idea," said Elizabeth. "Think vertical. We'll suspend the bag from the ceiling. I'm sure I have an extra plant hook around somewhere."

"That's a fabulous idea, Elizabeth. You see? This is the reason I didn't want you to help with the actual mundane rip-off. I needed your clear-thinking problem-solving ability after the fact."

Elizabeth briefly went back to her apartment to get the plant hook, a ladder, and her tools. When she returned, she said, "Before I do this, I want to pick out my bra."

"But of course."

It didn't take her long at all to choose a black and red lace bra. "This will do ever so swell," she said, holding it up to her chest.

"I don't mean to offend you," I said, "but I don't believe that bra is your cup size."

"Surely you don't think I'd wear the silly thing. It's the perfect motif for my new feminist paintings."

Elizabeth was much more sure-footed than I on a ladder and quite handy with a hammer and drill, so I left the hook-mounting task to her. While she worked, I put the rest of the bras back in the bag.

"This ought to hold," she said.

She passed down the tools. I handed her the bag. She hung the tie end over the hook, gave it a couple of test pulls, then climbed down from the ladder. "A successful installation, if I say so myself."

"Very nice," I said.

The bag swung in the breeze from the air conditioner.

Jackhammer gave it the evil eye and growled.

Even though, thanks to Elizabeth, the bra storage problem had been solved without rearranging my closets and throwing away a lot of junk, I was inspired to clean out my apartment.

I tossed out some stuff, thinking all the time about my long-term plans for the bras, or, more precisely, the fact that my plans were rather vague. I'd have to give them back to Lemmy eventually. But how? Anonymously? Or would I tell him I'd taken them and hold them hostage for money and then donate the money to . . .

The phone rang.

It was Johnny. "How's the little burglar?"

"Gloating over the fact that she pulled off the job without a hitch. Thanks for keeping Lemmy occupied."

"I was a big help, then?"

"You sure were. I couldn't have done it without you."

"Then you won't be mad when I tell you."

"Tell me what?"

"It's about my lunch with Lemmy. I ordered a superior

lobster ravioli and Lemmy went positively apeshit over the meatballs and spaghetti. He said it was the best he'd ever had."

"How nice for both of you. But I don't understand. Why would the fact that you two liked your food make me mad?"

"The restaurant has beamed ceilings, lots of rough-hewn dark wood paneling, big impressive leather chairs. Manly, you know, like an exclusive men's club."

"That's great, Johnny. I'm still not mad."

"It's a power lunch spot, set up for heavy-duty deal making. The atmosphere and the wine and later the brandy are all conducive to a serious discussion of business. Know what I mean?"

Oh no. I had a glimmer of what he might be trying to say. "Get to the point, Johnny."

"It's like this, Brenda. In the end, after a lot of talk, after all was said and done, I really did sort of rehire Lemmy."

And just when I'd been thinking about me and Johnny and . . . Oh well, it didn't matter what. That was now past history. I had only one thought at the present, and it was best expressed with a firm "Good-bye, Johnny."

"Wait. You've gotta let me explain. Lemmy's got this brilliant idea how we can resurrect New York City."

I lowered the receiver slowly, then slammed it down hard.

It occurred to me that the repercussions of my marriage to Lemmy cleaned out a lot more than my apartment. I'd gotten rid of all kinds of dead weight.

11

I save up household tasks for rotten moods, when getting down on my hands and knees, plunging my hands into vile, disgusting chemicals, and exposing myself to particulate can't possibly make me feel any worse.

My mood appropriately rotten, that's how I spent the rest of the day on into the evening. I scraped and scrubbed and cleaned until all the dirt in the apartment was gone, and then I called it a day.

I flopped down on the mattress flat on my back and was trying real hard not to think about Johnny and how goddamned mad I was at him or about Lemmy and Winfield and how goddamned mad I was at them when the goddamned phone rang. Too goddamned mad to talk to anybody, I let the answering machine do its thing.

After the allotted fifteen seconds for my outgoing message, Chuck's voice rattled out of the speaker, and I remembered I should be goddamned mad at him too. He had to be the one who'd told Fuzzy I'd married Lemmy.

"Hey, Brenda, you there? Come on, pick up. I know you're home. In bed, probably, ashamed to admit you conked out at such an early hour. In the wrong hands, such information could destroy your reputation as a trend-setting designer in the city that never sleeps."

Chuck sounded excited. Then again, Chuck pretty much

always sounds excited. I rolled over and burrowed my head under the pillow.

"Okay, Brenda," he said, "be like that. I'm calling to see if you happened to catch ol' Chrome Dome on the eleven o'clock news . . ."

The only person Chuck referred to as Chrome Dome was Lemmy. Lemmy on the news? What the hell for?

As if Chuck had heard my query, he continued, "Making a complete ass of himself."

I sat up and grabbed the receiver. "This is a nightmare, right?"

Wrong.

Well, actually, sort of right. It was a nightmare, but unfortunately not the kind I could wake up from.

"It's not like I was watching the news," said Chuck, "but I had the tube on droning in the background while I tested out a MIDI input contraption I built for Urban Dog Talk. I was screwing around with some construction sound samples I'd recorded earlier when all of a sudden I hear this sound, unpleasant yet eerily familiar, and then I realize it's not something of my own device, it's coming out of the TV and it's the whiny sniveling voice of your ex-husband-to-be, Chrome Dome himself, Lemon B. Crenshaw, so naturally I hit the record button on the VCR to capture the moment, and I thought maybe—"

"Stop. I've heard enough. I'm on my way."

"Bring a pizza, okay?"

Never in a million years would it have occurred to me that my little brassiere heist would make the news. Oh sure, it was newsworthy in a cute, human-interest sort of way, but I hadn't thought it would even get reported. A few years ago Lemmy had a little problem with a couple of cops I know. It got straightened out, but to this day he still holds a grudge, and he extends that grudge to all cops.

Knowing this, I assumed Lemmy would not report the missing bras. I also assumed he'd know it was me behind the theft. And I further assumed he wouldn't want me to get in any real trouble.

Lesson learned. Never assume.

And never underestimate the treachery of a publicity-seeking estranged husband.

It seemed Lemmy had twisted my scheme around. Instead of me dishing out the mental torture, it was him.

Another hot, steamy summer night. Once again throngs of zombied-out residents stalked the hazy side streets, some seeking a breath of fresh air, some obviously up to no good, and a hell of a lot of them going for pizza.

Dodging the water dripping out of the above-door air conditioner, I made it inside my favorite pizza parlor. Despite the weather and the fact that the air conditioner was doing a lousy job, the joint was hopping, full of hungry, pizza-crazed masses.

The workers were revved up. One guy spun out the dough. Another sprinkled toppings of cheese and onion and garlic and pepperoni. Another shoveled the pies in and out of big ovens. Another sliced them into sixths when they were cooked. Way in the back, blobs of dough rose. It was an efficient operation. The line of late-night pizza eaters moved fast.

The counterman recognized me. "Small garlic to go?"

"Not this time. Medium pie. Half and half. One side triple pepperoni, the other side garlic."

"Hot date with a carnivore?"

"Hardly."

"Fifteen minutes."

Jackhammer clamored to get out of his canvas bag, so I took him outside to wait. Midway down the block I found a comfortable stoop with a good view. I sat and watched the frightening interaction of pedestrians and bicycles and cars and trucks and buses, all mixing it up together, cursing and honking, but miraculously not at the moment slamming into one another.

As I waited, my imagination took off, running hog-wild, obsessed, one crazy out-of-control thought after the other. I envisioned myself serving hard time for the bra heist.

How long did first-time offenders get sent up for? Would the prison have a vegetarian option on the menu? Was it really up the river? If so, which river? East? Hudson? Mississippi? What if I didn't get along with my cellmate? Or, in a system crowded with hard-core offenders, would it be cellmates?

And what about Jackhammer? Elizabeth would be more than happy to take care of him, that was no problem, but I'd sure miss the little guy. I simply could not imagine life without him. I scratched the special spot between his ears. He licked my face, then jumped out of my lap and scrambled down the stairs, straining against his leash.

Oh, right. Reality. The pizza.

It waited for me on the counter top.

I paid the man and left.

On the cab ride to the East Village a halfway comforting notion managed to sneak its way into my fast and furious paranoid thoughts. I'd been so anxious to see the tape of Lemmy, I hadn't even asked Chuck what the news story had been about.

Maybe it had nothing to do with Lemmy's bra collection or the fact that it was missing. If it had been a slow news day, Lemmy could have been on for just about anything. It was possible that Lemmy had not yet returned home. He might not even know his bras had been stolen. He could have gone straight from lunch with Johnny to some random newsworthy event, a client's opening, perhaps. Yeah, I liked that. It would be like Lemmy to hog the camera. Maybe Blanner Doosen's new movie had premiered this evening. Or that sexy lounge singer, I couldn't remember her name, she might have had a performance. It could even have been one of those man-on-the-street interviews, a newsperson soliciting Lemmy's opinion on the upcoming mayoral election, and no doubt sorry to have asked.

There were a million reasons Lemmy might have been on the news that in no way involved his bra collection—or me. I'd find out soon enough.

"Welcome," said Chuck. He grabbed the pizza box and cracked it open. "Mmmmm mmm. Love the smell of red sauce and pepperoni."

Jackhammer squiggled in his canvas bag. He liked pepperoni too. Living with a vegetarian, he rarely got any kind of meat. I let him out of the bag. He bounced alongside Chuck over the thick carpet of cables and wires and stuff that crisscrossed Chuck's floor, connecting twenty or so computers to each other and to weird input and output devices and god knows what else.

Chuck put the pizza box on top of a stack of magazines on a table just out of Jackhammer's reach. "Don't worry, Squirt, your good buddy Chuck is gonna sneak you several greasy disks of pepperoni later, when Brenda's not looking."

He crossed the room and stood before a large, bulky object. Its function was not readily apparent; however from previous visits, I knew it to be his refrigerator. Chuck had encrusted every square inch of the entire surface with thousands of outmoded memory chips. He opened the door with his foot. "Orange soda? Beer?" He popped the top on a can of beer for himself.

"No thanks."

"Coffee? It's a fresh pot."

"Coffee would be good."

While Chuck scrounged around for paper plates and rinsed out a coffee mug, I sank down into one of his two matching red beanbag chairs. It squooshed up around me with a deep sigh.

"Chuck, what's this news story about?"

"Didn't I tell you?"

"No. Is it about Lemmy's stupid bra collection?"

I still clung desperately to a tiny glimmer of hope that Lemmy's appearance on the news had nothing to do with how I spent my afternoon.

Chuck handed me a steaming mug of coffee. "Yeah, it has to do with his bras."

My heart sank.

"But mostly," Chuck continued, "it's about murder."

Murder?

Chuck aimed a remote control at his wall-mounted TV. "Wait'll you get a load of Chrome Dome."

12

And there he was, goddamned Lemmy, the man who was still technically my husband. On scene. On screen. Preening. Hamming it up in living color, the totally obnoxious, full-tilt version.

A raven-haired newswoman in a no-nonsense navy blue pin-striped business suit stuck a microphone in his face. They were standing on the sidewalk in front of his building. In the background a gaggle of neighborhood kids mugged for the camera and a conservatively dressed man, probably a resident, darted into the revolving door.

Lemmy snuggled up close to the newswoman, draped an arm over her shoulders, and leaned into the microphone. "Yes, Pammy," he said with a solemn nod of his shiny shaved head, "I've suffered a loss of tremendous magnitude."

Pammy wrenched herself away from Lemmy and turned on a practiced-in-the-mirror serious expression to convey her deep and sincere sympathy.

"Gone," Lemmy boomed dramatically. "All gone. My world-renowned brassiere collection, which has taken me the better part of two decades to amass. Now ripped down from my walls. My priceless, irreplaceable bras."

He sniffled, wiped a fake tear away with a stubby finger, and then continued, all of a sudden sounding slightly less distraught and more businesslike. "And if that wasn't enough, the dastardly thief got my jewels too. Seven hundred and fifty thousand dollars' worth."

Jewels?

Chuck hit the pause button, looked at me, and raised his eyebrows. "Since when does Chrome Dome have three-quarters of a million dollars' worth of jewels?"

I shrugged.

Chuck restarted the tape.

Lemmy was laying it on thick. "And yet it could have been much worse. I owe my very life to my client, the wonderfully talented, fine actor Johnny Verlane. Had I not taken Johnny to lunch to talk over the latest offers pouring in from Hollywood—sorry, folks, I'm not at liberty to reveal the details, it's all very hush-hush—I would have been home at the very moment the killer was ravaging my apartment. I might have met the same brutal end as Adison Montgomery Shelton, my very close friend and neighbor. I shudder to think."

Adison Montgomery Shelton. Murdered. Holy flipping cow. No wonder the story made the news. The bra heist was a small footnote to the much larger story. Shelton was a very prominent citizen, a philanthropist. A long time ago I'd worked as a temp at a nonprofit organization largely funded by his donations.

While I struggled to absorb what all this meant, the camera cut away from Lemmy and dissolved into a montage of clips that showed Shelton making his entrance at various gala charity events while a voice-over told of his many good deeds. The camera loved Shelton's photogenic mane of prematurely silver hair, tanned, taut, nipped and tucked face, and the glamorous models he escorted.

Adison Montgomery Shelton was quite the man around town. He came from gobs and gobs of old money and had never worked a day in his privileged life. Yet he was generous. As I remembered, everyone at the nonprofit adored him. In my short time there, I never met him.

A quick cut back to Pammy. "And there you have it," she said. "Murder on the Upper West Side."

·

Chuck doused the TV.

"What do you think?" asked Chuck.

"On a grand scale I have no idea," I said, mostly to stall. I was busy trying to decide whether to tell Chuck that I took the bras. Of course Elizabeth might already have spilled the beans. "As pertains to Lemmy, he came off . . . well, like Lemmy. I can't believe that newswoman let him prattle on for so long about himself."

"Well," said Chuck, "from the pained expression on her face, I don't think that was the original plan. The technicians might have had trouble feeding the archival stuff about Shelton, and Lemmy just kept going, grabbing the free publicity."

"He's probably still going, too wrapped up in himself to notice the camera crew has gone and he's no longer on the air."

"Odd that I never knew Adison Shelton lived in Lemmy's building. You'd think Lemmy would have mentioned it, the way he's always dropping names of the rich and powerful."

"I knew it. Shelton lived directly above Lemmy, in a much larger apartment of course. He combined several smaller units. You're right, though. For some reason Lemmy didn't talk about it. It was Johnny who told me."

"And what's this bit about jewels? The only jewels I've ever seen anywhere near Lemmy is that dopey sapphire ring he wears on his stubby pinky."

We pondered the jewel question. It took all of about one nanosecond before we both reached the same blatantly obvious conclusion.

"You thinking what I'm thinking?" I asked.

Chuck nodded. "Insurance scam."

"Right. My husband, Lemon B. Crenshaw, is taking advantage of a tragic situation, milking it for all he can get."

"Nice to see 'ol Chrome Dome is keeping in character. I bet he made up the part about his bras getting ripped off too."

"Why do you say that?"

"Those bras are weird items to steal. They've no provable value and would be hard to fence."

Apparently Chuck didn't already know. I figured I might as well level with him. "Actually," I said, "Lemmy didn't lie about the bras. Somebody stole them."

"How would you . . . oh. I get it. You did it, right? You took those bras."

"I was out for revenge." I told Chuck about Lemmy's inheritance and Winfield's role. "He called me an unnecessary complication."

"Hey, you don't have to defend your actions with me. I think it's great what you did. And that's really funny about Winfield's pen."

"Yeah, well, looking back now, I should have quit while I was ahead, but I was so mad, I had to go after those bras."

"How'd you do it?"

"Easy. Johnny got rid of Lemmy, and Dweena got me into the apartment. I never intended for it to make the news. I wanted to keep it between me and Lemmy."

Chuck shook his head. "Smooth move, Brenda. Talk about rotten timing. You had to pick the very same day somebody got whacked in the building."

"Right, the same damned day."

I repeated that phrase several times to myself. The significance sank in, and my brain lit up. It had taken amazingly long. I'd been too crippled by anger, then stunned by Lemmy's TV appearance to think straight. My brain was running a little behind, but it finally put two and two together and came to an awful conclusion. "It's worse than the same day," I said. "I'm almost positive Shelton was killed while I was at Lemmy's."

"How do you know? Even the cops won't know the time of death or how he died until the medical examiner has had a go at the stiff."

"I don't need the official word. I heard this noise while I was at Lemmy's, sort of a thump. At the time I was scared

Lemmy had come home, but it had to be Shelton getting killed and dropping to the floor above."

"That sound could have been anything. Buildings are full of thumps and bumps."

Bumps. I jumped straight up off the beanbag and shrieked, "The guy! He's the killer!"

"What guy?"

"This asshole. In the stairwell. Very soon after I heard the thump, I left Lemmy's. I took the stairs, and this guy was running down so fast he slammed into me and I called him an asshole and he had to be the killer leaving the scene of the crime and—"

"That's great, Brenda. If this guy's really the killer—"

"No. Not great. Not at all."

I could actually feel the color drain out of my face. I must have looked terrible. Even Chuck, who usually didn't notice such things, commented.

"My god, Brenda, what's wrong with you?"

"The guy, the rude, arrogant asshole, the killer, he knows who I am. And he knows I saw him leaving the scene of the crime." Talking a mile a minute and probably not making much sense, I eventually succeeded in communicating to Chuck that soon after the stairway encounter I'd run into the guy on the subway and that Fuzzy had yelled my name and Midnight Millinery and I was truly in danger.

As I raved, Chuck's expression grew more and more serious. When I finished, he got up and got himself another beer. "So what are you gonna do?"

"I've got to go see Turner and McKinley."

"You know, Brenda, I never thought I'd say it, but in this situation, a visit to your local precinct detectives might not be such a bad idea."

I threw myself back down in the beanbag and buried my face in my hands. I deserved this mess. It was payback for my attempt at revenge.

Chuck tried to make me feel better. "You never know.

Turner and McKinley might be in a good mood. Even if
they're not, they have to take care of you. They owe you big,
after the way you saved their butts."

I waved my hand in the air to stop him. "Please, don't
remind me."

It was impossible to guess how the two detectives might
react. On the one hand, Chuck was right, they owed me. On
the other hand, they were totally unpredictable. That
Lemmy was involved further complicated the situation. The
very mention of his name was enough to piss off Turner and
McKinley something fierce.

I considered my other options. It didn't take long. There
were none.

And so, resigned to my fate, I called the precinct and
learned that neither detective was on duty that night but they
were both expected bright and early the next morning, which
meant I crashed in Chuck's beanbag chair with Jackhammer
sprawled out on my chest, because I was too scared to go
home, where I'd be a sitting duck for a murderous asshole.

Sometime in the middle of the night I woke up with an idea.
I knew what the killer looked like. I could draw. I'd make a
mug shot to help win over Turner and McKinley.

Except for the tiny lights from all the electronic equipment, it was pitch black in Chuck's boarded-up storefront
apartment. I called out his name, but he didn't answer. I
groped my way into his bedroom.

He wasn't in his bedroll.

I called his name again, this time louder. No answer. I
was already ill at ease, so it didn't take much to scare me. I
screamed at the top of my lungs, "Goddammit, Chuck,
where the hell are you?"

A muffled voice from somewhere: "Nineteen sixty-six or
thereabouts."

That made absolutely no sense. But I was so happy to
hear his voice, it didn't matter.

"Chuck?"

"I'm over here, in my time machine."

"I told you all about it," said Chuck, "at your wedding brunch."

"Sorry. Guess I didn't pay a whole lot of attention."

"You were drunk as a skunk."

"Wrong. I was sick as a dog."

"Whatever." He gestured toward a dull metal person-sized tube that looked an awful lot like a sewer pipe tipped up on end. "So this is it."

"A time machine?"

"Uh-huh. I don't have all the bugs worked out yet."

"When you said nineteen sixty-six—"

"I'm aiming for that decade. My plan is very simple. I'm sure you know how I feel about Elizabeth."

I nodded.

"And you know how she feels about being old enough to be my mother. My goal is to go back in time so I can meet her when we're almost the same age."

"I thought that kind of stuff was against the rules."

"What rules?"

"The rules against changing history."

"No such rules exist. Even if they did, I'd be quite willing to break them."

I've known Chuck Riley a long time. This was yet another of his many weird phases. Harmless, I hoped. "I wish you luck."

"Thanks. I'll need it. Damn tricky work this time travel stuff."

"As long as you're stuck in the here and now, I need your help."

"Sure. What can I do for you?"

"Fire up your best graphics computer. I've got a mug shot to produce."

"Hey, that's a great idea."

I made a detailed pencil sketch of the guy on the staircase.

Chuck scanned my drawing into the computer and opened it in his favorite paint program. "This is a killer application."

"Very funny, Chuck."

Chuck manned the mouse. I art-directed a bunch of tweaks of the guy's features and made the overall shape of his face a little longer. When an idea didn't work, Chuck made it go away.

After a lot of pixel pushing, a slight narrowing of the nose made a huge difference. "That's good," I said. "Now, if you could just arch his bushy eyebrows higher and scoot them a bit closer together."

"Piece of cake," said Chuck.

A few seconds later it all came together.

"That's him," I said. "The asshole on the staircase. The killer of Adison Montgomery Shelton. Print it out."

"You hungry?" asked Chuck.

"Starved."

He ripped open a jumbo-sized bag of generic bright orange barbecue potato chips, made a fresh pot of coffee, and proclaimed it breakfast.

"Got anything suitable for Jackhammer?" I asked.

"Leftover pizza crust."

Jackhammer was thrilled.

13

Early in the morning the heat hadn't yet settled over the city. The air was actually somewhat refreshing. I figured the walk from Chuck's to the precinct would wake me up and shake out a crick in my neck, a nasty reminder that I'd spent most of the night corkscrewed in a beanbag chair.

The East Village streets were coming to life as Jackhammer and I passed through. Merchants clattered open graffiti-covered gates. An occasional junkie lurked. Packs of new media workers rushed to the subway. The homeless moved along.

Not until I crossed crazy, gridlocked, honking Broadway did I become alert enough to realize that strutting boldly through the streets might not be such a great idea for somebody who was hiding from a killer who knew who she was and what she knew and might want to eliminate her before she ratted on him, which she was on her way to do.

Screw the fresh air. I sprung for a cab.

Most of the uniformed cops hanging out in the lobby of the precinct had seen me before. None of them bothered to ask my business. I trooped straight through to the back and up the stairs to Turner and McKinley's floor.

I paused outside the grim cubicle the two detectives shared to gather my thoughts.

Before I finished, Turner spotted me.

"Hey, there, whoa-ho, if it isn't Ms. Midnight! And you've got that cute little Jackhammer with you too. So good to see you both so bright and early on this beautiful a.m." He had a gigantic smile on his face.

Strange. True, the man was unpredictable. Still, that was not the kind of greeting I would ever expect from Detective Spencer Turner. I was thrilled to find him in such a jolly mood.

I unsnapped Jackhammer's leash and bent over to put him down on the linoleum tile floor. He immediately trotted off to go sniffing under the desks, probably seeking out doughnut crumbs. When I straightened up, I saw that Turner still had the big smile on his face.

Keeping the smile in place, he removed his well-shod feet from his desk and stood up. He took two strides over and slapped me on the back real friendly-like. I backed off when he made a move to pinch my cheek. I mean, enough already.

Detective McKinley's behavior was more typical. He was leaning up against the cubicle wall, arms folded, frowning.

Turner said to McKinley, "See? I told you so." He sounded more like a kid in grade school than a police detective.

McKinley scowled and mumbled a gruff "Goddamn."

"All right," said Turner to McKinley, "hand it over."

As if it caused him great pain, McKinley very slowly reached into the inside pocket of his custom-made, expertly-cut, fine dark gray summer-weight wool suit and plucked a crisp twenty-dollar bill from a silver money clip. He held the twenty between his forefinger and middle finger and waved it around in the air.

After a couple of failed grabs Turner snatched the bill and shoved it into his pants pocket.

As this little drama unfolded, I began to catch on as to what was happening. Even big city police detectives watch the eleven o'clock news. Obviously Turner and McKinley already knew about Lemmy's peripheral involvement in Shelton's murder. Man, oh, man, did these two piss me off. They were as bad as Lemmy and Johnny.

"Don't think I'm not on to you," I said. "I know what the deal is."

"Why, whatever are you talking about, Ms. Midnight?" said Turner, cranking up the sarcasm.

"You two made a bet on whether I'd be involved in that murder, just because Lemmy—"

Turner shook his head. "On that, Ms. Midnight, you're one hundred percent wrong. My partner and I did make a friendly little wager, but not as to *whether* you'd be involved. We bet on *how soon* you'd show up at our humble precinct with yet another one of your cockamamie stories. My esteemed partner did not recall that you are an early riser. He put his money on a post-noon appearance of our favorite neighborhood milliner. I, on the other hand, remembered."

Was I really so predictable? First Johnny and Lemmy bet on me, now Turner and McKinley. Furious, I wasn't about to stand for this crap. With Jackhammer following close on my heels, I stomped out of the cubicle and stormed into the stairwell.

Yeah, right, the stairwell, which of course reminded me of the purpose of my visit. Not only did I plan to give the detectives the mug shot I'd drawn, more importantly I wanted to get some protection for myself until the killer was behind bars.

I had to go back.

And so I swallowed my pride and returned to the detectives' cubicle, stuck my head in, and said—actually I had to shout to be heard over their roaring laughter, "Excuse me, Detectives."

"Oh, it's you, Ms. Midnight. Back so soon?" Again the full force of Turner's sarcasm.

"If you could possibly bring yourselves to stop it with the

hee-haws, you might be interested in what I have to say."

"Yeah? What's that?" said McKinley.

"I know who killed Adison Montgomery Shelton."

In unison, the two detectives rolled their eyes toward the acoustic ceiling tiles. At least they quit laughing.

"I mean it," I said. "I saw the killer leaving the scene of the crime."

"She sounds serious," said Turner.

McKinley nodded. "She does at that. Please have a seat, Ms. Midnight. Go ahead and blab away." He gestured toward their notorious ugly green squeaky folding chair, the hot seat, an effective squirm monitor, which they frequently enlist as a personal low-tech off-the-record lie detector.

I hated that chair but sat down to appease the detectives. The slats dug into my spine. I shifted my weight. The chair squeaked.

"Speak freely," said Turner. He was giving me enough rope to hang myself.

I gave them an abbreviated version of the events of yesterday afternoon.

"To sum up," said Turner when I finished, "you claim you were in Crenshaw's apartment at the time of the murder."

"Yes."

"And furthermore, that you, scooping the highly trained experts at the medical examiner's office whose sole job it is to determine time of death, have decided it's gotta be the exact same time you heard a noise from the apartment above that belongs to the deceased, Adison Montgomery Shelton."

"Yes. I heard a thump. From above."

"And on your way out of the building, you took the stairs instead of the elevator, and an alleged rude arrogant asshole in an alleged big hurry plowed into you."

"That's right. He rammed my thigh with the corner of his briefcase and didn't stop to apologize."

"My, my," said Turner shaking his head.

This wasn't going so well. Time to bring out the heavy artillery. I reached into my purse for the printout. "This is what the killer looks like." Surely they'd be impressed.

McKinley took the printout, gave it a quick once-over. "What's this supposed to be?"

"It's a mug shot of the killer. I drew it. My friend Chuck Riley—you remember him, don't you?—he helped. We tweaked my original drawing on his computer until it came out right."

Turner let out a big sigh. "So now you've added composite artist to your long list of abilities."

"I can draw."

"So could Picasso. Yet it never would have occurred to me to turn to him to solve a murder."

"I went to art school. I have an excellent visual memory. I'm telling you, this picture looks just like the guy."

McKinley paced back and forth in front of me. "Okay, for now, we'll give you that. What makes you think this man is the killer? The fact that he's rude? This isn't Cupcake, USA, you know. It's New York freaking City. We thrive on rude."

"That's a cliché," I said.

"So it is, so it is," agreed Turner. "Yet another cliché is the ridiculous idea that civilians solve murders."

"It happens."

"Rarely. And certainly not based on a thump and a jab in the thigh by a briefcase."

"It makes perfect sense to me. If you'd been there, you'd understand."

"How old is Crenshaw's building?" asked McKinley.

"It was built in the thirties, I think."

"Then we can agree it is old."

"Yes."

"Old buildings generate a plethora of strange noises," said Turner.

"Some noises *so* weird," added McKinley, "they might deceive an intelligent, well-meaning civilian, like, say, a

milliner with a very vivid, overactive imagination, into
thinking she's hearing somebody getting murdered."

"I didn't think that at the time. I didn't think that until I
found out that someone did get murdered in that apartment
sometime that day."

"What about Crenshaw? Did he comment on the sound or
did he think it was something else, like maybe water knocking in a pipe?" asked Turner.

I'd feared it would come down to this. I also knew better
than to lie. If they didn't already know, they'd find out soon
enough that Lemmy was at lunch with Johnny most of yesterday afternoon. "Well, no," I said, trying to appear so
casual that maybe the fact would slip right on by them.
"You see, Lemmy wasn't actually home at the time."

"So you were alone in Crenshaw's apartment?"

"Yes."

"What the hell for, Ms. Midnight?" said McKinley.
"Were you perhaps watering the plants?"

I shifted my weight in the chair.

"Go on, Ms. Midnight."

I waited two beats. A couple of more, then went for
broke. I revealed all. "No. I was taking Lemmy's brassiere
collection off his living room wall."

It took quite some time to explain. Amazingly enough,
neither detective knew Lemmy had a brassiere collection.
They hadn't even heard that Lemmy and I were married. I
had an awful lot of territory to cover.

The telling, along with the strain of editing out Dweena's
part in the bra heist, left me totally pooped. I slumped back
in the chair. It squeaked again.

"Is that all?" asked Turner.

"Yes."

Turner raised his eyebrows at McKinley, who raised his
and cocked his head toward the door. Together they exited
the cubicle.

"Stay put, Ms. Midnight."

I wasn't about to leave. I still wanted that protective custody. During the seemingly interminable questioning Jack-hammer had curled up under Turner's desk to take a snooze. He roused himself with a mighty shake and bounced over to me. To kill time I wadded up a piece of paper, and we played fetch.

Turner and McKinley came back with good news.

"We've concluded," said Turner, "that since at the time of the brassiere burglary you were married to Crenshaw, with a little bit of luck and a good attorney and two helpful police detectives who might put in a few words where they'll do the most good, the entire sorry affair will go down as a domestic dispute."

The detectives had come through for me. It pays to have friends in the right places.

"One more question," said McKinley. "Last night on the news I believe Crenshaw also said something about stolen jewels."

"Oh yeah," said Turner. "Now that you mention it, I remember that too. You didn't take any jewels, did you, Ms. Midnight?"

"Uh, no."

"How do you explain the missing jewels?"

I shrugged.

"Insurance scam, huh?"

Another shrug.

Miraculously, the detectives backed off that subject, no doubt saving it for a rainy day.

I brought up another subject. "Will you fax the mug shot to the proper precinct?"

"It's not standard procedure," said Turner, "but I suppose it won't do any harm. McKinley, take care of that, will you?"

McKinley's eyes lit up. He squirted a hit of breath spray into his mouth, picked up the drawing, and left the cubicle, a definite spring in his step.

"What's with him?" I asked.

"He's got it bad for a new officer," explained Turner. "Just so happens her desk is located a couple of inches away from the department fax machine."

"Speaking of romance," I said, "how's Gundermutter?"

Nicole Gundermutter was Turner's main squeeze, a former cop who gave up the force to open a motorcycle repair shop. Through a bizarre chain of events she'd become a friend of mine.

"Former Officer is fine."

"Do you call her Former Officer to her face?"

"Absolutely. She loves terms of endearment."

McKinley strode into the cubicle, smiling from ear to ear. "Mission accomplished." He handed me back the mug shot.

"That's it, then," said Turner. "You're free to go, Ms. Midnight."

Now, wait just a minute. Something was very wrong with this picture. "You're kidding, right?"

"Not at all. Much as we enjoy your company and Jackhammer's too, as public servants we have a shitload of paperwork to get done."

"I can't just up and go," I protested.

"Why not? Leg cramp?"

"I thought until this blows over you'd put me in protective custody."

"What do you need protecting from?"

"From the killer! Didn't you hear what I told you? He knows that I know he did it, and thanks to my friend Fuzzy, he knows who I am. Remember?"

Turner looked at me like I was nuts. "I'm afraid your experience doesn't justify protective custody."

"You can't mean that."

"Afraid I do, Ms. Midnight. A direct threat by a known violent criminal would help us out. I fear somebody who most likely didn't kill anybody possibly overhearing somebody else's name shouted over the din of the subway is not gonna cut it."

"He's right," said McKinley. "But if you like, since we're sort of friends and because you came forward on your own with information you perceived as important in a murder investigation, Detective Turner and I will be more than happy to escort you to your apartment building."

14

It was a half-assed offer, the detectives knew it and I knew it, but it was plainly the only offer I'd be getting, so I went for it, which seemed to surprise the hell out of Turner and McKinley, who didn't seem to be taking my concerns very seriously.

I hate when people do that. And they frequently do. It must be my goddamned upbeat attitude. My stiff upper lip. Fools them every time.

Don't they know it's all a front?

Did they really expect me to venture out onto the mean streets of Greenwich Village perhaps to walk straight into the arms of a killer?

Apparently.

The detectives certainly expected me to walk two blocks to where they'd parked their unmarked cop car. For chrissakes, that was halfway home already. I might as well walk the whole way with five-pound Jackhammer my sole protection.

I hung back, reluctant to leave the safety of the precinct. I liked it there. The place was lousy with good guys packing heat.

"We don't have all day," said Turner. He held the door open for me. "Let's move it along."

"No way," I said. "Too much exposure. The way I see it, the killer already knows my name and where I live and work. He might be smart enough to figure that if I were gonna rat on him, this is the place I'd do it, my local precinct, where I might possibly know somebody. Besides, I wouldn't want to deprive you of this golden opportunity to serve and protect and to use the private drive-through."

Turner cleared his throat and seemed poised to make a sarcastic comment.

McKinley shushed him with a look that I interpreted as "Humor the milliner who once saved your ass."

With a shake of his head and a disgusted "harumph," Turner strode over to the main door and shoved it open. "Wait here. I'll bring the unit around."

"Glad you finally see it my way, Detective." I knew he didn't, but it seemed the right thing to say.

A side door opened from the precinct lobby onto the drive-through. McKinley and I waited inside. To keep from having to make small talk, I conducted a one-way discussion with Jackhammer about how the nice handsome strong tall brave well-dressed policemen were our friends.

To avoid interfacing with a civilian, McKinley puckered up his lips and whistled—a familiar melody, a Broadway show tune maybe. I couldn't quite place it.

Jackhammer, sick of my babbling, wiggled. He probably had to pee, but I didn't dare put him down in the precinct lobby. Fortunately he was paper-trained. Once we got home he could make do with that until I arranged for Elizabeth to take him out. I had definite plans to stay inside until somebody assured me the killer was off the street.

I was beginning to realize the repercussions of that. No work; no play. In fact, not a whole hell of a lot of anything. It was a terrible situation I'd got myself into, and all because I hadn't been able to contain my anger at Lemmy.

Turner pulled the unmarked but blatantly obvious dark blue police vehicle into the drive-through and blasted the horn.

McKinley went out first. With a flourish he gallantly

opened the back door for me. I scurried in and sank down low in the seat and put Jackhammer on my lap.

I know it sounds silly, but during the ride home I covered my face with my hands, so if anybody—most especially the killer—saw and recognized the car for what it was, they'd think I was an apprehended perp getting carted off to parts unknown of the criminal justice system.

Because of how the one-way streets run it would have been natural for Turner to drop me off at the corner. By now he must have appreciated my fear, because he took the time to loop around the block so he could pull up directly in front of my building.

"I appreciate this," I said.

"You take care now, Ms. Midnight," he said.

McKinley came around and opened my door.

I started to get out, then waited a beat for the detectives to say what they had to say, but they kept mum. I couldn't believe they'd missed their cue. "So . . ." I said, lingering.

"So what?" grumbled Turner.

"Well, aren't you going to say it?"

"Say what?"

"You know. What you always say."

"Oh, that," said Turner. "Under the circumstances, I didn't think it necessary, but if you insist, I will do the right thing, stick to the rule book, and admonish you to keep out of this, Ms. Midnight. Be a good little milliner and go make some pretty hats. Leave the police work to the police."

Turner was right. I didn't need to be reminded, but it felt good anyway, comforting simply because it was so normal.

I replied in the normal way. "I wouldn't dream of interfering in a police investigation." Only this time I meant it.

McKinley escorted me to the door of my building.

"Thank you, Detective."

"S'all right."

Ralph, my doorman, wrinkled his brow in concern. "You okay?"

"Yeah. Sure," I lied. "Why do you ask?"

"Well, I don't mean to be nosy, but that car you rode up in sure looked like a cop car to me, and if that man who walked you to the door isn't a cop, I don't know who is. And forgive me for saying, but Brenda, you don't look so hot."

Having caught my reflection in a pane of glass in the front door, I knew he spoke the truth.

"You're damned sharp, Ralph. Very perceptive. I didn't want anyone to know, but since you noticed, I may as well be straight with you. You see, I've been having a bit of a problem."

"I knew it. What's wrong?"

"Some crazy guy has been harassing me, and so for the next few days the cops want me to lie low. I'd appreciate it if you wouldn't send anybody up. Buzz me first."

Ralph's usual practice was to send up any visitor he was familiar with without checking first with me. He'd buzz my intercom and announce after the fact that whoever was on the way up. This had been fine in the past. Now I wanted extra protection.

"Not even Johnny Verlane?" asked Ralph.

"That's right, not even Johnny."

He shrugged. "Whatever you say."

I thought it would feel great to be home, but I was wrong. At Chuck's and then later at the precinct, I was scared because intellectually I knew I should be. Now, supposedly safely holed up in my apartment, with the dead bolt in place and the chain lock fastened, for the first time I felt primal fear deep in my churning gut.

I quickly surveyed the apartment with fortification in mind. I checked all points of egress and ingress, although I was too scared to remember the difference, not that it mattered. Like most New York apartments, mine had one door leading in, and that same door led out. I also had two windows in the room and one in the kitchen. They were already locked, but the latches were a joke. I dug out some wooden canvas stretchers from the back of the closet, broke them off to the proper length, and crammed them between the top of the bottom window and the window frame.

And then I sat down cross-legged in the middle of the floor and contemplated the nature of fear.

Killers of men like Adison Montgomery Shelton did not get away with it for long. Whether or not the mug shot I'd drawn helped, the cops would nab the killer fast.

But until they got him, I was stuck home.

With a dog full of pee who didn't seem too pleased with the newspapers I'd spread out on the kitchen floor.

I called Elizabeth.

"What's up?" she asked.

"I need your help. Would you take Jackhammer out for me?"

"Love to. What's wrong? You didn't get that summer flu, I hope."

"I'm healthy but immobilized by fear."

She demanded details.

In the 1960s, that decade Chuck wanted to return to, Elizabeth got burned by the media. Ever since, she's boycotted all radio, television, newspapers, and magazines. Chuck reconfigured her Internet service provider's welcome page so she can avoid the headlines of breaking news stories. All of which is to say she hadn't heard about Shelton's murder until I told her.

"I knew it," she said when I'd finished. "If you'd taken me with you to snatch Lemmy's bras, none of this would have happened."

"I don't see the logic. The murder still would have happened, and I'd have had the added pressure of keeping your name out of it too."

"You've got to look at the big picture in a small way."

"You sound as abstract as Chuck."

"That may be so, but it's a fact that everything, and I do mean every teeny little thing, impacts every other teeny little thing. It's like if you'd dragged my molecules along with you and Dweena, the entire atomic structure of the universe would be different. Some stuff that happened wouldn't have. Some stuff that didn't happen would have, and you wouldn't have been on that staircase at the same time as the killer."

"Elizabeth Franklin Perry, if I didn't know better, I'd swear you'd been smoking dope." Or cruising in Chuck's time machine.

"Nope. Never did, never will. Deep-breathing exercises."

"I think you need some fresh air."

"You might be right. I'll be over in a sec for Jackhammer."

While Elizabeth and Jackhammer were out, I called my friend Pete. He owns Pete's Café, which is in the building next door to Midnight Millinery. Against the building code and without the knowledge of either of our landlords, we had knocked a hole in the wall and share a basement space.

"Pete, can you do me a favor?"

"Name it."

"I'm gonna be indisposed for a couple of days and I'd rather nobody knew."

"Not that summer flu, is it?"

"Very mild case. It would help me out a lot if you could stick a sign on Midnight Millinery's door. Say I'm in Paris on a buying trip—no, make it a selling trip, that sounds better."

"It's always good to put a positive spin on things."

"So you'll do it?"

"Good as done."

"You're a sweetheart, Pete. Any problems at the shop, customers lurking around, give me a call, but leave a message. I'll be monitoring."

"I'll keep my eye out. Feel better."

"Thanks."

*   *   *

If you've got to hide out, New York City is a great place to do it. With a phone call and a credit card, you can get the world delivered to your door within an hour. I'm not talking pizza and Chinese food or groceries. I mean seven-course meals from the very finest dining establishments, served with a flair by tuxedo-clad messengers.

Want a massage? Any kind imaginable and a few you probably can't imagine. Manicure. Pedicure. Video to go. A personal trainer to oversee pushups. Clothes, books, wine, kibbles for Jackhammer, bottled water.

But I didn't want any of that stuff. What I really wanted was a quickie divorce.

Brewster Winfield's answering machine picked up.

"Winfield, it's me, Brenda."

The lawyer got on the line. At least I think it was him. He didn't utter a word, just breathed hard into the phone. It was to be expected. The last time I'd seen him had been the lucky pen episode. Which reminded me, that messenger hadn't called yet. I'd have to follow up on that.

"Come on, Brew. You're a professional. Act like one."

More breathing.

"We have to talk."

Three quick bursts of breath, then at last he spoke. His normally well-modulated, deep, mellow voice had a high-stress, spiky edge. "I don't want to talk to you. I'm terribly distraught. That fountain pen meant a great deal to me."

"So terribly sorry for your loss," I said, hoping my insincerity was evident.

"Speaking of loss," he said, "my client's priceless bra collection has been stolen. I don't suppose you'd happen to know about that."

"Me? No. Only what I saw on the news. Lemmy came off pretty good, don't you think?"

"Would you mind telling me where you were early yesterday afternoon?"

"I was at the shop. Making hats."

"Hmmm, I wonder. That could easily be checked out."

"I get the feeling you're accusing me of taking Lemmy's bras."

"I didn't say that."

"Really. 'Cause it kinda sounded to me like you did."

"Well, I didn't. In fact, I take your thinking so as a direct insult to my professional integrity."

"Then we're both pissed. Agreed?"

"Agreed."

"So in the end it all evens out."

"I suppose. May I inquire as to the purpose of this call?"

"You may."

"Assume it done."

"Okay dokey. Let's talk divorce. I changed my mind. Despite the fact that I know all about Lemmy's inheritance and how you two were trying to screw me, I can't bear to be married to that man one second longer than necessary. Bring those papers by my apartment. I'm ready to sign."

"That's wonderful, Brenda. I'm sure Lemmy will be delighted. But do you really expect me to make a house call?"

"Yes, I do."

15

Winfield surprised me. Not only did he agree to come to my apartment, he said he'd do it immediately. "Might as well get this mess over with once and for all," he said.

Fine by me, even though it left little time to find a new place to stash the bag of bras that still swung pendulum-like from the ceiling. I could hardly leave evidence of my crime in plain view of the lawyer.

I knew Elizabeth wasn't home. After walking Jackhammer, she'd headed down to her Spring Street painting studio. I no longer had keys to her apartment. She took them a while back after she lost her own set.

At a loss for an elegant solution, I cut the bag down, put it in the bathtub, and closed the shower curtain. It'd be okay as long as Winfield didn't have to use the facilities.

The intercom buzzed.

I picked up the handset. "Yes."

Ralph's voice crackled out of the ancient device. "Brewster Winfield . . . here . . . you." He sounded tense, although it was hard to tell for sure because of the bad connection.

"Send him up," I said. "And, Ralph, thanks for calling first."

". . . welcome."

A few seconds later the intercom buzzed again.

"Yes, Ralph, what is it?"

". . . to warn . . . sure you want . . . this Winfield fellow . . . he's got . . . neck . . . scared . . . bejeezus outta . . ."

"Thanks for the warning. It's okay. She's not poisonous."

The doorbell rang.

I knew damned well how Jackhammer would react to Myrtle invading his territory, so I picked him up and clutched him close, then proceeded into the foyer and looked through the peephole.

There was Winfield, big grin on his face and a certain orange and black thing draped around his neck. It wasn't a silk scarf or a string tie.

"Goddammit, Winfield," I said loud enough to be heard through the closed door. "You should have told me you were bringing Myrtle. Put her in the carrying case, then I'll let you in." This must be my payback for the pen incident.

"Myrtle goes everywhere with me." He disentangled the snake from his neck and lovingly placed her into her carrying case. "Poor little Myrtle-poo," he said, to the snake, "Mean Brenda doesn't love you."

"Now," I said, "zip it all the way up."

Once he'd done so, I opened the door.

"Myrtle freaked out my doorman."

"So I noticed," said Winfield. "It was a small diversion and one which I thoroughly enjoyed. It's not often I allow myself such an indulgence."

"Make sure she stays in her case. Jackhammer is very territorial. I don't want any trouble."

"Fear not. I wouldn't dream of letting my precious Myrtle roam around your little hovel. She might scratch her smooth, sensitive belly on a splinter." He cast his eyes down. "Don't you think it's time you had this floor of yours sanded and coated? Or perhaps you could purchase a rug? You live like a pauper."

"You know, Winfield, you're absolutely right. Thanks for pointing that out. I could afford more luxuries if Lemmy were to cough up some heavy-duty alimony."

That stopped Winfield cold.

I loved watching the change in his expression. His mouth clamped shut, and his big grin shrank. I let him sweat for a minute, then said, "You know I hate rugs. My apartment suits me. I'm not gonna ask for alimony."

"A wise and equitable decision."

"Can we get down to business?"

Winfield and I sat at opposite sides of my small table. Between us, like a bulletproof barrier, stood his mono-grammed leather designer briefcase. He snapped the latch, opened the case, removed a sheaf of papers, and pushed them over to me. "Having been through divorce more than once before," he said, "you surely know the drill by now. You sign here." He tapped a line with his finger. "Later Lemmy will sign here." He tapped another line.

I signed, using my own ballpoint pen that Bucky's millinery supply house had handed out at their sixtieth anniversary party.

Winfield took back the papers and squinted at my signa-ture. "Brenda *Sue*?"

"That's right. Sue."

Winfield gave a little chuckle. "Brenda Sue. It's so, you know, like a hick from the sticks."

"Speaking of sue," I said, "that reminds me of what I ought to do to Lemmy."

"No, no, no." Winfield shook his head. "I wouldn't advise such action."

"Of course not. Lemmy's your client. Look on the bright side, more billable hours for you. Breach of promise sounds pretty good to me. What do you think?"

"You'd be laughed out of court."

"Don't you think I should get some kind of compensation for my trouble?"

"You mean besides the heartwarming knowledge that you truly helped a friend in need."

"Bullshit. You and I both know that Lemmy was no friend in need. He wasn't about to be deported. It was all a scam. He tricked me so he could beat Johnny out of a god-damned brassiere for his stupid collection."

"Then you are a friend indeed."

"Oh, cut the crap, Winfield. You're damned lucky I haven't lodged an official complaint about your conduct with the bar association. Know what? I still can."

"Don't blame me for your woes. You married Lemmy of your own free will."

"I wouldn't be surprised to discover the entire hoax was your brilliant scheme."

"It was not."

"I don't know if you committed a crime, but what you did was sure as hell unethical, and that's enough to get you in serious trouble."

Winfield glared at me. "Interesting that you should bring up ethics and crime in your veiled and not-so-veiled threats. It reminds me that Lemmy would like his brassiere collection returned. Posthaste."

"I bet he would."

"I fear he is so upset about his missing property he might find it difficult—perhaps, impossible—to sign his designated dotted line on these divorce papers. That would be an unnecessary complication in the dissolution of this, the latest in your long line of failed marriages."

Those goddamned words again: unnecessary complication. Now I was really pissed. "Go to hell, Winfield."

"Don't get so hot and bothered. I merely suggested that you might somehow, in your day to day wanderings on the streets of our fair city, stumble upon Lemmy's brassiere collection. Stranger things have happened."

"And if I do?"

"Simple. Return the collection. You'll receive a token reward. No questions asked. Until the collection is recovered, I'm afraid your divorce might possibly be, in the parlance of the law, contested. Dig what I'm saying?"

"Only too well."

"Good. And while you're making an effort to stumble

across those brassieres, it would be nice if you were also to stumble across a silver replacement pen for me. That might speed up the wheels of justice."

Winfield scooped up the papers I'd signed, slipped them into his briefcase, grabbed Myrtle's carrying case, and stood to go. "It's been a real pleasure."

Yeah, right. I didn't budge. "You know where to find the door. Let yourself out."

Despite my calm level-headedness, goddamned Winfield had managed to get the best of me. I was sorry I ever considered him my friend.

I stood with my back to Winfield and stared out the window, fingers crossed that the lawyer didn't stop off in the bathroom on his way out.

"Hey, what's this?" he asked.

My first thought was, oh no, he's spotted the bag of bras, but then his voice sounded too strong to be emanating from the bathroom.

Best to play innocent and hope for the best. "What's what?" I asked.

"This picture. I had no idea you knew Frankie Tibble."

"Who?"

"My god," he said, "all this time I thought your talk of lawsuits was a lot of bullshit. Don't tell me you hired Tibble to represent you. The man's a total incompetent. But hey, if that's what you want, go right ahead, it makes my job all that much easier."

"I don't know what you're talking about." I turned to face him.

He was shaking his head in disbelief, holding the mug shot of the killer I'd drawn.

"Do you know that man?"

"Frankie Tibble and I went to law school together. He was a couple of years ahead of me. An idiot. He got caught cheating on exams. They should have booted him out. When they didn't, everybody figured he either had an in with the dean or something on the dean."

A positive ID! I'd lucked out big time. I now knew who the killer was. I could have kissed Winfield. Instead, I suppressed my glee. I couldn't tell Winfield where I'd seen this man and what I knew he'd done without admitting I'd been in Lemmy's building at the time of the murder, thereby implicating myself in the bra heist. "What did you say his name was again?"

"Frankie Tibble. But surely you already knew that. You hired him. How come you've got his picture? It's a drawing, right?"

"I drew it. But it's not who you think. It's my cousin Joey. I drew it for a family reunion book."

"Well, it has been a few years since I last saw Frankie Tibble. Sure looks like him, though."

I urged Winfield to the door. "See you later, Brew." I bent down so my face was even with an airhole in Myrtle's carrying case. "Take care, you gorgeous snake, you."

I love New York. So many connections. The air positively sizzles. Still, I'd never expected to hook up so fast and with so little effort.

So the rude arrogant asshole murderer was a lawyer. Somehow that didn't surprise me one bit.

I yanked my phone book from the top of the closet, flipped to the Ts. There was only one Tibble, Franklin, Atty. He was on Christopher Street.

Excited, I picked up the phone to call Turner and McKinley. Three digits into punching in their number, I had second thoughts and hung up.

Winfield could be wrong. He could even be lying, I couldn't imagine why, but you never know. I think sometimes lawyers lie for no good reason other than to keep up their chops.

Before I made a complete fool of myself, I wanted to make sure this Tibble really was the guy on the staircase. If he was, then I'd talk to Turner and McKinley.

If I was going to go check this guy out, I'd need a disguise.

* * *

"Oooh, how creepy," said Dweena. "No wonder you're hiding out. I wish you hadn't told me. It makes my flesh crawl. The very thought that at the moment I was perusing Lemmy's bras, somebody—some very rich and famous body—was getting whacked a few feet above my head. Yuck. Nightmare City."

"Actually," I said, "I think you were already gone when Shelton was murdered. I'd almost finished when I heard the thump. That had to be him hitting the floor above."

"Well, that's a relief," said Dweena. "It means I can sleep at night. You know how Dweena needs her beauty rest, *now* more than ever before. Brenda, better hang on to your many hats, you are not gonna believe *my* news."

"Wait," I said. "First, can I borrow one of your wigs?"

"Yeah, whatever. Okay, Brenda, now get this—"

"Dweena, I hate to be rude, but I really need a wig. Could your story wait until you get here?"

"First you don't want to hear my news, and now you want me to bring you a wig. I thought you were coming here."

"I'm hiding out, remember."

"Oh, right. Okay, I'll be over right away with a bunch of wigs. If I don't tell somebody soon what happened, I'm gonna bust."

Dweena's "right away" somehow turned into an hour.

I was getting ready to call to see where the hell she was when the intercom buzzed. "Miss Dweena to see you," said Ralph.

"Send her up."

"Sorry it took me so long," said Dweena. She handed me a Balducci's shopping bag full of wigs. "I was selecting wigs to bring when I got a call and had to change outfits. This is my new dress. Like it?"

She swooshed through the room in a stunning ice-blue silk taffeta gown, cleavage dramatically displayed, full skirt billowing.

"It's a knockout. Where'd you get it?"

"This fabulous boutique I found yesterday after you so rudely sent me away. In case you care, I'm not the least bit upset about that anymore. It turned out for the best, and not only because I missed that man getting murdered but because I found this dress to go with the bra. Perfect, isn't it?"

"It flatters you."

"For two thousand dollars it sure as hell ought to. Can you believe that price?"

"On Madison Avenue? Sure. What I can't believe is that you paid that kind of money for a dress."

"I didn't. Even filthy rich me has to draw the line somewhere."

"Oh, Dweena, I hope you didn't steal it."

"Shame on you, Brenda, to even think such a thing. Dweena may boost an occasional diplomat car or do a little breaking and entering for a friend, but shoplifting is a whole other matter."

"You didn't buy the dress, you didn't steal the dress. So how did you manage to get the dress?"

"Here's how the deal went down. I'm in the dressing room, trying to pull the dress over Lemmy's bra, and the zipper gets stuck, so I go out to ask for help, and the designer himself is there screaming at the manager because the dresses in the window are wrinkled. He helps me snuggle down into the dress, and when it's all on, he is amazed at how utterly fabulous the dress looks on me, and right on the spot he calls this really big famous fashion photographer, and she comes and takes a bunch of shots of me in the bra in the dress, and to make a long story short, I'm gonna be plastered on the side of a building on Houston Street with bosoms two storeys high. They'll be able to see them all the way over in Jersey."

"Cool."

"And the designer gave me the dress as payment and—oh no, will you look at the time? Sorry, Brenda, I've gotta run.

The photographer called, and they want to do some additional promo shots. Happy wig picking and be careful with this lawyer fellow."

With that, she flew out the door, leaving a vacuum in her wake.

I tried on several wigs and decided on a flaming red number styled into a short pixie cut. I was pleased that it didn't look a thing like me.

16

If Chuck ever finished his time machine and made it back to the 1960s, maybe I could convince him, as long as he was already there, to take a stab at changing millinery history. The industry took some hard hits that decade. Times changed, fashion changed, people changed, hats were no longer everyday items or even anyday items, and the milliners were a little slow to catch on. Hair was big and ratted and sprayed into helmets, wigs were big, and hairdressers and wigmakers were perceived as the enemy. Then along came the hat wig, a totally embarrassing moment.

These thoughts ran through my head as I tucked my hair under Dweena's bright red pixie wig. I was at home, in the privacy of my own bathroom, transitioning from milliner to wig wearer. You'd think I'd be used to seeing just about anything on my head, but the wig looked weird.

Jackhammer seemed to agree. He stood on top of the toilet and stared.

"It'll be better with the right makeup," I assured him, then proceeded to slather some on.

A final glance in the mirror showed that I was definitely not me. Good going. That was the point.

On my way out of the building Ralph did a double take.

"It's me," I whispered, "but don't tell anybody."

He smiled and nodded.

It was strange to walk through my very own West Village neighborhood not being me. I imagined this was how Dweena felt all the time. I began to understand the appeal. I was free to make a complete fool of myself, and nobody would ever know.

For now, I needed to gather my wits and get up the guts to go through with Plan A. Which was, at the most basic level, to peek through Tibble's window and see if it was the same guy.

Of course, he might not have a storefront office. In which case, I'd move on to Plan B, slightly riskier, because I'd have to go into Tibble's office and talk to him.

I had a story at the ready. Most lawyers, no matter what their specialty, are capable of banging out a simple will. I'd tell Frankie Tibble I wanted a will. To make it short and sweet, I'd say I was still shopping around and simply ask how much. All I needed was a quick look at his face and an excuse to get the hell out.

I, or rather the new red-headed not me, stood at the corner and gazed the length of Christopher Street. The address would be about halfway down the block, right under all that scaffolding.

Oh. Scaffolding. A bad sign.

My good luck had changed to rotten.

The building was empty, in the process of being gutted, no more than a shell. A curbside Dumpster brimmed over with chunks of plaster, old toilets, and pedestal sinks. I double-checked addresses on the adjacent buildings. I had the right place.

For this turn of events I had no alternate plan.

A raspy voice from out of nowhere startled me. "You lookin' for somethin', Red?"

At first, the "Red" didn't register. When I realized he was addressing me, I spun around and found my red-wigged self face to face with the speaker, an elderly man, very skinny, withered, pale as a ghost, and leaning on a wooden cane. Not too threatening.

"Yes, I am," I said. "Didn't there used to be a lawyer in this building?"

"Yep. Tibble's his name. Forced out by his greedy land-lord, who happens to be none other than me. No great loss, that one. He was always behind on his rent. He's some other landlord's headache now."

"Do you have any idea where he moved to?"

"Sure do. Just around the corner." The old man pointed toward one of those narrow, twisty streets even long-time Village residents don't know by name and no cab driver can ever find. "See that sign hanging? That's him, he's down in the basement."

"Thanks."

The wooden sign squeaked on its hinges as it swung in the slightly fishy-smelling breeze that blew in off the Hudson River. Stenciled in faded letters: "Franklin D. Tibble, Attor-ney at Law."

All my previous experience with lawyers—from temp work in huge corporate law firms to dealing with the likes of Brewster Winfield—has led me to expect a certain level of affluence not at all in evidence here. What kind of lawyer was this guy? I mean, besides probably being an asshole and a murderer. Winfield's low opinion of Tibble's lawyer-ing ability might be right.

I clutched a rusty rebar handrail and negotiated my way down crumbling concrete stairs. The basement-level office had a small window, but it was impregnated with chicken wire and too filthy to see through.

So much for the idea of sneaking a peek at the man's face.

I reviewed the Plan B story in my head and realized that yes, I'd reached another of those crossroads, a crucial turn-ing point, where I could still back out. Or I could plunge ahead into the unknown.

I was being overly dramatic. I'd be perfectly safe, in and out of his office in twenty seconds.

I tried the door. It creaked part of the way open and then got hung up on a gunky old rug that I tripped over on my way in.

"If that's supposed to be a limp," said a man slouched behind a dented metal surplus desk, "you're gonna have to do better."

It was Tibble, all right. Or rather, Tibble was the rude arrogant asshole with the briefcase.

I felt very uneasy in the presence of a murderer. Time to duck out.

But Tibble was saying, "Friend of mine's an actor. If you can't get the limp down pat, we'll call him in to coach. His fees are quite reasonable. So what happened? Cracked sidewalk? Private property?"

Apparently my man Tibble was an ambulance chaser turned killer.

His smile changed into a leer as he checked me out.

The man gave me the creeps. All I wanted was to run over to the precinct and tell Turner and McKinley I'd found the killer of Adison Montgomery Shelton.

I tried to sound casual. "It's not a limp. I tripped is all. On your rug."

"Um-huh," he said. "Then what can I do for you?"

I launched into my prepared spiel. "It's like this friend of mine died recently," I said. "Lung cancer. Inoperable. She smoked four packs a day, so some things you've got to expect, but still, it got me thinking . . ."

"Let me hazard a guess," said Tibble. He put his forefinger on his chin and tilted far back in his chair. "Faced with the tenuous nature of life, you desire a will."

"Yes. That's right. A will."

"You've come to the right place."

I was pretty impressed with myself. My story had worked superbly. I hadn't even delivered the punch line and Tibble had already caught on. "How much does it cost?"

"Well, now, that all depends," he said.

"On what?"

He gestured toward a wooden swivel chair. "Why don't you have a seat?"

I didn't want to have a seat or stay in this dank, disgusting office with a killer for one more second. Unfortunately, I couldn't think of a diplomatic way out.

"Thank you." I sat down and rolled the chair close to his desk, prepared to listen to a rundown of his fees. "I don't have much in the way of assets. All I need is a simple will. You know, boilerplate."

"I see," said Tibble. He grinned, showing too much gum.

"So," I said, "what kind of money are we talking about?"

Instead of answering, he pushed his chair back, got up, walked over to the front door, and to my great concern slid the dead bolt closed.

The sound it made was terribly final.

"What the—"

"Oh, don't be alarmed," he said. "I want to assure your privacy when we discuss such sensitive personal matters. We wouldn't want anybody to burst in here and disturb us, now, would we?"

It did sound reasonable when he put it that way. "No, I guess not." I hoped he didn't notice the slight quiver in my voice.

I needed an excuse to leave. I could say I forgot my list of assets and would be right back.

While I tried to figure out what to do, Tibble perused his cinder-block and wood-plank bookshelves. Good, I thought, somewhat relieved. Books. The lawyer really had fallen for my bit about the will and had locked the door precisely for the reason he claimed, and now he needed to look up some weird probate law.

He gathered up several large volumes and brought them over to his desk, but before he put them down, he did a fast about-face and dumped them onto my lap.

All of a sudden, all of them, all at once.

What a surprise.

One by one the big, heavy books slid off my lap and

crashed to the floor. Instinctively, I grabbed at them.

Tibble whirled my chair around—and around and around and around. The last few books fell off my lap and went every which way.

I was totally dizzy.

Tibble stopped the chair.

I started to get up. He pushed me back down and snatched the red pixie wig off my head.

"Aha," he said.

I'm afraid after that some of the fine details of what occurred next are lost to me.

I must have screamed, but all I can definitely remember is the feeling of complete and total terror.

From somewhere Tibble produced a roll of duct tape. He slapped a length over my mouth, then reeled off more and bound me to the chair. He wound the tape around my waist, got my arms pinned down, then taped my feet together, all very fast.

Once I was immobilized, Tibble planted himself in front of me and said, "Did you really think that ridiculous disguise would fool me?"

Mouth taped shut, I didn't attempt to answer.

"I know who you are, Brenda Midnight, and what you do and where you were the other day. And I've got a damned good idea why you're here. Guess I foiled your little plan, didn't I?"

He sure had. I desperately needed another plan.

Tibble paced around his office, scratching his head and mumbling to himself. "I've got a good mind to . . ." His voice trailed off into a big sigh.

I didn't need to hear the words anyway. It was pretty obvious. Tibble knew what I knew about him, and now, to save himself from prison or worse, he had to get rid of me. Simple.

Time compressed then expanded. My reference points disappeared, and I had no idea how long he paced or what to do about it.

He did stop pacing—it had been either seconds or hours—and his inner conflict seemed to have ended. His mind now made up, he strode purposefully over to his desk, snatched up the telephone, and punched in a number. I couldn't make out what he said, but when he hung up, he addressed me loud and clear. "It won't be long now."

I am sorry to say that I wasted part of what I believed to be my last moments on earth trying to decide who to blame for my dire predicament. I reached far into the past for possibilities. In the end Lemmy came in second, far behind my first. Much as I hated to admit it, the blame was mine alone. I was the one who had opened Tibble's door.

How long ago was that?

Thoughts rushed into my head about Midnight Millinery and the many more hats I wanted to make and the future I might have had with Johnny. Faced with certain, possibly painful death, his ugly yellow and orange shag rug seemed a whole lot of fuss about nothing. Given another chance, I'd do it much differently.

I thought of Elizabeth. And Chuck. And . . .

The worst of all was Jackhammer. I got all choked up thinking of him. Already I missed him, the best little dog I knew, the best little dog in the world. He's so good and brave and strong and . . .

I tried to be good and brave and strong but couldn't pull it off. I shivered and shook. A single tear escaped my eye and trickled down my cheek.

It was goddamned irritating not being able to brush it away.

17

Now wait just a goddamned minute.

In the midst of all this self-indulgent whining I got bored. Enough with the if-only musings and of half-assed attempts to fix the blame. I knew better than to feel sorry for myself.

All right, Brenda, get a grip, pull yourself together, and let loose some focused, rational thought on the very pressing, grave problem of how to escape Tibble's creepy basement office.

Okay, so I couldn't move and I couldn't scream. I also wasn't about to go down without a fight. There had to be a way I could make a break for it.

To my advantage, Tibble hadn't yet made a move to kill me. He'd rolled me into the corner and turned the chair I was taped to so that I faced a brick wall. I couldn't see him, but I heard him drumming his fingers on his desk.

He seemed to be waiting for something—or more likely someone. Probably whomever he'd talked to on the phone. "It won't be long now," he'd said after hanging up.

He must have needed help to kill me. From what I've read, it's not all that easy to bludgeon someone to death. According to the latest, that was how Shelton died. Maybe Tibble had help with that too.

Would they do it right here in Tibble's office? Certainly it was convenient. I was already on the scene, gagged and immobilized. The downside was all that messy forensic evidence that would be left behind, not that anybody would notice in this hellhole.

On the other hand, if he wanted to do it in an out-of-the-way location he couldn't be linked to, he'd have to risk moving me. That would attract attention, even in the Village. A lot of attention if I could somehow figure out a way to free my hands and peel the goddamned duct tape off my mouth.

At the moment that did not seem possible.

It's amazing all the crap that went through my mind. What I needed was an escape route, a viable plan. Instead, my brain rebelled. I lost focus and started to think about duct tape. I remembered the time I ran out of pushpins and I tried to use duct tape to hold a buckram crown on a hat block. It had failed miserably. Too bad the tape was working so goddamned great now.

Boom boom boom.

Three loud, room-shaking whacks on the door jolted me back to the immediate bad situation. If I could have, I would have jumped straight up. Unable to move, I absorbed this new level of fear.

I heard Tibble hurry across the room. He threw the dead bolt and opened the door. "Took you long enough," he said.

Not nearly long enough, I thought. My time had done run out.

From my position I had no way to see who came in, but from the heavy footsteps it sounded like a big man. No, it was even worse. Two big men. Me against three. I didn't have a snowball's chance in hell.

"What seems to be the problem?" The voice was stern.

"Her," said Tibble.

I felt eyes on me. I hated being the center of attention. I hated not being able to face the enemy. I'd always heard it was harder to kill if the victim could look the killer in the eye.

Nobody said a word.

I held my breath, waited, and tried to have nice thoughts, since any one could be my last. I thought of Jackhammer, and then of Johnny.

Rrrrrp.

My skin stung like hell, but in a miraculous turn of events, I was free. I had no idea why and no time to ponder. All that mattered was that the goddamned tape was off.

Operating on total instinct, pumped on adrenaline, with no plan whatsoever, I jumped out of the chair, put my head down, and made a dash for the door. I aimed between two really big blurs.

"Stop her!" screamed Tibble. "Don't let her get away."

The larger of the two blurs reached out a big hand and latched onto my shoulder. "Oh no you don't, miss."

I whirled around to face the big man, my current captor, all that stood between me and the safety of the outside world. I struggled against his brute strength, tried to wrest away from his iron grip. He was well over six feet tall, dark hair, beefy, with a mustache, and dressed in . . .

The guy was a cop.

Or maybe not. It could have been a cop costume.

I twisted my head around so I could see the other big guy. He too was dressed like a cop. He had blond hair, twinkly eyes, and was clean shaven.

Quick review of the situation: Tibble had recognized me. Tibble had captured me. Tibble had taped me up. And then Tibble had called the cops. Or men dressed as cops. Either way, it made no sense.

Not that I was complaining. I was alive and untaped and apparently safe at least for the moment.

"She calls herself Brenda Midnight," said Tibble. "I think it's an alias she uses for business. She murdered Adison Montgomery Shelton."

"What makes you say so?" asked the blond, clean-shaven cop.

" 'Cause I saw her, it must have been right after it happened, acting guilty as hell, cowering in the stairway of Shelton's building, and then later I saw her again transporting stolen items. I assume someone has offered a generous reward for her capture."

"I wouldn't know about that, sir."

I pointed my forefinger at Tibble. "He did it. I saw him running away from the scene of the crime. He's trying to frame me."

"She's lying!" shouted Tibble.

From that point things escalated.

Yelling and accusations.

I said Tibble did it.

Tibble said I did it.

We were getting nowhere, a fact the cops soon recognized.

The dark-haired cop with the mustache stepped between Tibble and me. "This is bullshit. I say we run 'em both in."

His partner agreed. "Do you two think you can behave like good girls and boys?"

I crossed my arms over my chest.

Tibble grunted.

" 'Cause if not, we're gonna have to cuff the both of you."

I cooperated. My movements had been restricted enough for one day.

The two cops waited for Tibble to lock up his office, then escorted us outside and up the steps. Any lingering fears that they might not be real cops disappeared at the sight of their double-parked squad car.

The dark-haired cop opened the back door. "Okay, both of you, inside."

"No way," said Tibble. "If you think I'm going to sit next to a cold-blooded killer, you're dead wrong."

"Ditto," I said.

"Will wonders never cease?" said the blond cop. "We seem to have struck on something our little lovebirds agree on."

"Yeah, well," said the other cop, "according to the laws of probability, sooner or later it had to happen."

"Is this the way you always treat concerned citizens?" said Tibble. "You public servants ought to be thanking me and writing out that reward check, not carting me off to the precinct, seated next to a homicidal maniac."

The blond cop negotiated a compromise. He sat in the back with me. Tibble sat up front with the other cop. I liked the arrangement because I could keep my eye on Tibble. He apparently felt the same way about me, because he turned his head around and glared at me the entire time we were in the vehicle.

I met his glare with my own.

He blinked first.

The cops hustled Tibble and me into the ground floor of the precinct. This time I saw no familiar faces. The cops I knew must have been out keeping the West Village safe.

On my own, I made a beeline for the familiar staircase in the rear of the lobby.

"Where do you think you're going?" asked the blond cop.

"Upstairs. I'll only be gone a second."

"No," said the dark-haired cop. "That's not the way it works."

"But I really should let Detective Turner and Detective McKinley know I'm here on the premises."

"You know Turner and McKinley?"

I stretched the truth a bit. "Yeah, we're friends."

The officers went off to the side and spoke to each other in hushed voices. Then the dark-haired one went upstairs.

A couple of minutes later he returned. And a couple of minutes after that McKinley came chugging down the stairs to my rescue.

"So good to see you, Detective."

"You again?" he asked, wrinkling his brow.

"Not my choice," I said.

"Killer," said Tibble. He jutted his jaw at me.

McKinley gave Tibble a puzzled look, then turned to the dark-haired cop. "What's this all about?"

The cop shrugged. "Murder, to hear them tell it, but we think it's some kinda domestic dispute or a drug deal gone bad."

McKinley frowned.

I'd heard enough. "Don't you recognize this man?" I asked. "This is the guy in the mug shot."

Tibble screamed, "Mug shot!"

I ignored his outburst. "He's the guy who bumped into me after he killed Shelton."

McKinley thanked the two cops for their trouble and pulled rank. "I'll take care of them."

"I must agree with you, Ms. Midnight," said Turner. "Mr. Tibble does look remarkably like the composite sketch you brought us this morning." He held up a copy of my drawing.

I was happy when they put Tibble in the hot seat.

He shifted his weight. The chair squeaked. "I want to see that drawing."

"Fair enough," said Turner, handing him the picture.

Tibble gazed at it. "It doesn't mean diddly. I'm an attorney. I'm on the right side of the law."

Even Turner rolled his eyes at that.

McKinley led Tibble off. To lock him up, I hoped.

I stayed in the cubicle with Turner and explained that Brewster Winfield had seen the drawing of Tibble and that I wanted to check him out before running to the detectives with the information. "In case Winfield was wrong, I didn't want to waste your time."

Instead of thanking me for my trouble, Turner sighed. "Won't you ever learn?" Then, not even waiting for a response, he launched into a bunch of questions. They all seemed trivial to me. But then, fresh from the trauma of believing my life was about to end, anything would have seemed trivial.

I had no patience for Turner's questions. He went on and on. All I wanted was to go out and celebrate the fact that I was alive. And so every so often, whenever I could squeeze it in between one of his stupid questions and one of my one-syllable answers, I'd pipe up with, "Can I go now?"

His reply each time I asked was a gruff "No."

Finally I screwed up enough courage to ask, "Why not?"

"Because," said Turner, "a colleague from the precinct in which the murder occurred will soon join us. I'm sure he'll be interested in what both you and your friend Tibble have to say. Maybe he can sort out the bullshit, because quite frankly I've had enough."

"I suggest he beat a confession out of Tibble."

"That is not the least bit amusing, Ms. Midnight. Why so glum anyway? Isn't this what you wanted?"

Yes, it was what I wanted, I supposed, way back when-ever, but this was not the way I wanted it. Now all I could think about was exactly what I'd been thinking about when I thought I'd be dead before the day was done. I'd brought Tibble to the attention of the cops. Now I wanted to get on with my life.

"Is it okay if I call Johnny?"

Turner pushed his phone across the desk. "Make it snappy."

It was totally wonderful to hear Johnny's voice, even the outgoing tape on his answering machine.

When his message played out, I spoke. "Johnny, it's me. Are you home?"

He picked up. "Brenda."

"Do you have dinner plans?" I asked.

"I hope this means you're not mad at me anymore."

"It means I'd like to see you."

"I don't have any plans, so sure, dinner sounds good. Angie's?"

"No. I was thinking maybe some place a little fancier, like La Reverie."

"You've got to be kidding. La Reverie gets booked up more than a month in advance. We'd never get in on such short notice."

"I thought maybe you could pull some strings."

"Well . . ." said Johnny.

Turner growled. "That's about enough, Ms. Midnight."

"Sorry, Johnny," I said. "Gotta go. I'll call you later. Try and get that reservation."

"Where are you? Is that Turner I hear in the background? Are you in some kind of trouble? Brenda, talk to me."

18

Turner's questions finally fizzled out.

After a halfhearted attempt to make small talk about the blazing-hot summer—"Yep, it's a bad one, all right. Uh-huh. A real humdinger."—we both called it quits.

He shuffled papers around on his desk, occasionally banged a couple together with a big old stapler.

I sat and waited and wondered if I'd have to reveal to the detective from uptown the real reason for my visit to Lemmy's. I was calculating how much trouble I could possibly be in when I perceived a definite change in the atmosphere.

Turner pushed back his chair and got up.

In the doorway stood an extremely handsome man—tall, dark, terribly dashing. He had that undefinable something that knocked my socks off. And he was better dressed than Turner. This was the uptown detective?

Wow.

He strode confidently into the cubicle.

It is absolutely true that Turner and McKinley coached Johnny in how to act like a cop to help him bring a dose of realism to his Tod Trueman TV series character, a tough job given the absurd plots.

It is absolutely not true, even though a lot of people think it is, that Johnny based Tod Trueman on Turner or McKinley or any combination of the two.

Because I know Johnny, I know the truth. Tod Trueman was modeled on Johnny's seventh grade algebra teacher.

If I hadn't known better, I would have sworn Tod Trueman was modeled on this uptown detective. I mean, the man out-Todded Tod Trueman, he out-Todded Johnny Verlane, and I was willing to bet he out-Todded the algebra teacher.

I was riveted. Whatever drivel I had been thinking about was blown straight out of my mind. I was in major crush at first sight. I caught myself thinking crazy, happily-ever-after kinds of thoughts.

Too bad he turned out to be a total jerk.

"Mike Duxman," he announced. With a gorgeous heavy-lidded pair of deep-set dark liquid eyes he looked down his strong yet perfect nose at Turner's outstretched hand and shunned it. "If we could dispense with the formalities and get on with it. I've got a press conference in"—he made a big show of checking his diamond-encrusted Rolex—"forty-four and a half minutes."

Turner withdrew his hand and glanced in my direction.

I quickly looked down, opened my purse, and pretended to be searching for something deep inside. I didn't want Turner to know that I knew that he'd just lost round one of the dance of the macho male detectives.

Round two began a second later when McKinley returned to the cubicle and Duxman brushed off his attempt at a handshake also. "You don't mind if I use your desk," he stated. It was not a question.

McKinley appeared dumbfounded. His eyes darted from Turner to Duxman and back to Turner. Tension crackled in the air. "Uh . . . no, I guess not." He leaned up against the doorjamb.

Anybody who knows McKinley knows that this is his preferred stance when people are in the cubicle, but only when it is of his own choosing, not because some uptown jerk with an attitude decides to commandeer his desk.

I don't know a goddamned thing about rank within the police force, but it was kind of apparent that Duxman carried a much bigger stick than either of my detective pals.

Duxman, now seated at McKinley's desk, finally took notice of me. "She's the one?"

Turner told him my name and that yes, I was the one who had identified a possible suspect in the Shelton case. "Brenda, why don't you tell Detective Duxman what—"

Duxman cut him off. "I'll do the questioning. All the lady has to do is answer."

Funny, that was quite similar to the line Turner and McKinley always use on me whenever I try to volunteer information. It sounded much crankier coming from the full, luscious lips of Mike Duxman.

He proceeded to move those lips to question me.

Much as I wanted to help the investigation and see Frankie Tibble go to prison, in the short time I'd observed Duxman's behavior, I came to dislike him so much I felt less than my usual cooperative self.

The man was plain old mean. He made me nervous.

I froze up.

McKinley tried to help me out. "Ms. Midnight," he urged, "answer the detective."

"Uh, could you please repeat the question?"

Detective Mike Duxman grilled me for twenty-two minutes by his own estimate. Turner and McKinley stayed with me throughout. I appreciated that, especially near the end of the session, when Duxman summed up. "And so, while in the process of committing a felony, you observed a man and for some reason you came to assume this man was a killer leaving a crime scene."

I didn't know the precise technical legal definition of felony, so I kept quiet and wondered if I needed a lawyer and if so, would it be a conflict of interest for Winfield to represent me.

"If I may have a word?" asked Turner, ever so polite.

Duxman scowled. "Go ahead."

"There is an extenuating circumstance."

"Yeah?" Duxman challenged him.

Turner rose to the occasion. He efficiently reduced the long, sad, complex tale of my getting tricked into marrying Lemmy and all that followed into a brief statement.

"You're saying you vouch for the lady?" asked Duxman.

"Yes," said Turner.

"Me too," said McKinley. "Brenda Midnight is one of the good ones, not nearly as flaky as you might think."

Somewhere in the universe, something had forever changed, patterns had altered. Chuck would probably say a one had flipped to a zero or a zero had flipped to a one. I swear I heard the whoosh of the cosmic wind as cascading events altered course.

"What's Duxman's problem anyway? You'd think he'd be thrilled I found the killer. The man's got some nerve."

McKinley was escorting me through the long, murky, fluorescent-lit corridor.

"You don't understand. There's a lot more to this than meets the eye. This is a high-profile investigation under intense scrutiny from higher-ups, not to mention the media. Duxman can't afford to make a mistake."

"I still say he's a jerk."

"You may be right. But think how difficult it would be for him if a civilian were to solve his case."

"So he'd rather it not be solved at all."

"That's not true."

We neared the end of the corridor. I had a good idea where we were headed. "Please, not this," I said.

"I'm sorry, Ms. Midnight." McKinley stopped in front of the utility closet and unlocked the door.

Resigned to my fate, I stepped inside. After all I'd been through, I supposed it was not such a big deal.

Inside on an upside-down slop bucket sat Frankie Tibble,

Esquire, all alone in the middle of the small, smelly room, surrounded by mops and industrial-sized drums of cleaning fluids and deodorizers and cartons of toilet paper. He seemed unhappy but was obviously not under arrest.

Didn't anybody pay any attention to me?

"Your turn," said McKinley to me. He jutted his chin at the bucket. Then, with a jerk of his thumb, he indicated that Tibble was to come with him.

With a sweep of his hand Tibble offered me the bucket.

"Thanks so very much," I said.

"My pleasure."

Alone in the room, which reeked of too-sweet chemical deodorizer, I whiled away my time recapping my terrible day.

It was hard to believe that only an hour or so before, I was positive I'd be dead by nightfall. Back then at the height of my fear I'd had some pretty nutty thoughts about Johnny and me that had culminated in me telling Johnny I wanted to go to La Reverie tonight.

Not a simple desire.

La Reverie is not just any old fancy restaurant with reasonably good food, fabulous attentive service, lush decor, tons of fresh flowers, and flattering peach-colored lighting. It is an institution. La Reverie is known throughout the entire metropolitan area as the restaurant to pop *the* question. According to popular myth, a vending machine in the men's room is loaded with cubic zirconium rings for romantic emergencies.

I've been to La Reverie a couple of times but always in ridiculous circumstances, never as question poppee or popper. Today I'd stared death in the face and survived and thought maybe it was time to resolve this thing between Johnny and me. I felt the time had come to propose to Johnny and goddammit, cliché or not, I wanted to do it at La Reverie.

Now alive, relatively unharmed, and alone with my thoughts, I developed a serious case of cold feet. It was

Detective Duxman's fault or rather my head-over-heels reaction to him. If I could so utterly lust after a complete stranger, even for only a moment, especially one who turned out to be such a jerk, I must not be ready to marry Johnny.

Another deterrent to marriage popped into my now more rational mind. I was still married to Lemmy. Call me old-fashioned or superstitious, but if I'm gonna propose to somebody, I'd prefer not to be married to somebody else at the time.

The problem was that I'd already told Johnny I wanted to go to La Reverie. What must *he* be thinking?

My butt sore from sitting on the bucket I got up, stretched, walked over to the sagging shelves, and passed the time reading the small-print warning labels on the chemical containers.

I was puzzling over the proper pronunciation of a twenty-eight-letter word when Turner unlocked the door. "Let's go."

"Thought you'd never ask."

Turner ushered me back to the cubicle. He sat down behind his desk and put his feet up. I plopped down in the hot seat and marveled that it was actually worse than the bucket. McKinley stood, arms crossed, and leaned against the doorway.

Detective Duxman and Frankie Tibble were nowhere around.

"This is great," I said. "The arrogant jerk arrested the arrogant asshole."

Turner smiled. "Your assessment of the personalities involved is quite good, Ms. Midnight, but I'm afraid no arrest was made."

"Why the hell not?"

"As always," said McKinley, "your efforts are greatly appreciated, but as it turns out, Mr. Tibble could not have killed Adison Montgomery Shelton. Tibble has an alibi, which Detective Duxman quickly checked out."

"I can't believe it. How'd he do that so fast?"

"Couple of calls."

"That's police work?"

"Sometimes it is."

"Is that what you two would have done?"

The detectives both cleared their throat. Neither answered.

"What exactly is Tibble's alibi?"

"He claims to have been meeting with a client who lives in the building. He had every right to be on the premises."

"A conference with a client does not explain why he was running down the stairs like a bat out of hell and bashing into me."

"You're not in Belup's Creek anymore," said McKinley. "Once you've got a couple more decades of New York City under your belt, it'll sink in that New Yorkers are quite frequently in a big hurry."

"Tibble says he was late for another appointment," said Turner. "As so often happens in older buildings, the elevator was slow to arrive. Frustrated, he opted for the stairs. He admits he slammed into you, says he was all set to apologize when you called him an asshole."

"He *is* an asshole!"

"Calm down, Ms. Midnight. He may or may not be an asshole, but Frankie Tibble is not a killer."

"Tibble's story stinks and you know it. How convenient. A client in the building. You know damned well that Duxman fell down on the job. He should have checked out Tibble's alibi in person."

"I agree," said Turner.

"You're kidding," I said.

"No, I'm not," said Turner.

"Not kidding in the least," said McKinley.

"Our hands are tied," said Turner. "Duxman is a boob. But he is a high-ranking boob with friends in high places and a wife who's some big hoo-ha in city government."

"I'd sure like to talk to this client in person."

McKinley frowned. "I bet you would." He raised his eyebrows at Turner.

Turner gave him a slight nod back. Then with a sigh he swung his legs down off his desk, got up, and walked over to McKinley. "Step outside with me for a minute, partner. I need to confer with you in private."

"Oh," said McKinley with mock surprise. "Surely." He turned to me. "I assume you'll be all right in here alone. We'll be only a minute."

"One minute," said Turner. "Precisely sixty seconds."

I caught on quick.

Left behind, placed front and center on Turner's desk, was a yellow legal pad turned to a page of scrawl headed with today's date. I saw my name and Duxman's and Tibble's and one other name, Maureen Kenyen. This had to be Tibble's supposed client. Out to the side of her name were two numbers and a letter. If I interpreted correctly, she lived two floors above Lemmy, one floor above Shelton, but in a different line of apartments.

Turner and McKinley returned.

I was already back in the squeaky chair, looking innocent.

This time when I asked if I could go, they said I could.

"Thank you, Detectives," I said.

"Think nothing of it," said McKinley.

"*Say* nothing of it," said Turner.

"I understand."

Home at last—and alive.

I scooped Jackhammer up and hugged him so hard he squeaked. "I was afraid I might never hug you again."

He licked my cheek.

I put off calling Johnny, afraid he'd be making a big deal out of my desire to go to La Reverie. I didn't know how to explain I'd changed my mind without first telling him what had been on my mind, which he probably assumed anyway, but to confirm it would be courting big trouble.

As it happened, Johnny had failed to get a reservation at La Reverie. "Ever since *Tod Trueman* got canceled," he said, "I've got no clout. I might as well be invisible."

I assured him it was really okay. "After the kind of day I've had, invisible sounds pretty good."

"You up for Angie's?"

"Absolutely."

19

Tommy slid a glass of red wine to me across the top of the bar. He nodded toward the back room. "Johnny already went back. Said he wanted to be sure to snag *your* table."

"Thanks, Tommy." I picked up the wine and started to move away from the bar.

"Brenda?"

"Yeah?"

"Is something going on?"

"What do you mean?"

"Oh, I don't know, it's just that Johnny seemed strange, like nervous maybe."

"No reason I know of."

"Well, it's good to see you two back together. And I'm glad you guys' table is here at Angie's."

"Me too, Tommy."

As always, the joint was crowded. The juke box was cranking out a great old Muddy Waters number. I elbowed my way into the back room. I soon spotted the back of Johnny's head at our table.

"Hey, Brenda." Johnny stood up and pecked me on the cheek.

Here it was, another steaming-hot summer night, and he had on that black leather jacket of his, the one he knew drove me wild. Johnny always looked great, but this particular black leather jacket went way beyond great. It was as if the entire genre of garment had been invented just so he could put it on and be utterly cool. Underneath the jacket he wore a light blue T-shirt that made his dark eyes seem even darker and perfectly faded jeans that flattered his butt.

Johnny Verlane is no fashion dope. He's an actor who knows his stuff. This was intentional. He wanted to wow me and he'd succeeded.

How I wished I'd never mentioned La Reverie. What can I say? After a perceived brush with death, I'd had a weak moment.

"Hey, yourself," I said, sliding into my side of the booth. Jackhammer pushed himself out of his canvas bag, climbed up on my lap, and rested his chin on the table.

"Good to see you too, Jackhammer," said Johnny. "I need that superior nose of yours to help me sniff something out."

Jackhammer vibrated his tail stub.

"Sniff out what?" I asked.

Frowning, Johnny shook his head and peered down at the table. "Remember a long time ago I carved a heart with our initials inside?"

"Sure, I remember," I said, nonchalantly, like it was no big deal. I wanted to avoid romantic subject matter. Even so, I was thrilled that he remembered. "It was a very nice heart. Round in the right places, pointy at the bottom."

"Thanks. I am rather proud of my handiwork. I could swear it was right about here, but I don't see it." He tapped the table.

"That's the spot," I said. "When the light's exactly right and you bend your head precisely the right way, you can just barely make it out."

"I'm amazed that you know that." He twisted his head this way and that, raised it, lowered it. "I still don't see it."

"Light's not right tonight."

"I figure we're about due for a new heart anyway. Next time I'll bring a penknife."

Raphael swooped down on our table and delivered a special little burger ball for Jackhammer (courtesy of the house), a cheeseburger for Johnny, and a grilled cheese with a thick slice of juicy tomato for me.

"Johnny ordered you the regular," he said. "Is that okay?"

"Perfect," I said. "Nobody in the world does a grilled cheese better than you, Raphael."

"Thank you. At Angie's, we aim to please." He turned to Johnny. "Ready for another beer?"

"No thanks, not yet. Tonight I want a clear head."

A man at a table across the room caught Raphael's attention, and he hurried off.

"This isn't quite La Reverie," said Johnny.

"Food's much better here." I wanted to get the conversation away from my sudden urge to go to La Reverie and all the between-the-lines stuff that evoked. "So," I said, "have you talked to Lemmy?"

"Yeah."

"I hope he's really irked about his missing bra collection."

"He is, but there's a lot more to the story. Don't you know what happened?"

Of course I knew what happened. I was probing to see how much Johnny already knew. Not much, I hoped. He had a tendency to worry about me. "What do you mean?"

"That's right. I suppose you have no way of knowing. You almost never watch the news and you're hardly on good terms with Lemmy, so he wouldn't have told you."

"Wouldn't have told me what?"

"Don't get upset, Brenda, but about the same time you were in Lemmy's apartment taking the bras, a rich guy who lived in Lemmy's building was murdered. And get this: The killer also broke into Lemmy's and took his jewels. The good news is Lemmy thinks the killer stole his bras, so he doesn't suspect you."

"That's good."

"The bad news is you and Dweena were in great danger. You must have just missed meeting up with the killer in

Lemmy's apartment. I would have been worried sick except I talked to you before I found out and knew you'd made it back okay." Johnny cocked his head about twenty degrees to the right, flashed a stupid tooth-baring grin.

You wouldn't necessarily pick up on it from watching *Tod Trueman, Urban Detective*, but Johnny is an extremely talented actor. So good that it was hard for me to tell if he was acting dumb because he knew that I knew and he wanted me to tell him on my own or if I had him snowed.

It was even possible he'd gotten all the poop from Turner. They were friends. Johnny already suspected I was at the precinct. He might have followed up with a call to Turner. Keeping my eyes on Johnny, I took a big bite of my grilled cheese and then a long sip of wine.

He didn't say anything, and that dopey grin didn't fade. He was waiting. He knew. At least we weren't talking about La Reverie.

"Oh yeah," I said, "I heard about that. What's awful is I saw the killer."

"Oh, really? How interesting."

He definitely knew. "You talked to Turner, didn't you?"

"Maybe I called him. Maybe I became concerned when you called and I heard him in the background telling you to get off the phone. Maybe I wondered what the hell you were doing at the precinct. Yeah, maybe."

"I didn't want you to worry."

"Apparently I had damned good reason to worry. I hear you were duct-taped to a chair earlier today."

"It was nothing."

"Right."

"Okay, so I was scared."

"You're damned lucky, Brenda. What if you'd been right about this lawyer fellow, uh—"

"Frankie Tibble."

"Yeah, that's the name Turner mentioned. What if Frankie Tibble really had turned out to be the killer?"

"I'm not totally convinced he isn't. Even Turner and

McKinley—" I stopped myself. If Johnny knew what I had planned for tomorrow, he'd try to stop me.

"Turner and McKinley what?"

"They don't think the uptown detective did a very good job with Tibble's alibi. Turner actually called him a boob."

"Then he probably is."

"Speaking of boobs and bras and such, you don't believe that crap about Lemmy's jewels, do you?"

He got a pained expression on his face.

"Well?"

Johnny sighed. "You're right. I don't believe it. I think he's after insurance money."

"Your agent, Lemon B. Crenshaw, is pond scum. As Dweena would say, he's lower than a snake belly in a wheel rut in hell."

"You're the one who married him."

"Let's not get into that. Besides, it's almost history. I signed the divorce papers."

"Good. That means you'll be divorced soon."

"I guess. Unless Lemmy stalls. I'm willing to surrender the bras if he needs more persuading."

Johnny raised his eyebrows. "Is that why you wanted to go to La Reverie? To celebrate that you'll soon be a free woman?"

I shrugged, tried to make light of the issue. "I don't know why I wanted to go to La Reverie. Temporary insanity maybe."

Johnny seemed about to say something, but he must have changed his mind. He downed the rest of his beer. "I better get going. I have an early day tomorrow."

"Yeah, me too."

Leaving Angie's, I caught, out of the corner of my eye, the handsome face of Detective Mike Duxman on the late news. I shouldn't have been surprised, but I was. "Oooh, that's him," I said. I pulled Johnny back so he could see.

"Who?"

"The uptown detective, the boob."

"So he's the one. I see him on the tube a lot."

I waved my hand to get Tommy's attention. "Tommy, can you turn the TV up?"

"Will do."

Tommy aimed his remote control. The sound came up in time to hear Duxman give a brief statement that contained no solid information. He claimed the investigation of the murder of Adison Montgomery Shelton was moving along as well as could be expected. The department was following up on several leads and hoped to make an arrest soon.

A natural, he looked very good on camera. He looked like he knew it too. Boy, did I ever want to discredit that jerk.

20

Once we were out of air conditioned Angie's and into the heat, Johnny took off the ultimate black leather jacket and slung it over his shoulder.

I put Jackhammer down, and the three of us walked a ways together. Eventually we arrived at an intersection. My building was two blocks straight ahead; Johnny's four blocks to the left.

"Want to come up?" I asked.

He shook his head no.

"Okay, catch you later." I turned to go.

"Wait a second, Brenda."

I paused. "Yeah, what is it?"

"I want you to know I tried my damnedest to get us into La Reverie tonight."

"Is that bothering you?"

"Of course. I feel ineffective. Back when *TTUD* was number one, I could get a last-minute reservation anywhere in town."

"It's all right. Really. It was a crazy idea to go anyway."

"Not so crazy. I think it's a good idea. We'll go someday soon, right?"

"Sure. I guess so."

He smiled. "See you."

When Jackhammer and I got to the front of my building,

I turned around. Johnny was still standing at the intersection, as I knew he would be. He always watched out for me.

I gave him the thumbs-up to let him know I was home safe.

With a hearty wave he disappeared around the corner.

The little light on my answering machine was blinking when I got home. It showed two incoming messages. One was from Chuck, who wanted to know how the hell things had gone with Turner and McKinley and why the hell hadn't I called to let him know. The other was from Dweena, who wanted to know how the hell things had gone with the wig and why the hell hadn't I called to let her know.

I returned Chuck's call first.

"How could you keep me in the dark?" he asked.

"Sorry, I lost track of the time."

"I was worried. I don't trust Turner or McKinley."

"The mug shot did the trick, though in a way you'd never believe. Unfortunately, the killer has an alibi. It probably won't hold up, and I've got a way to blow it out of the water, believe it or not, with Turner and McKinley's blessing."

Chuck pumped me for more information. I begged off, telling him the truth, that I was dead tired.

Next I called Dweena, but she didn't answer, so I didn't have to tell her about the tragic failure of the red pixie wig.

On the way to the garbage room later that night I ran into Elizabeth in the hallway.

"You look tired," she said.

"I've had a very full day."

"Working on your fall hat line?"

"Actually no. I was held prisoner in a dank basement office by a rude, murderous lawyer, then taken into police custody. At the precinct I developed a severe crush on a cop that was over before it began, and I just got back from dinner at Angie's with Johnny, and I think he nearly asked me to marry him, but it's kind of hard to tell."

"Not very perceptive of you."

"If you'd been there, you'd understand my confusion."

"How *is* Johnny? I haven't seen him in the longest time."

"He's fine."

"Then he's not upset about his TV show."

"He's devastated but trying not to show it. How about you? How're the new paintings?"

"I've got to tell you, I love that bra. It's the perfect motif, jam-packed with symbolism—an empty container for an empty society."

"Heavy."

"Oh, and I'm also painting a little portrait of Chuck. He commissioned me. Isn't that weird?"

"What's weird is Chuck's time machine. Have you seen it yet?"

"No. I thought he was kidding about that."

"Afraid not. He's dead serious. I saw it at his place."

"How does it work?"

"I don't think it does, nor do I think it ever will, except inside Chuck's head. He told me he was in 1966, but he was really inside an old metal pipe."

"Why 1966?"

"I don't know."

"It was a lousy year."

I sprang out of bed early the next morning with a vague plan in mind, pleased that for once Turner and McKinley were behind me all the way. They actually needed my help. I could go where they couldn't and get the goods that would discredit Duxman and prove that Tibble had killed Shelton.

The detectives and I had come a long way.

To tell the truth, after a good night's sleep and some hard, down-to-earth thought, a hefty dose of doubt had diminished my conviction that Tibble had killed Shelton. He genuinely seemed to believe I'd killed Shelton, which he wouldn't think if he'd done the deed himself.

Even if he hadn't killed Shelton, I was damned sure Tibble knew more than he'd told the cops. I hoped whatever he'd held back would be revealed when I discredited his alibi, his so-called client, this Maureen Kenyen person.

My best bet would be to pass myself off as Tibble's paralegal and drop by Kenyen's apartment. After yesterday's debacle with Dweena's red pixie wig, I'd had enough of disguises to last me a lifetime. A business suit would be convincing enough, although not too easy to dig up. One of the many great perks about working for myself in a creative endeavor is that I never have to dress for that kind of success. Suits are in mighty short supply around my place.

I rummaged through the closet and dragged out some separates that might in dim light pass for a suit, although under close scrutiny the pitch-black skirt did not match the brownish-black jacket, and the white blouse was actually a ratty old T-shirt turned around backward to hide the Bucky's Millinery Supply logo.

I figured it would be fine. Anybody who did paralegal work for Frankie Tibble would hardly be expected to show up in Brooks Brothers.

Nothing like a recent murder in a building to crank up security procedures. It would be a long time before I could sneak into Lemmy's building while the doorman was at lunch.

To get in, I needed legitimate entry. The most direct way was through Lemmy himself. I dreaded the thought of dealing with him, but with no alternative I bit the bullet and made the call.

"We need to talk," I said.

"You can say that again, lovely wife of mine."

"Soon to be ex," I corrected him. "Can I come over?"

"Well, now, that depends. Are you gonna bring my brassieres to this powwow?"

"No."

"Aha. You admit you took them."

"I admitted no such thing."

"Gee, that's funny, Brenda, I thought for sure you did.

You answered no to my question about the bringing of the bras, implying you had the bras in your possession to bring, implying you took the bras. Guess I misheard you. My damn phone must be on the fritz again. Hold on a sec." A short silence was followed by a series of loud percussive thwacks as Lemmy repeatedly slammed the receiver on a hard surface, most likely his marble kitchen counter. He came back on the line. "You still there, Brenda?"

"So can I come over or not?"

"Yeah, all right."

I felt safe enough to leave my building and go out on the street. Even if Frankie Tibble were the killer, he was no longer a threat to me. I'd already told the cops what I knew. He wouldn't dare harm me now.

On the way uptown, I stopped by Midnight Millinery and took down the sign Pete had taped to my door: DEAR CUS-TOMERS, WE'VE GONE TO PARIS TO EXHIBIT OUR LATEST FALL HATS. SEE YOU SOON.

I dropped by Pete's Café. It wasn't open yet, but Pete was already hard at work, prepping for lunch. He gave me a con-spiratorial wink.

"Back from Paris so soon?"

"*Oui*. Did I miss much?"

"Nope. My egg man's wife had a baby girl yesterday, and he took the day off, and the guy he found to substitute got lost somewhere in Jersey, so yesterday I had to scratch the luncheon omelet special, but it was on the menu, and that pissed off one of my regulars, who claims she's gonna sue for false advertising, but aside from that it's been quiet as a morgue around here."

"Couldn't you have picked up a couple of dozen eggs at the grocery store?"

"Grocery store eggs suck. My reputation would have been ruined."

"I see."

"You gonna open up today?"

"I think so, but not until afternoon. I have an errand this morning."

"I wondered why you were dressed like that."

I missed Midnight Millinery and wanted get to work on a design that had come to me at Tibble's when I was taped up and in a big panic, thinking I was a goner. In the interest of speed, I took a cab uptown.

The cab driver got in the flow. He hit all the lights, and we zoomed to Lemmy's building in no time.

I paused for a moment outside to gather my wits, then pushed through the revolving door and proceeded across the lobby toward Stanley, the doorman.

When he saw me, he straightened his tie. "May I help you?" Despite the big smile that threatened to take over his entire face, his manner was more challenging than helpful. He didn't seem to recognize me from the other day. Good.

"I'm here to see Lemmy Crenshaw," I said. "He's expecting me."

"Your name, please?"

"Brenda Midnight."

He picked up a handset, jabbed a number into a console. "Mr. Crenshaw? Stanley here. There's a Brenda Midnight to see you, sir."

A brief pause, then he gestured in the direction of the elevators. "Mr. Crenshaw will see you."

I didn't have as much to hide as the time I'd snatched Lemmy's bra collection. But I decided to play it safe and got off the elevator on Lemmy's floor, then walked up two flights to Maureen Kenyen's floor.

It would have made more sense to see Lemmy first, but talking to him would put me in a foul mood, which would have made it really hard to pretend to be Tibble's paralegal.

Maureen Kenyen's apartment was at the end of the U-shaped corridor. I stood before her door, procrastinating. My forefinger hovered over the doorbell for a couple of minutes before I finally got up the nerve to push. Expecting

a nerve-shattering buzz, I was surprised to hear a sophisti-
cated, subdued bing-bong instead.

After that, silence.

I pushed again. Bing-bong.

Maybe she wasn't home. Could be she worked.

That would be okay, wouldn't it? If Kenyen had a regular
job with regular hours, she wouldn't have been home at the
time Tibble claimed to have been with her. That fact alone
would destroy his alibi. Of course, she could have been
home sick or—

Footsteps from inside the apartment.

With a friendly, nonthreatening smile plastered on my
face, I stepped back a couple of feet so she could see me
through the peephole.

I could feel her stare. In New York City it is highly irreg-
ular for strangers to drop by unannounced. I didn't expect a
red carpet.

"What do you want?" came a voice.

"Ms. Kenyen? I work for your attorney."

"Franklin Tibble is my attorney."

"Right. He sent me."

"Since when did Frankie get a . . . a . . . what exactly is
your position?"

"Paralegal. May I please come in?"

She opened the door about an inch, as far as the chain
lock allowed. Her left eye looked me up and down. I must
have seemed harmless. She released the chain and opened
the door all the way.

It was hard to guess her age. With dyed blue-black hair
and heavy, precisely applied makeup, she could have been a
well-preserved seventy-five or a hard-living, been-around-
the-block, haggard fifty-five.

"Do come in," she said graciously, then moved out of my
way so I could.

"Thank you," I said.

Sunlight streamed into a big living room. The apartment
was tastefully furnished, I supposed. Personally I hate

heavy upholstery, and she had a lot of stuffed stuff.

In fact she had a lot of stuff period. Flat surfaces were covered with framed family snapshots and little ceramic animals. Based on the decor I concluded she was closer to seventy-five than fifty-five.

She directed me to an ornate couch covered with striped silk. When she was sure I was comfortable, she sat in a matching chair opposite.

"A paralegal, you say."

"Brenda Midnight." I had no reason to lie about my name. I didn't care if Tibble found out.

"Frankie—er, Mr. Tibble didn't mention any paralegal."

"I'm a recent hire. Business is booming. His practice is really taking off."

"That's so good to hear. I'm pleased to meet you, Ms. Midnight. Your work must be quite fascinating."

"Yes, it is."

"Might I interest you in a cup of tea?"

"No, thank you."

"It's herbal. It'll only take a second in the microwave. We could chat a little and get to know each other."

She seemed lonely. I felt bad for her. "I'd love to, but I really can't stay. Mr. Tibble needs me at the office. He would have come himself, but he's terribly busy today. And since I live just a few blocks away, he asked me to stop by on my way to work. Didn't he call and tell you?"

"No, he didn't."

"That's odd. He might have been a little embarrassed. As you know, he is very competent."

"He is that."

"Even so, he seems to have misplaced an envelope. He thinks he might have left it here the other day." Proud of the way I'd dropped that so casually into the conversation, I relaxed and waited for her to take the bait and tell me Tibble hadn't been there and blow his alibi to hell.

"An envelope?" she said sharply. Her mood changed.

What had I said to upset her so?

In an instant she was out of her chair and standing over me. Her washed-out blue eyes flashed with anger. "You're lying. Frankie Tibble didn't send you. I know exactly who you are and what you want."

"I . . . I . . ."

"Get out! And tell whoever sent you that there will be no more envelopes. Did you get that straight? No more envelopes. That was all supposed to be taken care of. I won't put up with this bull any longer. I don't care anymore who knows. Go ahead and spread the word. I will not be blackmailed."

What?

I was stunned speechless. It sounded like she'd just accused me of blackmailing her. Had I heard right?

She repeated, screeching, "Did you hear me? I will not be blackmailed. Now get your ass out of my home."

21

Scared that Maureen Kenyen might call the cops or building security to stop me, I zoomed into the stairwell and clattered down the two flights, hell-bent to get to Lemmy's floor, not giving a flying hoot if anybody heard me or got in my way.

It struck me that I was doing exactly what Tibble had done the other day, but it was not the time to dwell on that curious fact.

I ran onto Lemmy's floor, sped around the corridor to his apartment, and banged on his door with both fists. Any port in a storm.

"Lemmy, it's Brenda. Open up! Hurry!"

From deep within the apartment he piped up, "Yeah, yeah, yeah. Don't get your panties in an uproar. I'll be there in a minute."

It seemed like a lot longer, but at last the door opened. Lemmy smirked at me.

I was so happy to see a familiar face I almost smooched his shiny, fresh-shaved chrome dome.

"Where've you been, oh wife of mine?" he said. "The doorman buzzed—it must have been a good ten minutes ago. He said you were on the way up. Did you get stuck in the elevator or what?"

"No, I was—"

"Holy shit, look at you. You're a mess, and in a business

suit too. Why are you dressed like that? What's wrong? What the hell is going on?"

I'd have loved to have known the answer to that myself. I attempted to calm down and gather my thoughts, but Lemmy kept rapid-firing questions.

"Lemmy, will you please shut up a minute? I need to think."

To his credit and my total amazement, he actually did stop the barrage. He waddled off to the kitchen. "Can I get you anything?"

"Yes, please. Water."

I stepped into Lemmy's groovy bachelor pad conversation pit, threw myself down flat on my back on his fuzzy white couch, and reviewed the recent events.

In all my confusion, one thing seemed clear. Although she'd played along for a while, Maureen Kenyen knew I was not Frankie Tibble's paralegal, and she'd probably known I was a fake from the instant she set eyes on me. Okay, that I could deal with. My costume sucked, my plan was lousy, and I had no contingency plan. I deserved to get caught.

But what was all this baloney about blackmail? I strained to remember her exact words. "Tell whoever sent you that there'll be no more envelopes." And then, "I will not be blackmailed."

Lemmy joined me in the conversation pit. He set a tall glass on the coffee table. "I hope you're not sick, because if you're gonna puke—"

"No, I'm not gonna puke." I sat up, grabbed the glass with both hands, and gulped. "Lemmy, do you know a woman named Maureen Kenyen? She lives two floors up."

"Black-haired old broad? Heavily penciled arched eyebrows plucked to hell?"

"Uh-huh."

"I wouldn't say we were friends, but sure, I know who she is. She's lived in the building forever."

"Do you have any idea why somebody might want to blackmail her?"

"That's a no-brainer, Brenda. Everybody's got something they don't want somebody else to know, and anybody with money is a target."

"So she's rich?"

"Rich enough, I guess. What's this all about?"

I summed up. I tried to gloss over some tricky parts, like how I happened to be in the building when Tibble ran into me, but Lemmy called me on it.

"Now hold on a freaking minute," he said, "You freely admit you were here in my building when Addy Shelton was killed."

I nodded.

"Gee, Brenda, that means you were mighty close by when my brassiere collection was ripped off."

"I guess."

"The irony blows me away."

"It's pretty weird, all right," I agreed.

"Tell you what, I'm gonna let it slide for the time being, because I'm intrigued by the ever-fascinating subject of blackmail. Tell me more."

"All I know is for some reason Tibble's alibi, that's Maureen Kenyen, thinks I'm a blackmailer."

"Why?"

"I'm not sure. It must have been something I said."

"Somebody once tried to blackmail me."

"Really?"

"Yep. Called his bluff. I told the dude to piss up a rope and thank you very much, go right ahead, I could use the publicity. The coward backed off."

It was hard to tell if Lemmy was kidding. "What did he have on you?"

"Nice try, Brenda. Now, here's the interesting part. Guess who the blackmailer was."

"I haven't the foggiest."

"Three guesses."

"This is stupid. I don't want to play guessing games."

"Humor me."

"Lemmy, you're obviously bursting to tell me, so cut the suspense, and get on with it."

Lemmy opted for the dramatic delivery. He climbed up on his coffee table so he hovered over me, held out his arms preacher style, spread his fingers wide, and boomed, "Adison Montgomery Shelton, that's who."

"Come on, Lemmy, that's not the least bit funny. I mean, Shelton's body is barely even cold and already you're making bad jokes."

"It's no joke."

It took a while, but Lemmy eventually convinced me he was telling the truth or rather what he truly believed to be the truth. I had serious doubts. The concept of Adison Montgomery Shelton as a blackmailer simply did not compute. Again I thought back to the time I'd temped for one of Shelton's non-profits. I had no behind-the-scenes access. All I did was type addresses, but I remember the place was well-run and doing good work—various programs to help the homeless. This made it all the more difficult to believe what Lemmy was saying.

"I don't get it, Lemmy. Why would a man like Shelton be involved in such a dirty, dangerous business?"

"Money."

"Shelton had piles of money."

"So he wanted more piles. Not so hard to understand. His entire life was about money. The man was obsessed. When he first contacted me for purposes of blackmail, he called himself John Dough."

"Cute. I still don't see why you're so sure Shelton was John Dough. Surely he didn't come to you in person."

"You're correct. The blackmailer called, told me what he knew, and suggested a ridiculous amount, which he claimed was non-negotiable."

"Did you recognize the voice as Shelton's?"

"No."

"You better not say you used the callback feature on your phone. No blackmailer would be so stupid as to make a threatening call from a traceable line."

"Geeze, Brenda, you must think I'm a real dope. Of course I didn't star sixty-nine him. What I did was turn loose my powers of observation. The blackmailer mentioned one specific indiscretion. So I asked myself, 'Lemmy, my man, who besides you and the babe in question would have known about that?' and I remembered me and her bumped into Shelton late one night in the elevator. But that's not all. After I told this John Dough character to bug off, whenever I ran into Shelton, he acted standoffish."

"Maybe because he'd witnessed your . . . whatever with whomever, your indiscretion, as you so delicately put it. He might not have approved of such goings on."

"Hey, we're talking about Adison Montgomery Shelton here. Big playboy."

"Oh yeah, right."

"Trust me, Brenda. After years of negotiating deals for my clients, I know how to read people. I could tell by the look in Shelton's eyes. And consider this: Shelton got whacked. Blackmail is one swell motive. Remember that *Tod Trueman* where—"

"Let's stick to real life. I presume you told the cops all about Shelton's attempt to blackmail you."

"Hell no. The way I see it, Shelton got what he deserved. If one of his blackmail victims did him, it's no skin off my nose."

"Hmmm," I said. I took another drink of water and let my mind go with the idea. Suppose Lemmy was right and Shelton really was a blackmailer. Maureen Kenyen was a blackmail victim. And the two of them just happened to live in the same building. Either that was a bizarre coincidence or Shelton was blackmailing Kenyen. Kenyen killed Shelton. No. Scratch that last. Kenyen hired Tibble to make payoffs. Or she hired him to kill Shelton. I was right back where I started, but with hard evidence of motive. That was better than a random smashup on the stairwell.

Yeah, great motive. Except I didn't believe it, because I still couldn't see Shelton as a blackmailer. I had no desire to even pursue the idea. Blackmail is too damned scary for this milliner. I didn't want to go anywhere near it.

I knew what I had to do.

"Lemmy, you've got to tell the police what you told me."

"No way."

"It's motive. More important, it's a motive the police probably would never dream of in this case. Shelton doesn't fit the profile of a blackmailer. Believe me, the cop in charge of the investigation, Detective Mike Duxman, would never in a million years connect the dots. He's lazy, too busy being the on-camera spokesman to actually conduct a proper investigation."

"Sounds like my kind of guy. Do you think he's got an agent?"

"Dammit, Lemmy, this is serious. If you don't tell the cops, I will."

"Oh, Brenda, better listen to your hubby. If I were you, I wouldn't run off and blab to the cops."

"Why not?"

"As it stands right now, the cops are convinced burglary was the motive for the murder. They think the burglar hit my apartment first, then Shelton's, and that Shelton interrupted the perp mid-burgle. If you get them thinking otherwise, they'll eventually figure out that the killer was never in my apartment and that—"

"Allow me to finish that thought. While such information might serve justice, might get a cold-blooded murderer off the streets and into prison, it would ruin your chance to collect insurance money on jewels you never owned. You're a scumbucket, Lemmy."

"Thank you, my dear. Don't forget, if I were to tell all to the cops, I'd also have to rat on you for filching my bras."

That wasn't nearly the threat Lemmy thought. Turner and

McKinley already knew. So did Detective Duxman.

Even though Lemmy knew and he knew that I knew he knew, it was not in my best interest to come right out and admit to him that I'd taken his bras. It was still a condition of our divorce. Instead of saying something I'd later regret, I flashed him a big smile and told him I had to leave.

"So soon? And we were beginning to have fun."

"Call Winfield, sign the divorce papers, then we'll have fun."

"Gee, Brenda, I'll get right on that, that is, just as soon as my brassiere collection is back on my wall again. I'm lost without my bras. I've become a sad man in an empty shell of an apartment, all meaning stripped from my life."

"Maybe you shouldn't be so attached to stuff. It's all transitory, Lemmy."

"Know what I'm gonna do? Once my collection has been returned unharmed, and you and I are the very happily divorced couple we were always meant to be, I'm gonna throw the biggest goddamned celebratory divorce party you ever saw. You'll come, won't you, as the divorcée of honor? If the weather holds, it'll be an afternoon barbecue on my lovely balcony."

"Lemmy, that's got to be the stupidest idea I've ever heard."

Much as I wanted to leave, I had reservations. I was afraid somebody would be combing the building, searching for me. I took off the jacket and turned the T-shirt around logo side out, but it wasn't enough.

"Lemmy, don't you have to go to the corner and pick up a newspaper or a bagel or something?"

"No."

"Oh."

"Why?"

"I was hoping you'd walk out of the building with me. Maureen Kenyen was extremely upset. I can hardly blame her. The poor woman thinks I'm a blackmailer. She might have alerted the authorities. You would be my safe passage out of the building. If anybody asks, you could tell them I've been with you the whole time."

He frowned.

"Please. I'd feel so much more legit with you by my side."

"That's a new one," he said, "almost an insult. But all right, I'll do it as a favor and as a little reminder that I want my bras back."

"I know you do."

No one lurked in the hallway. The elevator was empty. Lemmy and I sailed through the lobby. No problems, no cops, no second glances from the doorman, no Maureen Kenyen standing in the shadows.

Once on the street, I thanked Lemmy and hailed a passing taxi. Lemmy opened the door for me. After I was seated, he leaned into the cab and said, "About my bras. No questions asked. Remember that."

He slammed the door shut. The cab rolled around the corner and nosed into downtown traffic.

22

Instead of cutting over far to the west, the taxi driver plowed his vehicle right through the center of Times Square, a neighborhood I hardly recognized since its mutation into a squeaky-clean theme park. If Dweena had been along, she would have thrown a fit about the inefficient route. Me, I had too much on my mind to care.

I relaxed, sat back, and took in the flashing barrage of sights, confident that somewhere behind the bright, cheerful facades, underneath the millions of twinkling lights, beyond the glittery advertising billboards, still lurked the nasty perverted old soul of the former Times Square. It was no doubt laughing its ass off and ogling the rosy-cheeked tourists as they tripped agog through the corporate wonderland, forking over money for logo-embellished goodies.

Soon my thoughts of facades and artifice and dark souls led me to wonder if the soul of a blackmailer could possibly have lurked behind the photogenic public do-gooder face of the late Adison Montgomery Shelton.

Despite Lemmy's insistence, I didn't think so.

I could accept the possibility that Shelton wasn't quite what he appeared to be. I mean, who is? It just seemed to me that if this particular individual really was a bad guy, if he wanted to inflict evil on the world, the wealthy playboy philanthropist would not have picked blackmail. Too bad I hadn't stayed in touch with anyone who'd worked at his organization. I could have called and asked if their main benefactor was a creep.

Lemmy said Shelton was obsessed with money and wanted more. I suppose it is human nature to want more of whatever. Most humans don't turn to crime to get it, at least not that kind of crime.

My immediate problem was what to tell Turner and McKinley. I had to come up with something. They sure weren't going to forget they'd let me see Maureen Kenyen's name. They'd be dying know if I'd talked to her and would want a full report.

A message from Dweena waited on my answering machine. She desperately needed her wigs back and would I please be so kind as to drop them off?

Good. I wanted to talk to her. She knew more about money than anybody I knew. I bagged the wigs, snapped on Jackhammer's leash, and off we went.

On the way to Gansevoort Street, Jackhammer scored a chunk of garlic bread from his favorite Italian restaurateur, who reminded me that Johnny and I hadn't been in lately.

"My new pumpkin ravioli," he said. "Very special. Spiced the way you like. I make it just for you."

"Soon," I promised. I much preferred it to La Reverie. Great food. It didn't take a month to get a reservation or cost a fortune. And the best part—no pretense or romantic subtext.

Dweena gave the red pixie wig a vigorous shake, then placed it lovingly on a wig stand. "So this is the one you used. I must say, it wouldn't have been my first choice for you. Did it do the trick?"

"Well, not exactly." I filled her in on the terrible Tibble incident.

"Speaking from experience," she commented, "duct tape is a bitch. You must have been scared out of your everlovin' mind."

"I was pretty scared. I thought for sure I was a goner."

"Poor Brenda. I feel simply awful. Now that I see it and you in the same room, clearly the red pixie is not you."

"I thought that was the idea."

"Brenda, for a hip, with-it, finger-on-the-pulse-of-now designer you don't know a hill of beans about dress-up. First rule of disguise: It's gotta be believable. Kinda like it's not the real you but an alternate you, a you you really could be. And believe me, you could never be a red pixie."

"I see. Me but not me but not too much not me."

"It's abstract. You just know. Either you've got it or you don't, and judging from your choice of wig, I'd say you most definitely don't. I could kick myself for bringing that wig. I should have at least stuck around to help you choose. I could have been fashionably late for the session with the photographer."

"How did that go?"

"It was so cool. She showed me proofs of my billboard, and I must say, Dweena is very very lovely even when enlarged to twelve storeys high. I was a little concerned about pores in the oily nose zone, but I came out peach-smooth all over. It's hard to believe I'm getting paid gobs of money for having so much fun."

"Speaking of gobs of money, I have a question for you."

"Ask away."

"How does old money differ from new money?"

"That's easy. Taste and class. Old money people say new money people have neither. And new money people—well, hey, that's moi!"

"Aside from the snob factor is there any technical difference?"

"Old money has been around longer, like forever, in the same family, stuck away somewhere, festering interest. But technically, no. Old or new, money's money. It spends the same, piles up the same, gets frittered away the same. Why?"

"I was thinking about Adison Montgomery Shelton."

"Now, that money is most certainly old money gained by unconscionable exploitation of the working class by robber barons."

"How much do you think he had?"

"Multiple millions, I suppose."

"I heard a rumor he was running low on cash. Is it possible for somebody like him to be overextended?"

"Of course. You don't have to be dirt poor to have expenses exceed income. That can happen at any level. Or if he didn't spend it, he could have lost a pile through bad investment, the trusting yet naive investor led astray by unscrupulous broker types. Shelton was a big player. You know how it is, the bigger they are, the harder they fall. Now that I think of it, I kinda halfway remember maybe hearing he'd made some bad decisions. It's kind of hazy. Whatever I heard was third or fourth or fifth or sixth hand. My ear is not exactly to the ground anymore."

"Could you find out for sure? It's important."

"No. I'm afraid your pal Dweena has no more friends on Wall Street."

"Yes, but you have enemies on Wall Street. That's even better. People afraid of what you know."

"Good point, Brenda. Brilliant, actually. Naturally I've thought the same many times. With the stuff I know . . . man, oh man. Too bad I'm stuck with a powerful set of ethics. No matter how much some of those assholes screwed me over, I can't bring myself to return the favor. Why do you care so much anyway? I mean, the guy's dead."

"Lemmy says Shelton was a blackmailer. Weird, huh?"

"I'll say. What gave Lemmy that idea?"

"He claims Shelton once tried to blackmail him."

"No kidding."

"The only way it makes any sense to me is if Shelton needed money."

"I suppose it's possible. Despite the unreliable source, Lemon B. Crenshaw, blackmail is an intriguing thought. Rather gets my juices going."

"Does that mean you'll check into it?"

"Let me think on it a while. It is fun to think I could blackmail somebody to tell me if somebody else might have had motive to blackmail somebody."

"Do you think your ethics could handle it?"

"Like a tree that bends in the wind to maintain strength, those ethics of mine need to be flexible. I know of a very special someone from my old brokerage whom I'd love to intimidate. After the big insider trading blowup, to escape prosecution he ratted on a bunch of people, then managed somehow to wheedle his way into a startup e-trade firm. He is in a position to hear all the gossip."

From Dweena's, Jackhammer and I walked over to Midnight Millinery. I rolled up the gates, opened the door, and got a whiff of a bad odor. It was the strangest feeling, like the shop was mad at me for neglecting it. In the short time it had been closed, dust and grime had settled onto every surface.

Jackhammer, on cockroach patrol, trotted around the periphery. I opened the back window to blow in some fresh air and slung a rag around to dust off the surfaces. I got the place back to normal in no time at all. Soon I was happily draping a large piece of exquisite orange silk over a loose framework to make a close-fitting hybrid of cloche and turban.

It was great to be back and officially open for business.

Or so I thought until the bells on the door jangled and I looked up to greet my first customer of the day and it turned out to be customers in the plural.

Turner and McKinley.

They caught me. I'd been procrastinating about calling them, because I didn't know what to say. They were men of action. When I didn't act, they did.

"Greetings, gentlemen. Out enjoying the weather?"

"Can't say that I am," said Turner.

"Too damned hot," said McKinley.

Okay, so the small talk was done.

McKinley plopped his butt on my high counter and sat swinging his legs and smiling and admiring the excellent shine on his expensive shoes.

Turner sauntered over to me. "So?" he said.

I gazed up at him and smiled. "So what?"

"Come on, Ms. Midnight. We're all friends here. You can dispense with the innocent act. I assume you paid a little visit to Maureen Kenyen."

"Oh, so that's what you want to know about. Yeah, I stopped by to see the lady. I'd say she's somewhere in her seventies, dyed blue-black hair, heavy makeup, about five-foot-five."

"So much for your excellent powers of observation, but to tell the truth, Ms. Midnight, I don't give a good goddamn what Kenyen looks like. I want to know what you found out."

"Oh, you mean about Frankie Tibble's alibi?" I was stalling, all the while trying to determine how little I could divulge without pissing off the detectives.

McKinley apparently had had enough of my jive. He jumped down off the counter and joined Turner in glaring down at me. "Don't try our patience," he said. "Of course he means the alibi."

"All right, here goes. Frankie Tibble is Maureen Kenyen's attorney. That much is true."

"Did Kenyen substantiate Tibble's story that he had business with her on the day Shelton was murdered?"

Although the detectives couldn't say, I knew they were after an opening, a wedge, any little thing to discredit Duxman and prove he'd done a lousy job. "I am sorry to have to tell you we didn't get around to that. I wasn't with her long before Maureen Kenyen became extremely agitated."

Turner and McKinley sighed in unison.

I'd never seen them so depressed. They must have felt impotent. I hated that I'd let them down.

McKinley rallied. He slapped me on the back. "Don't

feel bad, Ms. Midnight. We know you did your best, but we're gonna need much more to convince our esteemed colleague Duxman to check out Maureen Kenyen in person." He walked out the door, shaking his head.

Turner started to follow his partner, then lagged behind. He turned and said, "Thank you."

"You're welcome."

Turner seemed so sad, I decided to go for broke.

"I did hear an interesting rumor."

That perked him up. "Yeah? And what's that, Ms. Midnight?"

"Somebody told me Adison Montgomery Shelton was a blackmailer."

At least it got a laugh out of him, a roaring one at that. "That's a good one, Ms. Midnight. Remind me of that next time I think the neighborhood milliner might actually come up with useful information."

This time he made it all the way out the door.

Screw it. I'd done my duty. It wasn't my fault nobody believed me.

I got back to my hats, delighted to put the last few days' events behind me.

Yeah, right. I should know myself better by now. I could not stop thinking about Shelton.

Obviously either he was or was not a blackmailer.

If Shelton was a blackmailer, then most likely one of his victims finally got fed up enough to kill him. Much as I hate to agree with Lemmy, I kind of did on that point. If a victim did it, Shelton only got what he deserved. Yes, there was a killer loose somewhere, but not a killer who posed a threat to anybody else.

The other possibility, and unfortunately the one I tended to believe, that Shelton was not a blackmailer, had more dire consequences. If that were true, then a killer was still on the street and this killer was dangerous.

So I guess I hoped Shelton was a blackmailer.

Hard to imagine in the heat of summer, but fall really was

just around the corner. I needed a cohesive collection. Feeling the pressure, I worked until I pooped out.

While putting away my supplies, I stumbled on a scrap of veiling, which reminded me of the final project in my specialty millinery course. I'd had to design the headgear for an entire wedding party. Not merely the bridal veil with a fifteen-foot-long train, but the bridesmaids' hats, the flower girl hat, the mother of the bride hat, the mother of the groom hat, and little hatlettes for the catering staff.

Why not design an ex-wife hat? This was an untapped market of ever-increasing potential. Plenty of ex-wives attend their exes subsequent weddings. Surely they deserve a special hat.

If I came up with a good enough design, maybe I'd even attend Lemmy's stupid divorce party.

Newly energized, I got out my sketchbook and turned to a fresh page.

23

I love the feel of millinery materials in my hand, the smell, the immediacy. And so I usually design directly on the block, by draping woven fabric or smooshing wet felt or slashing buckram and twisting paper-covered wire. When I come up with a good prototype, I refine whatever comes off the block and then draft an official pattern.

I rarely do preliminary sketches, but the ideas for the ex-wife hat gushed out of my head so fast and furious I had no choice. The pages of the sketchbook filled up rapidly. My graphite stick literally burned.

The hats were whimsical, gravity-defying shapes in hot, high-contrast colors. Designed not for the sad, embittered ex-wife but as celebration for the gleeful, happy ex-wife, somebody like me. For inspiration I thought of Lemmy and also my first ex, Nado. I don't see him often, but when I do, right away I remember why I married him. Five minutes later I remember why I divorced him.

Floating in the back of my mind was a vague idea about propellers, like on a little boy's beanie. It was the right attitude but I didn't like the verticality. I was wondering how hard it would be to make pinwheels that could go off in all directions when a loud bang at the door startled me.

The shop was closed, but anybody who walked by could see me at work.

Jackhammer leaped straight off his bed of piled-up fabric scraps, skittered over to the door, barked a few times, then ran to me and climbed up on my lap.

Hanging on to Jackhammer, I stood up to get a clear view.

Frankie Tibble, the rude arrogant asshole lawyer himself, was outside, hands cupped around his eyes, peering through the glass. He kicked the door with such intensity I knew he must be mad.

My first instinct was to think: Great, a pissed-off Tibble, the last person I ever wanted to see again regardless of his mood. My second instinct, which should have been my first and would have been if I hadn't been having so much fun with the ex-wife hat, was the realization that I might be in danger.

While I didn't think Frankie Tibble had killed Shelton, I also realized I could be wrong about that, and it seemed pretty obvious that he was somehow involved. I just hadn't yet figured out how.

I glanced at the clock. It was late. Turner and McKinley would have gone home hours ago. If I called 911, a bunch of cop cars and ambulances and fire trucks would screech up, lights flashing and sirens blaring, and Tibble would either run off or stick around. Either would be difficult to explain to the assembled authority figures and rescue teams.

I'm neither brave nor foolhardy. I like my life and am a great believer in self-preservation. I do not intentionally walk into dangerous situations.

Unfortunately, this situation had come to me and was presenting itself very loudly. If I didn't get Tibble to shut up soon, some angry neighbor would be putting in that call to 911.

Remembering how Tibble already had had the opportunity to send me on a long walk off a short pier and how he would be the obvious suspect should anything happen to me, I concluded that even though I didn't like the man, he probably wasn't nearly that stupid.

With Jackhammer still in my grip, I took a deep breath,

walked over to the door, and released the chain lock.

Tibble shoved the door open and pushed his way in and screamed at me, "Who the hell do you think you are to go harass my mother like that?"

The man's attitude sucked. And after I'd been nice enough to let him in. "I didn't harass any . . ."

Wait a minute. Had I heard right? His mother?

"You might as well admit it," he raged. "My mom ratted you out. I know damned well it was you poking around asking a lot of questions that are none of your business. You didn't even use a fake name. I mean, how stupid is that? Since you don't appear to be stupid, I assume your action was intentional. You wanted me to find out."

Find out?

My brain, spinning way ahead of my mouth, was trying to deal with Tibble's reference to his mom. Meanwhile, my mouth was spewing forth with "No, it can't be" while realizing that yes, it absolutely could be. Maureen Kenyen could very well be Tibble's mother. Underneath all that makeup was a face not unlike his. Both had blue eyes and also a similarity about the eyebrows. Maureen Kenyen obliterated hers by plucking, Tibble let his sprout to their fullest, but they had the same high-arched shape.

This would sure help explain how a cellar sleaze like him had an uptown client like her.

I attempted to hide my bewilderment.

Jackhammer, meanwhile, wanted down, but I hung onto him, afraid he'd attack Tibble. He was a lawyer and not very well off. The bastard would probably sue. I told Jackhammer to cool it, but he didn't. Instead he squeaked.

"Cute," said Tibble.

I thought he was being sarcastic, but he approached and leaned down at eye level to Jackhammer. "Boy or girl?"

"Boy. Jackhammer's his name."

"Hey, little guy, Jackhammer. You are so tiny." He held out his hand.

I couldn't believe it when Jackhammer licked Tibble's

knuckles. I could feel his tail stub vibrate against my chest. He usually had better taste in humans.

Tibble straightened up.

I saw that his expression had softened considerably.

"Just because you hang out with what has got to be the cutest dog I have ever seen," he said, "doesn't give you the right to bug my mom."

Way beyond coherent speech, I could only stare at Tibble and Jackhammer, flabbergasted.

Jackhammer squirmed again and I let him down.

Tibble walked over to my vanity. With a dramatic sigh he sank down on the bench. Before I knew it, Jackhammer was curled up in Tibble's lap.

"About my mom, did she invite you to dinner? She almost always does that, unless someone's a real loser, which"—he gave me a good, hard head-to-toe appraisal—"you're actually not. However, you're not my type, so don't go getting any funny ideas."

How weird. Here was a man intent on protecting his mom and slightly embarrassed to admit she thought he needed fixing up.

"I'm terribly confused," I said. "Are you trying to tell me that Maureen Kenyen is your mother?"

"You really didn't know, did you?"

"No. I had no idea. And to answer your other question, no, your mom didn't invite me to dinner, and believe me, I'm hardly getting any funny ideas. You're most assuredly not my type. You don't even come close."

"Oh," he said. "Well, that's good, then. I'm glad we got that straightened out."

"Me too."

"So why'd you bother my mom?"

I decided he deserved an honest answer. "I was checking up on your alibi." I braced myself in case he started screaming again.

He stroked Jackhammer and remained calm. "The cops already did that."

"One cop. One lazy cop. Detective Duxman. All he did was make some calls. That's not proper police procedure."

"So you decided to take the law into your own hands."

"No, Detectives Turner and McKinley asked me to step in."

He chuckled. "Oh sure. Big city police detective hotshots often go to milliners for help."

"The detectives and I have a long history. For them, it was a tricky situation. They knew Duxman had fallen down in his duty but weren't in a position to do much about it. I, on the other hand, a mere civilian immune to police procedures and interoffice politics, could. You're right, they didn't come right out and ask me, they hinted. You'll be happy to know I'm almost positive neither you nor your mom killed Shelton."

"Gee, thanks a lot."

"However, I suspect you were up to no good."

"Funny, I have the exact same feeling about you."

"Want to know what I think?"

Tibble didn't respond. His piercing look challenged me to continue.

I had to be careful. I didn't want to get him riled again, especially while he was holding Jackhammer, but I wanted more information. "I believe a man who called himself John Dough was blackmailing your mother. I don't know what for, and I don't care."

Stony silence.

I continued. "And you helped her out by making the payoffs." That, to me, seemed the most reasonable explanation.

Stony silence, part two.

That was as good as a yes.

I paused, considered what I now knew, and realized how well it fit with Lemmy's accusation that Shelton was a blackmailer.

"And then," I said, "after you made many payoffs on behalf of your mother, you eventually found out that John Dough was"—I paused to make sure I had Tibble's full attention—"none other than Mr. Adison Montgomery Shelton."

End of stony silence. Tibble looked as befuddled as I'd felt earlier. "How'd you . . . ? I mean . . ."

Amazing. Shelton really was a blackmailer.

Both Tibble and I, now parties to the same secret, fell silent. My brain clicked away synthesizing information. I suspect Tibble's brain was putting in overtime, trying to decide whether to level with me.

I smiled my encouragement.

At last he said, "Oh, what the hell. You're right. It was Shelton. How'd you find out?"

"Your mother wasn't the only person he was blackmailing."

"Who else? You?"

"No. Let's just say a friend who had a hunch who it was. How did you find out Dough's real identity?"

"Easy. If Shelton hadn't picked on my mom, I'd almost feel sorry for the guy, he was such a bumbling blackmailer. Didn't know his ass from a hole in the ground. I think he got his ideas from bad spy novels. He specified money drops in public places, always a different location, but he wasn't careful when he picked up the money. One night I simply stuck around after stashing the money in a freebie newspaper box. I hid in a recessed building entrance until John Dough made the pickup."

"Bet you were surprised."

"Oh yes. I could not believe my eyes. Adison Montgomery Shelton! Give me a break. To be sure, a week later I made another payment—in a trash receptacle outside of Penn Station—and hung around again. Only this time I followed him home. That confirmed it. I didn't know what to do. I continued to make payments, one a week. That's what I was doing the other day, but when I got there, Shelton was already dead. I panicked and ran down the staircase."

"That's where I came in."

"Precisely."

"Hmmm," I said. I believed him a little, but part of his story didn't hold water. Since he seemed willing to talk, I probed further. "I find it strange that instead of one of the public places you mentioned, all of a sudden you're making payoffs at Shelton's apartment. You must have confronted him and told him you knew who he was. How'd he react to that?"

Tibble gently placed Jackhammer on the floor, then stood up and stretched and rolled his head around so that his neck popped.

I know a stall when I see one.

Finally he said, "Did I say I was there to make a payment? Sorry, it's very late and I'm dead tired. What I meant to say was I made the drop and then followed Shelton back to his apartment and . . ." He paused, probably realizing this version also made no sense.

I nodded as if so engrossed in his gripping story I hadn't noticed the discrepancy.

He continued, real fast, spitting out words. "And Shelton was dead. It was so awful. The door was slightly ajar. I should have known that meant trouble, but before I could think, I pushed the door all the way open. I didn't have to go in, I could see Shelton from the hall. Clobbered. Blood and guts everywhere. It was all over, nothing I could do for him."

"What a close call. The killer must have been on the scene seconds before you showed up."

"Yes. That's why I thought you'd done it. Right after, I ran past you on the stairs."

More like plowed into, but I let it slide. Tibble was talking himself into a trap, and I didn't want to slow his progress.

Tibble went on, full speed ahead. "I should have known a puny hundred-pounder like you couldn't have done that much damage. It's not easy to bludgeon someone to death."

"Right," I said. "It takes lots of strength."

"It sure does."

"And lots of time."

He started to nod in agreement, then frowned.

"So," I said, as if puzzled, "how could you have been following Shelton and then find him already dead? Were you delayed?"

"Yes. That's exactly what happened. Shelton went right up because he lived in the building. I had to check in with the doorman."

"Now that I think of it, isn't it strange that you followed Shelton all the way to his apartment? You already knew it was him from the first time you tailed him."

A flustered Tibble tried to recover, but became entangled in a mess of excuses and gave up in defeat. "Okay, you got me. I admit I only followed Shelton that one time. And yes, I did go to his apartment on the day he was killed. I was going to confront him with what I knew, but like I said before, he was already dead."

"Oh, I see. You were gonna confront him, blackmail the blackmailer, cut in on some of Shelton's action."

Tibble took my accusation in stride. "Even if that were true—and it most certainly is not—it doesn't change the fact that Shelton was dead when I got there."

"Why didn't you call the cops?"

"I already told you. It was too late for Shelton. He was dead. No cop could change that. It would have been tough to explain my presence, so I bolted. You'd have done the same."

Maybe, maybe not. "Did you see anybody else around, anybody acting suspicious?"

"Only you. I apologize for bashing into you, but you know, extenuating circumstances."

"I guess we're right back where we started."

"Not quite. You already admitted you don't think I did it. Well, good news. I don't think you did it either. I hope you'll keep this between us. I wouldn't want Mom dragged into a murder investigation."

I didn't want that either. Unless I could find out the

names of Shelton's other victims, telling Turner and McKinley wouldn't do anybody any good. "I understand. Just tell me one thing. How much was Shelton into your mom for?"

"None of your business, but I'll say this much. To a guy like him, pocket change."

24

I slept like a rock. No dreams or night-mares or passing thoughts of Frankie Tibble, his mom, blackmail, or murder. Not even Lemmy and his goddamned brassiere collection disturbed my sleep.

Because of the extra-deep sleep, I woke up earlier than usual the next morning and jumped out of bed, excited that I could spend the entire day at Midnight Millinery. I couldn't wait to get back to the ex-wife hat designs.

I threw on a pair of cutoffs and a T-shirt. "Hey, Jackhammer, want to go out?"

He wagged his answer.

Jackhammer skittered down the hallway, stopping to sniff at any apartment where a dog or cat lived. I noticed that overnight somebody had slipped envelopes under all the doors so that only a corner poked out. Solicitation of any kind was not allowed, and except for take-out delivery menus everybody pretty much abided by the rules, so I figured it had to be a notice from building management. Not another burst water pipe, I hoped.

Thinking I'd walked over the notice on the way out of my apartment and anxious to know what management had to report, I went back to check, but found no envelope under my door.

Strange. Everybody else had one. Perhaps a computer error had dropped me from the main distribution list. I'd better tell somebody before the foul-up spiraled out of control.

Ralph was the doorman on duty. He smiled as I approached his desk and asked what he could do for me.

"I was wondering about the notice everybody got under their doors. For some reason I didn't get one."

Ralph's smile faded. He didn't reply, which I thought was weird. Ralph was generally quite a talker.

"So what's up? Another leak?"

Ralph shifted his weight in his chair. "Uh . . . no. Not a leak."

"Well, then, are they painting the laundry room floor? What a mess the last time. Remember? It was a full-scale urban disaster when the paint didn't dry for days and nobody could do their wash. You'd have thought it was the end of modern civilization."

Ralph creaked out half a smile, not much more than a twitch, and it quickly faded.

"What is it?" I asked, this time more insistent.

Ralph gazed down at his hands, cleared his throat, and muttered, "Rug shampoo."

"Rug shampoo?" I didn't get it. What rug could building management possibly be shampooing that they needed to tell the residents about? For that matter I didn't know of any rugs in the public spaces. The lobby floor was marble, the hallways were ceramic tile.

Ralph let out a big sigh. "It's my brother-in-law, Stefen," he said. "The man's a damned fool. Quit a good-paying stable accountant job with full benefits and bought into a rug shampoo franchise. And wouldn't you know my sister's pregnant again. I was only trying to help them out. Early this morning before my shift I slipped the envelopes under the doors. Inside is a full-color advertising brochure for Stefen's business, plus everybody got a ten dollar off coupon."

"Everybody except me," I said. It came out all wrong, paranoid, like I actually cared.

"Please understand," said Ralph, "color printing costs very much. You don't have rugs, so I didn't give you a brochure."

"That's logical."

"If you want, I have a couple of extra."

"No, really, it's okay."

"You sure?"

"Don't worry about it. But I am curious. How did you know I don't have rugs?" I was positive Ralph had never been inside my apartment.

Ralph relaxed, and his smile came back full force. "You know that lady who lives in the apartment below you, Marta?"

"The crabby old witch with the stubby whiskers and short, steely gray hair?"

He nodded. "All the time Marta's coming to me complaining about you and little Jackhammer."

"What in the world did we do to her? I hardly know the woman."

"She says you clomp across your hardwood floor like a three-hundred-pound linebacker and Jackhammer's toenails are constantly going click-click click-click and the two of you are driving her crazy. She wouldn't hear that if you had a rug."

"That's a brilliant deduction, Ralph."

"No rugs, no rug shampoo brochures."

"I hope your brother-in-law does well."

Jackhammer and I roamed around the Village for a while, taking advantage of the day before it got too awfully hot.

When we got back, I was surprised to see the light on my answering machine blinking and even more surprised when I played back the message. It was very early for Dweena to be calling. I returned her call right away.

"I cannot believe you're up before noon."

"You're assuming way too much," she said. "Dweena is not up before noon. What she is this morning is *still* up from yesterday. You see, Brenda, throughout the entire night, as a big fat favor to you, I've been hosting a brutal battle within. Dweena versus Dweena, not a pretty sight. Remember those ethics we talked about?"

"You mean about how to be strong they need to be flexible like a tree that bends in the wind?"

"Uh-huh. You might say my ethics bent over ass backward and twisted themselves into a pretzel worthy of a yoga master. To aid the cause of right, to see justice served, to help my pal—that's you—I did some digging, made some late-night calls, awakened some people, called in several favors, and threatened one of my favorite enemies, who coughed up the following scoop. Rumor on the street is that a couple of years ago Mr. Adison Montgomery Shelton blew the whole wad his family had amassed over many generations."

"Wow."

"He lost it all in less than a year on Internet start-ups, very tricky investments those little buggers."

"I thought that's where everybody quadrupled their money."

"Sextuple or more. But not everybody, and most assuredly not Shelton. He got screwed royally. He didn't know the territory. Actually nobody knows that territory, but some are good at making others think they do and become known as specialists. But the guy Shelton trusted was even worse than a so-called specialist. This guy was an out-and-out con man, now serving time, probably in the cell next to some of my former coworkers."

"Thanks, Dweena. I appreciate that you went out on limb for me."

"I hope it helps."

"It does. Evidence is piling up that Shelton really was a blackmailer. That he actually needed money makes a rather compelling motive. Somebody like him could hardly go out and get any old nine-to-five grunt job."

"Imagine his resume," said Dweena. "Qualifications: a

lifetime of experience as a filthy-rich playboy philanthropist."

"Given no choice, he turned to high-risk venture, the shadow world of blackmail."

"Hey, speaking of high-risk ventures, what's Chuck up to lately?"

"What do you mean?"

"One of the fellows I talked to last night heads up a venture capital firm. He's looking to throw some money at somebody."

"How about a hat designer?"

"Nah, he's into high tech. That's why I thought of Chuck. He's always a step or two ahead of the pack."

"Right now, Chuck is trying to be many, many steps behind the pack. He's developing a time machine to take him back to the nineteen sixties so he can meet Elizabeth when they're almost the same age."

"That is so romantic I can't stand it. I swear I'm getting weepy."

"Quite frankly, I think Chuck has finally stepped over the edge."

I opened the shop early and spent most of the day working on my fall line. It was starting to take shape.

Two regular customers came in to inquire about my trip to Paris. "Did you sell many hats?"

"Oh, *oui, oui.*"

I never show prototypes to customers, but I brought out a couple of the hats that I'd already finalized. They claimed they could see the Parisian influence and promised to return soon to place their orders for fall.

Weird how fibbing about a few sales in Paris increased sales on West Fourth Street.

Late in the afternoon I put away fall and turned to the ex-wife hat project and was totally engrossed, elbow-deep in bright yellow cotton duck, when the bells on the door jangled and Johnny walked in.

"What's that?" he asked.

"A hat," I said.

"I figured as much." He picked up a triangle of bright yellow fabric. "A new direction?"

I didn't think he'd find the ex-wife hat project nearly as funny as I did. "Special occasion."

"Oh, I see, special occasion. Speaking of which, tomorrow night, at the usual time, the network is rerunning a *Tod Trueman* episode."

"Johnny, that's terrific."

"Terrific for me. Not so terrific for the summer replacement show it is replacing. It also occurred to me that maybe I should make us that reservation at La Reverie. What do you think?"

I wondered how much, if anything, to read into that. Remember, this was the man who thought he'd proposed when all he'd done was apologize for a hideous orange and yellow shag rug. "Gee, I don't know, Johnny."

"You seemed up for it the other night."

"Let me think about it, okay?"

He frowned. "Yeah. Whatever."

I went back to my work, afraid to look him in the eye.

And so he left.

"Good-bye," I said as the door slammed shut.

I climbed into my display window. Half-hidden by several berets that hung at various levels on my hat tree, I watched Johnny stalk off. Without a glance back, he turned onto Bleecker Street and disappeared around the corner, probably headed toward his apartment.

I hadn't meant to hurt his feelings. I wished I'd never brought up La Reverie.

After that, I couldn't get back into the ex-wife hats. I put some stuff away, shut the lights, locked up, banged down the gate, and called it a day.

I went back to my rugless apartment and thought about making dinner, but the cupboards were mighty bare.

If I hadn't been such a jerk, Johnny and I would have had dinner together. But I was a jerk, so I went to Angie's alone. As some kind of punishment I didn't even bring Jackhammer along, and since I was so totally alone, I sat at the bar and munched grilled cheese and sipped red wine and ignored the news droning and flickering on the big TV over the bar.

That is, ignored it until I heard the voice of Detective Duxman.

What was it with that man? Every time I got anywhere near the TV at Angie's, his mug was on it.

The arrogant, lazy detective boasted to the newscaster that his men had nabbed the killer of Adison Montgomery Shelton.

Now, that was a surprise, but a good one. I was delighted. And relieved. It meant I was off the hook. I no longer had to worry about who had blackmailed whom or who knew what.

Duxman was saying, "A painstakingly thorough investigation proved to be the killer's undoing."

The newscaster intoned a cliché phrase about closure.

The camera pulled away from Duxman and dissolved into shots taken earlier of the perp walk. Some cop, not Duxman, paraded a grizzled guy in front of the cameras. The grizzled guy attempted to hide his face, but each time he put his arm up, the cop pushed it back down.

The newscaster continued in a voice-over: "The alleged killer, a man who goes only by the name of Daryl, was picked up earlier today in a routine roundup of homeless persons."

Next up, fire in a midtown tower.

I finished my grilled cheese and left Angie's.

My initial glee on hearing of the arrest soured considerably when I heard who had been arrested. What an insult to the memory of Shelton. Blackmailer or not, in the past the man had done a lot to help the homeless.

A homeless man sure makes a convenient scapegoat for an incompetent cop who needs to make an arrest in a high-profile case.

Violent crime is down, tourism is up, and New York City makes piles of money every time somebody from Iowa or Japan vacations in the Big Apple. We can't afford bad publicity. Whenever a prominent citizen gets murdered, the police are under incredible pressure to make a quick arrest. Truth and justice matter less than splashy headlines.

I wondered what Turner thought. Maybe I'd give him a call tomorrow and ask.

Marta, the woman who lived below me, made a career of griping. However, much as I hated to admit it, what Ralph said she'd accused me of was true. I clomp—though I can't imagine that it sounds like a three-hundred-pounder—and Jackhammer's toenails always need clipping.

In an effort to be a more thoughtful neighbor, I sat down on the banana-shaped couch. "Come over here, Jackhammer."

He leaped onto my lap. I rolled him over and tickled his belly. He kicked and thrashed about, having a great time, until he spotted the dreaded nail clippers on the back of the couch. He jumped down and tore off across the room.

In quick pursuit, I scooped him up and brought him back to the couch. "How about if we do one foot tonight?" I pleaded. My lack of authority was shameful.

Jackhammer refused to have any part of the clippers. He was amazingly strong for five pounds. I couldn't get a good grip on his foot. I gave up for the meantime, plotting to sneak up on him in his sleep.

25

Yesterday I got up early because I'd slept well. Today was a whole different story. I got up early because I couldn't sleep at all. At six o'clock in the morning I gave up the battle. Why toss and turn and fret about Johnny's hurt feelings and the arrest of a homeless man when I could be doing the laundry?

My red nylon laundry bag had been pressed into service for the transportation and storage of Lemmy's bra collection, so I gathered my dirty clothes, tied them up in a dirty sheet, and headed down to the basement.

As I rounded the corner to the laundry room, a loud racket coming from inside stopped me dead in my tracks. Somebody in there was smashing something against something else. No way was I going to confront a crazed vandal.

I picked up the house phone to alert the doorman and have him call security when the vandal shrieked. "Goddammit to hell!"

The voice, highly stressed out, was Elizabeth's.

I hung up the phone and dragged my clothes into the laundry room just in time to see her slam a big jug of liquid detergent into a metal box that was bolted to the wall.

"And a cheery good morning to you," I said.

Elizabeth's body jerked. She spun her head around. "Oh, Brenda, it's you. You scared the living daylights out of me. I didn't hear you come in."

"I sure as hell heard you."

"I imagine you did."

"What's wrong?"

"I've got three goddamned loads of goddamned sopping-wet clothes to dry, and this goddamned thieving machine ate my goddamned laundry card."

The organization that runs our laundry room had recently switched from quarters to debit cards, and the new system left a lot to be desired. The card recharger frequently failed, and the washers and dryers sucked value out of the cards seemingly at random.

"Technology marches on," I said. "Try pushing the black button."

She pushed. Her newly charged card popped out. "That's fantastic, Brenda. How'd you know what to do? I swear I've been reading these goddamned instructions forwards and backwards for the last ten minutes. They don't give a hint."

"The super showed me."

"Hmpf." Elizabeth started her dryers. She waited for me to throw in my loads of wash, then we took the elevator upstairs together.

"Since you haven't asked me to walk Jackhammer lately," she said, "I assume you're no longer afraid to go out on the street."

"Yeah, guess I overreacted."

"Better safe than sorry."

"They made an arrest in the Shelton murder, but I think they got the wrong guy."

"It won't be the first time the cops screwed up. Why do you think so now?"

"You'll probably find this hard to believe, but I've been poking around a little."

"I don't find *that* hard to believe."

"It turns out Adison Montgomery Shelton was a blackmailer."

"Get out of here!"

"It's true."

"Why would a man like that do a thing like that?"

"He needed money."

"He was rich."

"Not any more he wasn't. He made some bad investments."

"Easy come, easy go. In my book, blackmailers are the lowest scum. In my humble opinion if one of his victims killed the bastard, then he got what he deserved."

"My feeling exactly. The problem is the cops didn't arrest one of his victims. They don't even know about his victims, because they don't know he was a blackmailer."

"Who'd they pinch?"

"A homeless man."

Elizabeth shook her head in disgust. "Idiots."

"I think they were after a quick and easy headline."

By this time we were off the elevator and standing in the hall outside our apartments.

"Do me a favor and come inside for a minute?"

"Sure," she said. "What do you need?"

"Hold Jackhammer. I've got to clip his toenails and can't get him to sit still."

Elizabeth followed me into the apartment.

Jackhammer trotted into the foyer to greet us. Elizabeth bent down and picked him up. "Hey, Cutie Pie, what's this I hear about mean ol' Brenda trying to cut your pretty little toenails? Is she torturing you for the heck of it?"

"I'm not torturing him. I have good reason. I was down in the lobby talking to Ralph, and he told me that Marta, you know that witch down below"—I pointed at my floor—"complains all the time about noise coming from my apartment. She says I clomp and Jackhammer's toenails click."

"Oh, for chrissakes. Marta's a notorious troublemaker. Why do you care what she says?"

"I'm trying to be a good neighbor. You never know, she might some day lodge an official complaint with the board and they'll force me to carpet my floor, and you know how I hate rugs."

"Do I ever. It's too bad, too. If you didn't hate rugs, a

long time ago you and Johnny could have ridden off into the sunset together and lived happily ever after. You realize, don't you, that Marta's probably already informed the board of your grievous transgression. The board has no doubt ignored her. Complaining is her hobby. I'm surprised Ralph even mentioned it to you."

"It came up in conversation. His brother-in-law bought into a rug shampoo franchise."

"Oh yeah, I got a brochure under my door. I didn't know it was Ralph's brother-in-law's business."

Elizabeth and I sat on the couch. I put Jackhammer on my lap and turned him over on his back. She held him down and made kissy sounds to divert him. I clipped, and we got all four paws done. He jumped off the couch and ran into the corner, angry at both of us.

"Thanks," I said. "Couldn't have done it without you."

"You're most welcome. Now that I look around your place, I see something's missing. Where's the big bag of bras I hung up?"

"I had to cut them down. Winfield was on his way over. I hid them in the bathtub. Of course, I take them out when I bathe."

"I should hope so. What are your long-term plans for the collection?"

"I'll probably give them back to Lemmy."

"I'm sure having fun with my paintings. I decided to combine the bra motif with flashy motel neon and call the series Vacancies. I hope it's not too literal. The action is the abstract subtext."

"Interesting," I said. "Have you finished Chuck's portrait?"

"Not yet. I need him for one more sitting, but it's hard to pin him down and get him to commit to a time."

Oh, time. I checked the clock. "My wash is done. I've got to go."

"Too bad we're out of synch," said Elizabeth. "My dryers have another half-hour."

"It was fun doing laundry together while it lasted."

Speak of the witchy devil.

When I got down to the basement, Marta, my downstairs neighbor, was railing at the super. "People in this building are so rude," she said, glaring at me as I walked by. At first I thought she was complaining about me and considered telling her I'd clipped Jackhammer's nails, but her gripe du jour was the recycling bins in the incinerator rooms and how nobody separated their garbage properly. "They throw egg cartons in with the returnable cans and slimy, wet sesame noodles in with the glass."

She did have a point, but I kept my mouth shut and continued on to the laundry room.

Back upstairs, waiting for my clothes to dry, with time on my idle hands, I called Detective Turner and asked if he knew the particulars of the arrest of the homeless man.

Turner politely informed me that the Shelton murder was not his case, and it was most certainly not my case, because I was a milliner, not a cop.

"Did you even try to get Detective Duxman to look into the blackmail thing I mentioned?"

"Thank you very much, Ms. Midnight, for your concern," he said, "but Detective Duxman does not work for me. As McKinley and I have already told you, our hands are tied."

The next sound I heard was a dial tone.

I called back immediately.

"You again?" said Turner with a sigh.

"I was thinking," I said, picking up the conversation where he'd so rudely ended it, "I'm a taxpayer. Therefore Duxman works for me."

"So why don't you bug him?"

"Because I like you more. And because you know damned well Duxman is incompetent. And because I have a hunch you don't think the homeless man did it."

"You are quite perceptive, Ms. Midnight."

"Duxman is taking the easy way out, grabbing a headline."

"That is a distinct possibility."

"How can you sit back and let an innocent man go to prison?"

"Is that what you're so worried about?"

"Yes, and you should be too."

"Nobody's gonna go to prison. I doubt the case will even get to trial, but if it does, any dope of a public defender can convince a jury the homeless man is deranged. They'll lock the guy up in a nuthouse for a couple of years, where he'll get a warm bed and hot meals and an occasional bath, and everybody, most especially the homeless man himself, will be better off for it."

26

I left the finished laundry in a huge pile on the couch, snapped on Jackhammer's leash, took the roundabout way to Midnight Millinery, and opened up early for the second time in two days.

I was tending to one of my favorite customers, a publicist who'd been coming to Midnight Millinery since day one. Each season she ordered a brand-new custom hat.

Today she was seated at the vanity, agonizing over her reflection in the mirror. She'd already decided on a sexy, side-mounted beret but needed to choose a fabric.

She held a swatch of velvet to her face. "Don't you think green makes me look rather washed out?"

I knew better than to agree with that statement. I turned diplomat to say, "Blue brings out the color of your eyes better."

I rifled through my swatches and handed her a piece of blue silk. "Try this."

She held the new swatch to her face and scrutinized them. "You are so right. I guess that's why you're the designer. Problem is, I'm sick to death of blue."

"Pink flatters your skin tone." I offered another swatch.

She wrinkled up her nose. "Too girly."

Just then Frankie Tibble waltzed through the door, whistling a tune, looking like he had the whole world on a string.

"Good morning." He made a sweeping motion as if tipping a hat.

What the hell did he want?

"Hello," I said as warmly as possible under the circumstances. "Take a look around. I'll be with you in a moment."

"No hurry."

Jackhammer ran over to greet his new pal.

"New boyfriend?" whispered the customer. A trace of disapproval edged into her voice.

I shook my head no. No, no, no. Never. No way in hell.

"Good," she said. "I kind of like the old one, you know, that guy with the TV show."

She said that like she couldn't quite recall Johnny's name, which was total bullshit. She was trawling for gossip. It was her job. I didn't hold it against her.

I was trying to come up with a snappy yet unprintable response when I was saved by the bell—or rather the trill of her cell phone.

She took the call, mumbled into the small silver-toned device, clicked it closed. "Sorry, Brenda, I've got to run. One of my clients got himself in a heap of trouble."

"I'm sorry."

"Don't be. A million bucks couldn't buy this exposure. All I have to do is turn a negative into a positive. Check out tomorrow's Page Six to see how well I did."

"I'll do that."

"As to the hat, let's go with the blue." She shoved a hundred-dollar bill into my hand. "This enough for a deposit?"

"Absolutely."

She hurried out of the shop.

A fabulous customer. I wanted to clone her.

I tucked the money into my pocket.

Now that we were alone, Tibble ambled over to my work table. "Do people really wear hats in this day and age?"

"That they don't is a common misconception. A good example is that very stylish woman who was here."

"Don't think I didn't notice her. She's quite a babe."

"She rarely goes anywhere without a hat. Perhaps your mother would like a custom-made turban."

"I don't think so."

"Not even to celebrate an arrest in the Shelton case?"

"I wondered if you'd heard about that."

"I suppose that's why you're here."

"Not at all. I was passing by and thought I'd stop in and shoot the breeze."

"You can't possibly expect me to believe that. I know you're checking up on my mood because you're worried sick that I'll tell somebody about your mother. Well, I won't. Your mother's secret, or rather, the fact that she has one, is safe with me. Nobody will ever know Shelton blackmailed her or anybody else, unless of course you and she manage to acquire some scruples somewhere, decide to do the right thing, and tell the cops."

"You nuts or what? My mother has spent lots of money to keep her secrets secret. She's got no reason to talk."

"Sure she does. To right a wrong. To feel a special glow. To see truth and justice prevail. If the police could be convinced to investigate Shelton's career as a blackmailer, I'm sure they'd turn up a slew of suspects."

"Yeah, so what?"

"So the homeless man Duxman arrested will get off. You know as well as I that he didn't do it."

"I also know that the charges against him won't stick. He'll end up in a psych ward for a couple of months."

"Funny, that's pretty much what Detective Turner said."

"You talked to Turner?"

"I didn't mention your mother."

I didn't blame Tibble or his mother for the problem. In their shoes, I'd probably do much the same. Still, it made me mad, but more at the situation than any particular individual.

I threw my anger into my work. I slammed around and

made the blue beret for the publicist in one long sitting. Toward the end, when I was handstitching a nicely contrasting bright red headsize band inside, I finally slowed down and got into the natural flow of the work.

Hand work relaxes me into sort of a hypnotic state.

And it was there, some undefinable somewhere, tranced out, making neat little stitches, that I had a breakthrough that brought me back to the here and now.

Lemmy!

My sleazy ex-husband to be, Lemon B. Crenshaw, was the answer. When Shelton had tried to blackmail him, he'd successfully called Shelton's bluff because he didn't give a good goddamn if his indiscretion became known. He craved the publicity. Maybe he still did.

He kept the blackmail incident secret from the cops only because it would blow his little insurance scam. If the cops were force-fed the truth, they could no longer claim Shelton's murder was a botched burglary or that the same burglar had broken into Lemmy's and taken his bras and jewels.

All I had to do was convince Lemmy that the cops were on to him, which was true, and that it was in his best interest to come clean, which was also true.

His answering machine took my call.

When it was my turn, I said, "Lemmy, it's me. Pick up, it's urgent."

He answered. "Hello, wife. I'm sure you understand that to me 'urgent' equals a discussion about the return of my missing brassieres."

"Life and death, Lemmy."

"Not my life and death."

"No, but it might be about your freedom. I don't want to say any more over the phone. It's not a secure line. I must see you in person."

"Okay, Brenda, here's the deal. You bring my bras, and I'll listen to whatever you've got to say."

He hung up.

Good. Lemmy had reacted exactly as I hoped.

Not long after, I rested the laundry bag of brassieres on the shiny terrazzo floor of Lemmy's lobby. "I'm here to see Lemmy Crenshaw."

"Your name?"

"Brenda Midnight."

The doorman, Stanley, flashed an obsequious smile, then buzzed Lemmy. He didn't seem to recognize me, but it was definitely the same guy who had been on duty when I last visited, probably the one who'd been on his lunch break the time Dweena and I sneaked in. Considering all the bad stuff that had happened since, I wished he'd eaten a sandwich at his desk so he would have been around to refuse to let us in the building. But no one had stopped us, so here I was, returning the bras I'd taken that day.

"Mr. Crenshaw says he's expecting you."

"Thank you."

Lemmy didn't even say hello. He grabbed the bag of bras and clasped it to his chest.

"My brassieres."

He opened the bag and plunged his head inside. When he came up for air, he said, "My beautiful bras are back home where they belong."

From the way he spoke of the bras, you'd think they were lost puppies.

For a brief moment I lapsed into feeling sorry for the pain I'd caused poor, pitiful Chrome Dome Lemmy, then I remembered who he was and who I was and that we were married and was quite pleased that my heist had hit where it hurt.

I wasted no time in getting to the point. "You're in serious trouble, Lemmy."

"Whaddya talking about? My bras are back. All is right with the world."

"Turner and McKinley know what you did."

He ignored me and carried the bag down into his conversation pit and sat down on the fuzzy couch. One by one, he removed the bras from the bag and examined each carefully.

"I repeat, the cops are on to you."

Lemmy continued to ignore me until all the bras were out of the bag. Then he shot me an accusatory look. "Where's my pale pink 1950s satin super-padded bra? And the seventies black and red lace number is gone too."

The man certainly knew his collection.

"Lemmy, those two bras are destined for fame."

"What are you talking about?"

"Dweena's wearing the pink satin in one of those gigantic ads that hang on the side of a building. Isn't that fantastic?"

"Dweena! Disgusting is what it is. Is it some kind of freak ad?"

"Not at all. She's modeling a dress by a hot-shot designer who's on the verge of making it big."

"So the bra is *under* the dress."

"Dweena hasn't been too clear about that. She's mentioned cleavage and that her bosoms are two storeys high. I think parts of the bra peek out of the dress."

"I better get it back in perfect condition."

"It'll be fine. Dweena is very respectful of vintage clothing."

"And what, pray tell, happened to my other bra?"

"Elizabeth took the black and red lace style as inspiration for her new series of paintings."

"They both better credit the Lemon B. Crenshaw Brassiere Archives."

"I'll see what I can do."

"Do that. I can always have Winfield sue for unauthorized usage. Or something."

"I'm sure that won't be necessary. Now, are you ready to listen to what I came here to say?"

Lemmy crossed his arms over his chest and pouted.

I took it as a yes. "I was talking to Detectives Turner and McKinley."

"Primo jerks, the both of them."

"Whatever. But they're smart, Lemmy. Due to circumstances beyond my control the detectives are privy to the fact that I took your bras. From that they were able to determine that you maybe exaggerated a bit when you told the cops your jewels were missing."

"So what?"

"I know you don't care how that misinformation messed up a murder investigation, but you realize you could be in trouble with the insurance company. They frown on that kind of behavior. If Turner and McKinley drop a couple of hints to the right people about your bogus claim—"

"Not their job."

"That may be true, but it's one they'd love to do."

Lemmy rubbed his chin. "Okay, you made your point. I was thinking I might withdraw that claim anyway. Now that I've got my beautiful bras back, the money doesn't seem so important. I mean, hey, I could always go make some money, right? Get Johnny a new series, sit back, and take my percentage."

"That would be nice."

"Or revive *Tod Trueman*."

"What about New York City having been reduced to a pile of ashes?"

"I'm still working on that problem."

I steered the conversation back on subject. "So now we've established you will withdraw your false insurance claim."

"I believe I said I was thinking about it. I haven't made up my mind yet."

"You'll do it, because then you'll be free to go to the cops and tell them Shelton tried to blackmail you."

He hit the side of his head with the heel of his hand. "Huh? I must not have heard you right. Why would I want to do that?"

"Think about it, Lemmy. Free publicity. You'll piggyback on the high-profile story of Shelton. That virtually guarantees you front page news, and while you've got the media attention, you can slip in an interesting tidbit that it was actually Johnny Verlane who deduced that Shelton was the blackmailer, because he got good at that kind of stuff as star of the ever so realistic *Tod Trueman* show."

"Let me think." He closed his eyes, apparently deep in thought. A couple of minutes of that and he roused himself to say, "You know, Brenda, I'm liking it. I'm liking it a lot."

"That's great, Lemmy. I'll make all the arrangements. One more thing. Now that the bras are back, I suppose you'll be signing the divorce papers."

"I don't see why not."

Of all the rotten timing, on my way out I ran into Maureen Kenyen in the elevator.

I was afraid she'd scream bloody murder, but instead she smiled.

"My Frankie told me you were okay," she said. "He doesn't say that about too many women."

"Sorry I upset you the other day," I said.

"Please," she said. "You mustn't worry about it. Ever since . . . the situation, I tend to be on edge."

"I understand."

"Nice to see you again," she said, polite if absurd. "Frankie's the only good that came out of my first marriage. I really must have you two over for dinner. Next week perhaps? I make a killer pot roast."

The truth sprang to my lips. "Actually," I said, "I'm married."

"Oh." She seemed disappointed. "Who's the lucky guy?"

"Lemmy Crenshaw."

"Bald Lemmy from downstairs?" She sounded incredulous.

"It's kind of a long story. We don't live together."

"Well, you know what they say. There's no accounting for taste."

The elevator landed in the lobby.

" 'Bye," I said.

"Ciao," she said. She stopped at the doorman's desk. "You have a package for me, Stan?"

I walked through the Upper West Side. Mission accomplished, I thought, pretty damned pleased with myself. Now all I had to do was get Turner and McKinley to tell Detective Duxman that Lemmy had new information pertinent to his case. Or maybe I should go to Duxman myself.

While trying to determine the best approach, I passed by a charity resale shop. In the window, thrown on top of a filthy couch-bed, lay an ugly shag rug, very similar to Johnny's former yellow and orange atrocity, the one we'd fought over so long ago.

Ugh. I hated to be reminded.

I couldn't get thoughts of rugs out of my mind. Filthy, itchy dirt catchers, chock full of allergens, all the vacuuming and shampooing in the world wouldn't do a bit of good. One merely spits the putrid particulates into the air, the other grinds them in deeper.

In retrospect it's hard to track my thought process, but somehow rug vacuuming and rug shampooing led me to think of my doorman, Ralph, and how he'd figured out that I had no rugs and how doormen were in a great position to know all kinds of stuff about tenants—like who visits whom, who sneaks out in the middle of the night, who gets frequent deliveries from the liquor store—but all doormen probably weren't as sharp as Ralph. And then I thought of Lemmy's doorman, Stanley, and wondered if he were half as good as Ralph.

My thought process came to a sudden stop.

No, it couldn't be. Could it?

Well, why not?

A tattered leather club chair decomposed in front of the resale shop. I sat. I needed to concentrate.

Diverse facts clicked into place. My vague idea solidified and what had initially seemed far fetched kind of worked.

What if Lemmy's doorman Stanley was as good as Ralph at deriving conclusions from tiny bits of information? What if he supplied Adison Montgomery Shelton with information for blackmail? What if he hadn't been at lunch the time Dweena and I slipped into the building? What if he had something far more sinister on the menu? What if, like Tibble, he wanted a chunk of the blackmail action? What if, unlike Tibble, when he arrived, Shelton was still alive?

27

"Can I help you?"

"Huh? Oh. No, I was just . . . uh . . ."

Deep in thought, I hadn't noticed the proprietor come out of the resale shop.

"Fabulous chair, isn't it?" he said.

"Uh-huh. It's very comfortable. I must have dozed off."

"I can give you a good price."

"Much as I'd love to take it home, I live in a studio apartment. It's jammed up enough as it is."

"Well, enjoy your sit, then. I'll be inside if you change your mind."

I leaned back in the chair again.

Now, what had I been thinking about before the interruption? Oh yeah. I'd come up with the absurd notion that Lemmy's doorman had killed Shelton.

I thought now of my doorman, Ralph, and the others who worked in my building. Professionals through and through, extremely trustworthy. They had to be. It was their job.

There were lots of doormen in New York City. Probability alone would account for a few bad apples.

Still, it was a crazy idea.

I'd only ventured a couple of blocks away from Lemmy's building. It would be easy enough to go back and talk to Stanley the doorman and see how he reacted to a couple of questions devised to reveal what kind of guy he was. On the way, I came up with a perfectly plausible ruse.

From across the lobby Stanley seemed to be a man doing his job, meeting and greeting and directing and watching and enjoying himself at it. He did not look at all like a co-conspirator to blackmail or a greedy, cold-blooded killer.

In a way, that counted against him. Forget *Tod Trueman* reruns. In real life the bad guys often turn out to be the ones you least expect.

I approached the desk.

This time Stanley recognized me. "Here to see Mr. Crenshaw again?" He made a move to punch Lemmy's call button.

"Actually, no. It's you I want to talk to."

"Yes," he said, a little tentatively, I thought.

"This is a nice building," I said.

"Shipshape."

"And very well run, it seems."

"We like to think so."

I gestured at the bank of monitors sunk into his desk. "Is that your security system?"

"State of the art. Only the best for our tenants."

"That's wonderful."

Because it wouldn't serve my purpose, I didn't bring up the embarrassing fact that despite the super security system, one of the building's tenants had recently been murdered.

"Your name is Stanley, isn't it?"

He bristled at first, then relaxed, probably realizing his name was embroidered on his uniform. "Most people call me Stan."

"Okay, then Stan it is. So, Stan, you see, I've got this friend. He's very big on the west coast in the film business. He needs a pied-à-terre in New York. You know how all those movie people have finally wised up and want to spend part of their time here. Bi-coastal they call it."

Stan nodded.

"I'm sure my friend would find this building to his liking.

For him, good security, which you have, is essential. He also requires, well, I'm not sure how to put this, let's just say because of his lifestyle—he's quite the ladies' man—he simply must be assured of a high level of discretion."

Stan smiled. "No problem."

"That brings me to my next question. Do you know of any apartments available either for sale or rent?"

"Afraid not. This is highly desirable property. Most apartments are snagged before they're officially listed."

"It's a tight market, vacancy rate virtually zero, and people are desperate for full service pre-wars."

"You said it. If I do happen to hear of an apartment, I'd be happy to let you know."

"Come to think of it, a little while ago when I was with Mr. Crenshaw, he mentioned a vacancy. I think it was the apartment directly above his. Yeah, I'm almost positive that's what he said."

Did I detect a flicker of fear in Stan's eye? Hard to say, not knowing the man.

"That apartment is not on the market."

"But it will be, right?"

"Yeah, I guess so, sooner or later."

"I'm sure my west coast friend would be happy to pay a generous finder's fee. He's heard some scary stories about the brutal New York real estate market. He can well afford to smooth over some of the bumps. That is, if the apartment were to meet his requirements. Would it be possible for me to take a peek?"

Stan shook his head no.

"Come on, Stan, work with me on this. I bet you've got the keys. What time do you take off for lunch? I could meet you, and we could go up together."

"That's against the rules. I couldn't do that." He leveled his gaze at me, then cocked his head, as if waiting for me to say something or rather offer something.

I got the distinct impression a hundred-dollar bill might be all it would take to persuade Stan to break the rules. I actually had the cash—the deposit for the blue beret—but I couldn't afford to part with it to test my theory. "That's too bad," I said.

Stan looked disappointed, but after a moment he perked up. "Here's what I can do. Give me your telephone number or better yet your friend's, and I'll contact him directly if an apartment opens up."

"Oh, would you? That would be great. It's probably best that I stay out of my friend's real estate deals anyway."

Stan gave me a piece of paper and a pen. I made up a name, scribbled it down, and took extra care to assure it was illegible. "I don't have my friend's number with me. He's in the LA book."

Stan folded up the piece of paper and put it in the inside pocket of his uniform.

For the second time that day I left Lemmy's building. I planned to take the subway, but on the way to the station, a Number Ten bus pulled up to a stop, and I hopped on. A longer ride would give me more time to think.

So what had I learned? Lemmy was in love with his bras. Maureen Kenyen had forgiven me and now wanted to fix me up with her son, Frankie Tibble. Stan the doorman might be willing to take money for services rendered. Big deal.

I didn't have nearly enough to convince Turner and McKinley that if they plunged into the treacherous waters of interoffice police politics they could solve the murder and at the same time discredit Duxman.

Lemmy was still my best bet, which pretty much meant I didn't have a chance in hell. He'd probably go back on his promise to level with the cops. I'd already returned his bras to get him to talk, and now I had no leverage.

"End of the line."

What? So soon.

But no, I looked out the bus window, and we were most

definitely not in the Village. The bus had pulled up by Penn Station. I had to transfer to a Number Twenty.

It was a long wait.

I had more than enough time to come up with the idea that Shelton might have kept records of his nefarious transactions and that I should get Dweena to break into his apartment so I could take a look around for some reference to Stan. The cops would have already searched, but since they didn't know about the blackmail, they might have missed an important clue.

All I can say is thank goodness for gridlock.

By the time the Number Twenty bus finally shuddered up to the curb, I'd had a severe attack of sanity and rejected that incredibly stupid idea.

I called Lemmy as soon as I got home.

"Can't get enough of me, huh?" he asked.

"Right, Lemmy."

"I'm in the middle of rehanging my lovely bras. Once they're up, I'm gonna sit back and contemplate the beauty of the collection. Care to come back uptown and join me? We could indulge in a bit of predivorce marriage consummation. A little booze and maybe I could manage to get in the mood."

"No thanks, Lemmy. The reason I called was to emphasize how very important it is that you tell the cops about the blackmail."

"You know, Brenda, now that you mention it, I was kinda having second thoughts about that."

"Now that you've got your bras."

"Bingo."

"You're taking a risk. If Turner and McKinley—"

"Cut it with the scare tactics already. My favorite detectives can't touch me, not anymore. Thanks for the tip. I took what you said to heart. I called the insurance company and withdrew the claim. Turner and McKinley have nothing on me."

"Dammit, Lemmy. You promised."

"And you promised to love honor and cherish until death do us part."

"That's bullshit. We had a simple civil ceremony with none of that crap. Besides, you don't want to be married to me any more than I want to be married to you. Speaking of which, did Johnny ever give you that goddamned bra?"

"He did. I'd say everything worked out swell."

"A matter of opinion."

"You'll be happy to know that I told Winfield I'd sign the papers. You should be hearing from him soon."

For once Lemmy actually committed an act of truth. I was amazed and really happy when not long after I hung up, my phone rang and it was Winfield.

"You didn't happen to find my pen, did you?"

"No."

"Well," he said, "I suppose I must go ahead with this anyway. Subsequent to the return of his missing property, my client, Lemon B. Crenshaw, has agreed to sign the divorce papers forthwith. Brenda, before you know it, you'll be a three-time loser. Or is that four-time?"

28

I'd packed a lot of activity into my morning. After I got off the phone with Winfield, I was surprised to see it was only one o'clock. Time moves in weird ways. Chuck could probably provide hours of technical discourse on the subject. Me, I was happy to get over to Midnight Millinery at a reasonable hour.

My plan was to spend the rest of the day making hats, but in truth, once I got settled down, I spent more time worrying.

I was able to accept that it was kind of maybe sort of morally okay to let things slide if one of Shelton's blackmail victims had killed him. I agreed with everybody else on that subject. Despite his good work in other areas, Shelton got exactly what he deserved.

It was damn tough for me to accept that it was in any way okay for the homeless man to get blamed just because he'd probably get released and suffer no ill effects. How arrogant to assume the man would be better off after a run through the system and a stay in a psych ward.

However, if Lemmy's doorman Stan really had killed Shelton, my position was not the least bit ambiguous. I couldn't rationalize away inaction.

When I simply could not sit on the information one more second, I called Turner and, after a quick discussion about the miserable weather, told him what I had to say.

"That is so precious," he said. "I thank you for telling me the doorman did it. Hang on a minute, let me share this crime-solving nugget with Detective McKinley."

In the background, uproarious laughter.

Then McKinley came on the line. "Golly gee, Ms. Midnight, we were so sure the butler did it."

I hung up, not bothering with a formal good-bye.

A little later the phone rang. I picked up immediately, hoping it would be Turner telling me he'd reconsidered what I'd told him and maybe it wouldn't be such a bad idea to look into it, but it was Johnny.

"I wanted to remind you about tonight."

Tonight? I had no idea what he meant by that. I chose my words carefully. His feelings were already hurt. Walking on eggs, I said, "Oh, yeah, right. Tonight."

"You didn't forget, did you?"

"How could I?"

Please, I thought, don't let this be about La Reverie. What if Johnny went ahead and made a reservation and then forgot to tell me? La Reverie was too touchy a subject for me to come right out and ask. "I can't find where I wrote it down. What time was it again?"

"Ten o'clock. Like always. Prime time. Tonight they're rerunning Episode Sixteen. That reviewer in Iowa said it was my best work."

What a relief. He was talking about the *TTUD* replacement of the summer replacement that got canned.

"A very good episode," I said. "You were spectacular when you single-handedly rescued the big-breasted platinum blonde from the clutches of the evil drug kingpin."

"Thanks. I thought I did a pretty good job rappeling out of that helicopter. Lemmy says when the important decision-makers see Tod back in action, they'll wake up."

Goddamn Lemmy. I hated to see him get Johnny's hopes up over nothing. I doubted the decision-makers would be glued to their sets. This time of year, they were in their Hampton hideaways, fretting over the fall lineups.

"I hope so, Johnny."

"Thanks, but in a way, I'm not so sure I do," he said.

"What do you mean?"

"You'd never get me to admit this in public, but lately I've been thinking that maybe the world is a better place without *Tod Trueman, Urban Detective*."

"How can you say that? Your Tod always comes up on the side of good and right."

"That's the problem. Tod wasn't edgy enough, Brenda. I should have played him tougher. I should have sneered more, talked out of the side of my mouth, smoked, swilled whiskey, gone beyond the chaste kiss with the gorgeous gal. I should have given Tod more gray area. Life is not all black and white, you know."

It sure was on my television set, a nine-incher, which I wrested down from its storage place way high in the very back of the closet.

It was also a world without sound until I hooked up an audio cable and ran it through the stereo, a pain-in-the-ass procedure that saved me from ever watching too much TV and falling under its stupefying influence.

The hookup procedure reminded me of how Lemmy's doorman Stan watched the ebb and flow of life and who was doing what with whom on his desk full of monitors. Unfortunately those thoughts led me to a frightening possibility that should have occurred to me before and proved beyond a doubt that I'd not been thinking straight.

Lemmy's building was wired for video security. I didn't know which areas the cameras covered. The monitors were set into the doorman's desk at an angle, slanted toward whomever was seated at the desk, away from inquiring eyes of passersby. But you've got to figure the stairwell would be a good place to put a camera to see who was lurking about.

In other words, me.

I was probably overreacting, not all that unusual.

Once I got started, the train of thought rolled along faster

and faster, out of control. If cameras monitored the stairwell, and if Stan had killed Shelton, and if he was already
back at his desk after doing so, he'd have seen me lingering
in the stairwell and witnessed my run-in with Tibble.

Then again, Stan, if he was a killer, probably wasn't too
professional about it, so after killing Shelton, he would have
had a lot on his mind—moral issues, getting-away-with-it
issues, losing-his-job issues. He wouldn't have paid much
attention to what else might be happening in the building.
But he might have an inkling, a memory waiting to be
jogged.

And that's exactly what I might have done a little while
ago when I fed him that bullshit story about my so-called
friend, the heavy in the film industry who needed an apartment. Unless Stan was a complete fool, he'd have caught on
that I was probing, and if I was right about him, he wasn't a
complete fool, and being a doorman, he probably had a
good memory for faces and he might remember that he'd
recently seen mine not only in person but also on his monitors at that very crucial time in his life immediately after
he'd whacked Shelton, and he might conclude that I knew
more than I should, and he could always go back to the
video tapes to check for sure.

If that wasn't enough, he knew my name too. I'd given it
to him freely each time I'd visited Lemmy legitimately. My
fake friend might not be in the LA phone book, but I was
sure as hell in the New York book.

Of course, those cameras might not have archived the
action, they might only display events as they happened in
real time, in which case, even if Stan's memory did get
jogged, he couldn't check to be sure it was me that day in
the stairwell.

I finished setting up the television.

Next I tried to convince myself my latest fears were
unfounded, but of course I couldn't.

The *Tod* show wouldn't be on for a few minutes. I used
the time to call Chuck.

"Chuck, what do you know about surveillance cameras?"

"They're easier to build than time machines."

"You're not seriously still on that kick, are you?"

"It's not a kick. It's what gives my life meaning, the possibility of being reunited with Elizabeth."

"Reunited, that's how you see it?"

"Um-huh. We were together in the era of preconsciousness."

"Oh, that era. I thought you wanted to go back to the mid-nineteen sixties."

"That's right. My calculations show that as the best time to intervene. The planet was in such turmoil, nobody will notice my little ripple."

"I'll miss you."

"No, you won't. If I pull this off, you won't even know me and therefore you can't possibly miss me."

"I'll sense a vacuum, a gaping hole. I'll have nobody to sneak pepperoni to Jackhammer, nobody to fix my computer, nobody to tell me about surveillance cameras. So while you're still part of my life in the here and now, talk."

"Okay, sure. Could you like narrow it down? Surveillance is a huge field. You talking infrared?"

"No. Nothing special. Just regular everyday kind of snoop equipment, the kind of stuff a big apartment building might use."

"A building like yours, perhaps?"

"Sort of, except mine doesn't. More like Lemmy's building. I need to know if those cameras record what they see."

"Well, that all depends."

"On what?"

"On whether they're hooked up to recording devices."

Oh. "I guess I should have thought of that."

"The sound of your 'duh' resonates all the way through time and space to my humble East Village hovel. The fact that you didn't think of that leads me to believe you didn't think at all, which means you're preoccupied and up to no good."

"Thanks for the info, Chuck. I owe you a pizza. Gotta go."

Once again, full-tilt paranoia on a rampage.

Whatever the next step was, I had to take it, and I'd better do it soon for my own good.

The *Tod Trueman* theme song came on. The familiar melody comforted me a bit. After a quick opening scene, a teaser, they cut to a commercial.

When the show came back on, I'm afraid I didn't give it my full attention. Except for Johnny looking ultra cool and the weird feeling I always get seeing him passionately kiss somebody who isn't me, I didn't miss much.

Johnny was too quick to blame himself for *TTUD*'s cancellation. The writers should have come up with a new plot twist, something besides the drug kingpin and the beautiful woman half undressed and in distress. Changing the kingpin's ethnicity and the woman's hair color each episode didn't quite cut it.

Silly as it was, one part rang true. Every week Tod would rid the world of yet another drug kingpin, send the evildoer up the river, but by the very next week—same time, same station—another drug kingpin would have risen up to take his place, showing the awful truth that evil never dies. There's always somebody else anxious to take over.

And that's what gave me my idea.

29

Many long, hard hours of intense thought later, when slashes of pink and orange stained the eastern sky, my glimmer of an idea had blossomed into a ready-to-execute plan to trap the killer of Adison Montgomery Shelton.

After that, the contingency plans.

Then Jackhammer and I went outdoors, sucked in lots of fresh morning air, and ran—fast but not too far. At that hour the streets were relatively deserted. We saw one other dog walker, then passed by a man asleep in a government-issue canvas mail cart, and a block farther on dodged a threesome of club kids as they staggered up the avenue, drumming on store gates with a stick.

Back in the apartment Jackhammer snarfed up a bowlful of kibbles. I downed a cup of coffee and ran through my plan several more times backwards and forwards, testing it with every worst case what-if I could conjure.

Forced to accept the cold, hard fact that the plan might fail, I had to make dead certain that whether or not I successfully trapped the doorman, at least I would be in no danger.

I needed to enlist some help.

It was still early, so I gave Tibble a call to be sure he was already in his office.

It took him several rings to pick up. "Tibble here."

"It's Brenda Midnight. I need to talk to you. Mind if I drop by?"

"Not at all, but do me a favor and pick up some bagels and coffee on the way."

"Sure."

The all-night deli on the corner was empty except for the counterman. Behind him was a drip-style coffee machine. The liquid inside the pot looked suspiciously pitch-black and thick.

"How long has that coffee been festering?" I asked.

"Fresh-made, I swear. You want?"

I nodded. "Two extra large. And half a dozen bagels."

When he gave me the bag, I reached inside to take out a cup of coffee. I pried open the lid and sniffed the rising steam for that telltale burned odor. It seemed okay.

"Told you it was good."

Tibble answered his door dressed in plaid cotton pajamas. Stray tufts of hair stuck out from his scalp.

He grabbed the bag from the deli out of my hand. "Mmmm, I can smell the coffee."

Me too, in more ways than one. "You live in this office, don't you?"

I could relate to such an arrangement, having lived at Midnight Millinery, sleeping in a bedroll beneath my blocking table, for quite some time.

"It's only temporary," he said. "Just until my eight-million-dollar Upper East Side penthouse gets remodeled. Right now, as we speak, workmen are carving a small den out of the central ballroom and installing a nine-foot claw-footed antique porcelain tub in the master bath and landscaping the wraparound terrace. You know how it is. These contractors take forever."

Yeah, right.

He took the two coffees out of the bag, handed me one,

and put the bagels in the center of the desk. "How much do I owe you?"

"My treat," I said.

"Thank you."

"You're most welcome."

He bit into a bagel, tore off a chunk, and washed it down with a gulp of coffee.

"Now," he said, "if I might hazard a guess as to the purpose of your visit—you want to hassle me until I give in and get my mom to go to the cops and tell them about the blackmail."

"I know who killed Shelton."

"Not, I assume, the homeless man they arrested."

"Nope. It's the doorman, Stan."

Tibble wrinkled his brow and shook his head. "What makes you think so?"

"I believe Stan was feeding Shelton information to use for blackmail. They must have had a disagreement, perhaps about the size of Stan's cut, and in a fit of anger Stan bludgeoned him to death."

Tibble shook his head so violently he had to stop in order to speak. "Back up. Start from the beginning."

I began to detail the thought process that led me to my conclusion.

Tibble interrupted with a totally irrelevant comment. "When Mom told me you were married to that Lemmy Crenshaw guy, I nearly bust a gut laughing."

"As I told your mother, it is a long story, and quite frankly, Frankie, none of your goddamned business."

"Okay, be that way, but you've got to admit, it is funny."

Not to me.

"You visit your mother frequently," I said, returning to the subject. "Did you ever see Shelton talking to Stan?"

"I suppose. Nothing unusual about that. It's a friendly building. I tell you Stan didn't do it. I've seen pictures of his family. He's a faithful husband, a good father."

"He may be, but he's also a killer. Do you know how long

ago those security monitors were installed in his desk? Stan told me they were state of the art, so I assume they're relatively new."

"Yes, they are. They put them in when the lobby was renovated. That must have been a couple of years ago. I remember because there was a huge flap over the project. They had to have a desk custom-made to accommodate the monitors. The first contractor screwed up the job, the monitors didn't fit, and he ran off with the money. The board had to get another contractor who could do the job fast and got stuck with all kinds of rush fees, and they went way over budget."

"When did Shelton start blackmailing your mother?"

"I'm not going to answer that."

I hadn't meant to anger him. "Believe me, Frankie, I couldn't care less who your mother had an affair with."

"She didn't have an affair! What a terrible thing to say. You take that back right this minute."

"I'm sorry, I just thought—well, it doesn't matter what I thought."

"It does matter. In honor of my father and the love he and my mother shared, I want to set the record straight. There was no affair."

"I understand. I apologize."

"What Mom does is—"

"Don't say another word. I truly don't want to know." Of course that was a lie. For the first time, now I was really itching to know what the hell Maureen Kenyen had done. If not an affair, then what? Did she ship goods out of the country in a duty-avoidance scheme? Or receive stolen items? Did she pickpocket people in the elevator? Steal laundry from the clothes dryers?

Tibble seemed anxious to unburden.

It took all my willpower to control my curiosity. "Really, I only need to know if the blackmail started before or after the new security system was installed."

"Oh. I see what you're driving at." Tibble pulled a folder

out of his desk drawer and rifled through the papers. "Um-huh. Interesting. It all began about two years ago, which would coincide with the new security system. I always assumed Shelton caught her, but I suppose Stan could have figured it out. Still, it's damned hard for me to see him as a killer. I've known the man for years."

"I've got a foolproof idea of how we can prove his innocence or his guilt."

"We?"

"Yes. I'm afraid I might have already tipped my hand to Stan. I don't want to make him suspicious. You're the perfect one to help. You know the man. You frequently visit the building."

I told him what I wanted him to do.

He told me I was out of my mind if I thought he would.

I could tell pleading would be a big waste of breath. "At least do me one favor."

"Maybe."

"There's a telephone on Stan's desk. Do you happen to know the number?"

"Sure."

He flipped through a Rolodex on his desk and wrote down the number for me.

"Thank you," I said.

"Good luck, but I hope you're wrong. I like Stan."

Okay, the plan remained the same. Only the players changed. I was now in the starring role.

I would need Lemmy's cooperation, which would have been difficult to get except I figured out a way that Lemmy wouldn't even know he was helping.

As an added bonus I'd have a chance to test-drive my ex-wife hat.

I made the call.

"Good morning, Lemmy."

"Yes, it is," he said, "a very good morning indeed. My bras are back on the wall."

"Thanks for signing the divorce papers."

"My pleasure."

"You know, now that our marriage is almost ended, I've changed my mind. I think a divorce barbecue is a terrific idea."

"Yes, it is."

"I'd love to be guest of honor."

"Good. It's only fitting."

"I have one request."

"Which is . . ."

"Have the party real soon."

"Like how soon?"

"Tomorrow would be fantastic."

"Are you crazy? It takes time to make a party."

"Okay, then, how about the next day?"

"I don't know, Brenda. It's not proper to have a divorce barbecue bash before the divorce is finalized, and that won't be for another couple of weeks. It's not like Winfield has only got to bribe one person or call in one favor. He's got lots of palms to grease and lots of butts to kiss to speed up our happy divorce. And he's still pissed about his pen."

"I'm working on getting that back."

"You know where it is?"

"I ran into the messenger who took it. He said he'd call after he found out what the pen was worth."

"And you believed him? You are way too trusting, Brenda."

Lemmy was right about that. I was concerned that the messenger hadn't yet called, but I didn't let on to Lemmy. "He'll call," I said. "I promised to make him a good offer."

"Well, don't hold your breath."

"Can we just get back to the divorce party?"

"Yeah, I guess."

"It's a brilliant concept, and, Lemmy, you get all the credit. Since you invented it, you get to define what's proper. I say we do it now. The weather's perfect. Waiting until the divorce is a done deal will put us right in the middle of hurricane season, a lousy time for a barbecue. Just think. Wind and driving rain. The balcony door opening and closing. More wind and driving rain. People going in and out. Even more wind and driving rain."

"Will you stop it with the wind and driving rain?"

"Well, you wouldn't want to subject the fine, delicate vintage fabric of your brassieres to such horrific weather conditions."

"All right, Brenda, you made your point. We'll do our divorce party the day after tomorrow. You'll have to help with the invites, though."

"Of course, Lemmy. I wouldn't have it any other way. You call your friends. I'll call mine."

It was crucial to call Turner first. If I couldn't convince him to show up, my plan would be a bust.

When I invited him to the party, he was less than enthusiastic.

"I know it's late notice," I said, "but hey, it's a party."

Turner growled, "Divorce sucks. The breakup of a marriage is a goddamned poor excuse to celebrate."

"At first it struck me that way too. But you've got to take into account who I'm divorcing."

"I see what you mean. Divorcing Lemon B. Crenshaw does call for a celebration. You say this little barbecue affair is at *his* place?"

"Yes. He has a balcony. It'll be fun."

"I'm surprised the shaved-head smarmy agent has agreed to have *me* in his home. He hates my guts, I hate his. Remember?"

"How could I forget? The thing is, Lemmy doesn't know. As guest of honor, the blushing divorcée to be, I get to invite anybody I please. And I want you. McKinley too. Is he around?"

"Yeah. Hang on a minute."

I heard him tell McKinley about the party. Turner came back on the line and told me McKinley would be delighted to attend.

"Terrific," I said. "Do you think Gundermutter can make it?" I had to ask but actually hoped Nicole Gundermutter couldn't be there. It would have been great to see her, but my plan required that Turner come alone. I'd formulated contingency Plan B in case Gundermutter was available, but as it turned out, she was on vacation.

"I'm sure Former Officer would love to help you celebrate, but she's in Milwaukee this week."

"Milwaukee? What the hell for?"

"Harley-Davidson museum. Heaven on earth for Former Officer."

"Too bad she'll miss the party."

"I'll make it up to her somehow."

"I'll bet you will." I still had to make sure Turner didn't come with McKinley. Unable to think of a way to put that diplomatically, I said simply, "You and McKinley come separately, okay?"

"Why?"

"I'm afraid if the two of you show up together, it might be more than Lemmy can handle."

That must have made sense to Turner. He agreed to come alone. "It's probably better if McKinley and I each bring our own car anyway."

Want to learn a lot about your friends? Invite them to a divorce party and see how they react. I imagined Lemmy was going through the same with his friends.

The oft-married Elizabeth was keen on the concept but wished she'd come up with it. "I myself have had so many divorces and have absolutely zip to remember them by. Such a rotten shame."

Bachelor Chuck Riley, on the other hand, was so offended he snootily claimed to have other plans for the day, but when I emphasized food grilled on a real live barbecue and pointed out that Elizabeth would be in attendance, he rechecked his computer calendar and suddenly realized his other plans were actually for the same day in another decade.

"Whenever I finally get this time travel thing perfected, I'm gonna need a kick-ass scheduler."

Dweena thought the idea was a hoot. "I do adore a theme party, though I'm not sure if it's appropriate to bring a gift to such an occasion."

"We're not exactly registered at Tiffany's," I said.

"Hmmm, flowers maybe. I wonder if there really is such a plant as stinkweed."

"I don't know."

"Which direction does Lemmy's balcony face?"

"South, I think. Why?"

"My billboard will be up by then. This is so exciting. I'll bring a high-powered telescope. All the guests can take turns ogling my bosoms. Did I mention they're two storeys high?"

At first Frankie Tibble was suspicious. It was too soon after I'd asked him to help me trap Stan. But I assured him he was not part of the plan and all he had to do was eat, drink, be merry, and roast a marshmallow. He agreed to attend.

"Bring your mom too," I said.

30

Propellers or pinwheels?

A difficult choice, but an excellent way to keep my mind engaged. Otherwise I'd have been a nervous wreck thinking about tomorrow.

I had to get over my aversion to surface embellishment, which as a rule I take extreme measures to avoid. To me, a hat should be a sculptural whole, not a shape decorated with add-on crap. However, for the ex-wife hat, it seemed appropriate to break that rule.

After much agonizing between the traditional propeller and the jauntier, happier, more feminine pinwheel, the pinwheel won.

Next I had to figure out how to make the things, not an easy task, but again, I was happy to keep occupied.

I made experimental pinwheels out of various millinery materials. I tried wired felt, canvas-covered buckram, starched straw. Most of them looked okay, but none of them spun worth a damn. Eventually I gave up and chased around town until I found pinwheels at a party goods store. I bought two dozen in bright colors, went back to Midnight Millinery, and finalized the design.

The results, if I say so myself, were absolutely stunning. The finished ex-wife hat was a small, close-fitting bright yellow canvas duck cap that curved around the head with a bouquet of spinning fire-engine-red pinwheels. I attached a strong piece of elastic so the entire structure could be worn tilted dangerously and quite sexily over my left eye.

The results so inspired me, I considered developing an entire collection of ex-wife hats. I hate pastels and fluff. I don't do weddings. I don't make veils. Why not specialize in the flip side of wedded bliss? The market was half as huge and potentially a lot more fun. Even if Lemmy's idea of divorce parties didn't catch on, I could think of many other occasions to wear an ex-wife hat, such as showing up at the restaurant where the ex is dining with his new flame or making an unforgettable entrance at the ex's next wedding.

I wrapped the finished ex-wife hat in tissue paper, nestled it down into a Midnight Millinery hatbox, and took it back to the apartment.

Late that afternoon when the phone rang, I let the machine take the call. I'm lousy at keeping secrets and feared if I talked to my friends I'd end up blabbing my real plans for the next day and blow the whole thing. But the call wasn't from a friend. It was from the bicycle messenger who'd run off with Brewster Winfield's good luck antique silver pen. It was about time.

I grabbed the receiver. "Don't hang up. I'm here."

"Are you ready to make me an offer I can't refuse?" he asked.

"How much?"

"The online bidding currently stands at three hundred seven dollars and seventy-four cents. The auction closes in thirty-seven minutes. There is always some risk involved that the high bidder will flake out or send a rubber check. So as a special service to you, who will pay today in person in cold, hard cash, I offer the pen at three hundred. Take it or leave it."

Did I feel three hundred dollars' worth of guilt at heaving the pen out the window? No. Winfield deserved it. But I did feel three hundred dollars' worth of guilt for my loss of control. I shouldn't have done that, no matter how mad he made me.

"Okay. I'll take it."

Two hours and a stop at the ATM later, I took Jackhammer to Washington Square Park. The messenger was already at our appointed meeting spot, the eastern leg of the arch.

He flashed the pen. I showed him the money. Real quick, like a drug deal, we made the exchange.

Back home in time for dinner, I boiled some bow-tie pasta, served it with butter and Parmigiano-Reggiano and a huge pile of fresh steamed broccoli on the side. Then, after a rousing game of catch the chewy toy with Jackhammer, I dragged out the mattress and conked out early.

I wanted to be in top form for tomorrow.

My radio alarm clock went off not long after sunup. I jumped out of bed, eager to start the day I couldn't wait to see end.

Clear skies were predicted, a perfect eighty-degree day. Jackhammer and I checked it out in person. Circling the block, I looked to the west, that part of America where our weather comes from, and saw not a cloud in the sky. It would be a fabulous day for a divorce barbecue.

It took me quite a while to get up the nerve to do the one last thing that would set the wheels of my plan in motion. It's not that it was scary or put me in any danger, I just didn't want to screw up.

I couldn't predict Stan's reaction, so a prepared script was out. I'd have to think on my feet.

I did some deep-breathing exercises, then dialed the number Tibble had given me.

"Desk."

It sounded like Stan, but it was crucial to make sure. I asked, "Is this Stan?" I tried to sound like it didn't matter much to me one way or the other.

"Stan it is, at your service," came the reply.

So far, so good. "Stan, am I correct in assuming this is a secure line?"

"I'm not sure I know what you mean."

"Let me explain," I said, a stern edge creeping into my voice. "What I mean is we wouldn't want anybody eavesdropping on a very important conversation we're about to have. We need to keep this between us. You know, like private."

"I'm quite busy. If you don't mind—"

"Stan, I wouldn't want to alarm you, but I highly encourage you to make the time to talk to me."

He didn't say anything, but he didn't hang up either.

"So," I said, "secure or not?"

"No one can listen in."

"Good. You see, Stan, it's like this. Mr. Shelton—"

"Shelton?"

"Yes, Adison Montgomery Shelton. I believe you knew him, a former resident of the building you're in right this minute."

"Of course I know—uh, I mean I knew—Mr. Shelton."

"I was pretty sure you did. Mr. Shelton told me to call you at this number in case anything ever went wrong. I suppose him being dead qualifies as pretty goddamned wrong. What would you say about that?"

I heard a rapid intake of air. Other than that, no response.

"Actually, Stan, I should be thanking you. Bet you had no idea replacements waited in the wings. Now that Shelton is, shall we say, quite permanently out of the picture, and we do thank you for that, you've got yourself a couple of new partners."

"I don't know what you're talking about."

"I'm talking about partners, Stan, with an 's,' plural, as in me and my colleague. You'll be meeting us soon. Naturally, as with any new relationship, there will be a period of adjustment. Us getting to know you, you getting to know us, that kind of thing. Before you know it, we'll all be real comfortable with each other, snug as bugs in a rug."

"I still—"

"Come on, Stan, you can't fool me. We both know what we both know. My colleague and I were thinking that to show good faith all around, we ought to do a quick deal with you—money for information. What do you say?" The tone of my voice made it clear he had no choice.

"Uh . . . okay."

"Glad we agree on that, Stan. My colleague and I, we want to do this deal soon. Today in fact."

"I don't get off until four. I can't leave the desk."

"That is perfectly understandable. Believe me, my colleague and I certainly realize the importance of you keeping your job. So here's what we're gonna do to make it easy for you. My colleague will come to you this afternoon, say around twoish. He'll announce himself as Turner. That's not his real name, it's a code. You don't have to say anything. Give him an envelope with information, he'll slip you an envelope with money. That's it. Easy, no?"

"What kind of information?"

"Information we can use."

"I see."

"That's good, Stan. Let's hope we have a long and prosperous working relationship."

I hung up the phone, glad that part was over with.

Stan seemed to go for it. Not until much later would I know for sure.

Meanwhile I had a divorce party to get ready for.

I slipped into a backless black clingy dress, chose a pair of high-heeled strappy black patent-leather pumps, and topped off the ensemble with my new ex-wife hat. A quick glance in the mirror, an adjustment to get the hat tilted just right, and I was all set.

As guest of honor I got to Lemmy's early.

Stan was on duty in the lobby, sitting over his deskful of security monitors. I thought he looked a little nervous.

He recognized me, waved the back of his hand toward the

elevators. He didn't even bother to call Lemmy to tell him he had a visitor. Poor Stan, he acted like he had more to worry about than a guest attending a party in the building.

I hoped so.

Lemmy fluttered around his dark apartment, adjusted pillows, set out bowls of nuts, skewered marshmallows, and straightened his bras on the wall.

"This last-minute stuff is a bitch," he said. "I want everything to be perfect."

"You've done a good job, Lemmy. The apartment looks wonderful, but don't you think it's kind of dark?"

"You know I can't expose my bras to much sun. I'm not gonna open the drapes until the last minute."

At two o'clock Lemmy opened the drapes.

Moments later Elizabeth arrived. "What a spectacular hat," she said.

"Why, thank you. It's an ex-wife hat. I made it all by myself."

Lemmy bussed both her cheeks. "I'm so happy you could be part of the celebration." He laid on the charm extra thick, aware that she still had one of his bras.

"I wouldn't miss this event for the world. Congratulations, you two. You make a charming . . . uh, whatever."

"Divorced couple," I said.

"Soon to be," Lemmy said.

After Elizabeth, the guests seemed to arrive all at once. People poured through the door, offered hearty best wishes, and wandered off in search of food and drink. I recognized a few of Lemmy's clients, various starlets, even one of his ex-wives.

She hugged me like we were long-lost sisters. "Oh, you poor dear."

"It's not what you think," I said.

"It never is," she said.

Everybody I invited showed up—my stylist friend Margo, part-time amateur stripper and full-time real estate broker Irene Finneluk, feather and trimming merchants

Naomi and Norbert Needleson, noodle designer Lance Chapoppel, Frankie Tibble and his mom, Maureen Kenyen. All in all, a great crowd.

Winfield was there, of course. I pulled him off to the side and presented him with his pen.

It was worth the three hundred to see the normally articulate lawyer struck speechless with gratitude and with tears in his eyes.

Chuck bopped in and didn't even notice my ex-wife hat. In fact, he was so busy checking out the Elizabeth of this decade, it took him five full minutes of staring before he made it to the balcony, where Brewster Winfield and Maureen Kenyen had teamed up to grill hot dogs and toast marshmallows.

Dweena, being Dweena, arrived fashionably late, emphasized by the fact that her bra arrived a full second before the rest of her. After a quick hug, she hurried out to the balcony, where she set up her telescope and encouraged everyone to take a gander at the gigantic image of herself stretched over the entire side of a building miles away on Houston Street. I had to admit, it was impressive. And yes, her bosoms really were two storeys high. A bit of the bra peeked out of the top.

Lemmy saw the ad and beamed with pride. I can't remember ever seeing him so genuinely happy. He stood next to Dweena and posed for Tibble, who was the only one who thought to bring a camera.

When McKinley strode in, Lemmy was in such a great mood, he didn't even flinch. He was actually nice to McKinley and proudly showed off his big wall of brassieres, but all good things must come to an end. In the middle of a discussion about uplift and separation, McKinley received a call on his cell phone.

Turner, I suspected, calling from the lobby.

McKinley had to run off somewhere. "Police business," was all he would say.

I assumed it was a little problem Turner was having with Stan the doorman.

On his way out McKinley grabbed two toasted marsh-mallows.

About half an hour later I couldn't stand it any longer. Curiosity got the best of me. For privacy I stole away into Lemmy's bedroom. He really did have a round water bed beneath a mirrored ceiling. I flopped down on the bed so I could see myself call down to the doorman's desk.

"Desk."

The voice did not sound like Stan's.

"Isn't Stan on duty now?" I asked.

"S'posed to be. Stan had to leave. I'm filling in. Can I help you?"

"That's all right. It's a matter only Stan can handle. Guess I'll have to wait until his shift tomorrow."

"I wouldn't count on it, lady. I got a hunch Stan won't be back tomorrow. In fact, Stan might not be back for a long time."

I clicked off.

My plan had worked. Relieved now and very self-satisfied, I bounced on Lemmy's bed and gloated.

Was I ever in a party mood. I went out and circulated among the guests and eventually migrated out to the balcony. Maureen Kenyen rubbed a bunch of spices on an ear of corn, and with Winfield's help she barbecued it especially for me. It was delicious. Maybe I'd take her up on that dinner invitation.

While I chomped away, Winfield asked, "Where's Johnny Verlane? I thought for sure he'd be here."

"*The* Johnny Verlane?" said Maureen.

"The one and only," said Winfield. "He and Brenda are sort of—"

"Friends," I said. "Just friends. Actually I haven't seen him yet. He must be inside. It's so crowded I can't tell."

I finished the corn, then searched for Johnny. I couldn't wait to tell him how I'd caught the killer.

"Have you seen Johnny?" I asked Elizabeth.

"Can't say that I have."

Chuck hadn't seen Johnny.

Dweena hadn't seen Johnny.

That was weird. Six-foot-tall Johnny was hard to miss.

I elbowed my way over to Lemmy, who was pontificating to a small group about the sociological ramifications of brassieres. I waited patiently until he broke for breath. "I've been looking all over for Johnny," I said. "Couldn't he make it?"

"How the hell would I know?"

"Didn't you call him?"

"Not me. I thought you were gonna. He's your boyfriend."

31

A little later I sneaked off once again into Lemmy's bedroom. This time I called Johnny. His machine answered. I expected it would.

"Johnny, it's me, Brenda, please pick up." I swear I could feel him brooding in the background. He must have somehow found out about the party. "Dammit, Johnny, I can explain."

I could have explained right then, but there was always the possibility he really was out somewhere and hadn't heard about the party and wasn't mad he hadn't been invited, so it seemed best to leave a vague message.

I rejoined the party, but it was hard to have a good time while worrying that Johnny was devastated, and so not too long after, I told Lemmy I had to go.

Before I knew it, Lemmy had jumped up on a table and was dinging a wine glass with a fork. He pulled me up beside him. "Quiet, everybody," he said. "My blushing ex-bride has a statement she'd like to make."

"I do?" I whispered.

"Sure you do," he said. "Say anything. It doesn't matter what."

The room had fallen silent, and our guests had gathered around Lemmy and me. I was stuck with no way out.

Stumped for the profound, I grasped at cliché. "I'd like to thank each and every one of you for your love and support through good and most especially these recent really bad times."

Everybody clapped.

"Aren't you forgetting something?" shouted Elizabeth.

"I am not gonna kiss Lemmy, if that's what you mean."

"No, not that," she said. "Toss your hat."

"Oh, I get it, like a bouquet."

I turned my back to the crowd, yanked the ex-wife hat off, and threw it into the crowd.

Despite Chuck's efforts, Dweena caught it.

I didn't even want to think what that might mean.

On my way out of the building I was pleased to see a uniformed policeman stationed in the lobby. The area around the doorman's desk was cordoned off with yellow crime-scene tape.

"What happened?" I asked the cop.

"Watch the news," he said.

As soon as I got home, I called Johnny again and got his machine again. Positive he was home, I snapped on Jackhammer's leash and walked over to Johnny's apartment building.

I had my keys with me, so I let myself in the outside door, crept up the stairs to Johnny's floor, and stuck my ear up against his door. He was in there all right. And mad. I could hear him all the way down the hallway in the kitchen, slamming pots and pans.

I considered knocking, rejected that idea, and very slowly and quietly unlocked his door.

"Hey, Johnny, it's me."

I dropped Jackhammer's leash and let him run through the apartment. He headed straight for the kitchen. The pots and pans stopped banging.

I peeked in and asked, "What are you doing?"

"What's it look like I'm doing?" said Johnny. "I'm bending over so I can scratch Jackhammer between the ears.

Before that, I was preparing a gourmet dinner—for one."

"I've been calling."

"Oh, really, I hadn't noticed."

"You found out, didn't you?" I asked.

"Found out what?"

"The party. Who told you?"

"What difference does it make who told me about your and Lemmy's divorce party that I was not invited to?"

"I'm really sorry. It was a big screw-up, a miscommunication. I thought Lemmy invited you, he thought I did."

"I couldn't have come anyway. I was so terribly busy. I felt compelled to sort through a box of my old newspaper clippings. I organized them by degree to which the reviewer thought *Tod Trueman, Urban Detective* sucked."

"Sarcasm doesn't suit you, Johnny."

"Aside from my full social schedule, a celebratory divorce barbecue has got to be the stupidest idea I've ever heard of."

"I thought so too, at first. I have to admit though, it was kind of fun—except I missed you."

"You don't take divorce very seriously, or marriage either."

"Not this divorce, not this marriage." I was beginning to feel less defensive and perhaps a little pissed off myself. "Remember, Johnny, it was you who started this whole thing when you bet Lemmy he couldn't get me to marry him."

Johnny frowned. He had no reply to that. He squatted down next to Jackhammer. "Can you believe it, Little Guy, somehow Turner and McKinley got invited, and you know how Lemmy despises them?"

Now I knew who'd spilled the beans. Johnny must have run into one of the detectives.

"It was important they be there . . ." I trailed off, to avoid making him even more angry. Much as I wanted to tell him how I'd devised a great plan that had resulted in the arrest of a killer, I realized that now maybe wasn't the best time to bring it up.

"Great," he muttered. "It was important to have the detectives at your party, men you wouldn't even know if I hadn't introduced you, but not me. Very well, Brenda. It's been swell knowing you too. Now, if you'll excuse me, I must get back to my dinner. I'd invite you to join me, but I'm having an all-meat meal, including the beverage and dessert."

I watched the news that night. The story didn't make the ten o'clock news or even the eleven, but sometime in the middle of the night I woke up and heard it on the radio. Police, having turned up additional evidence, had made another arrest in the Adison Montgomery Shelton murder and released the homeless man, who stated through an advocate that the system was unfair. Duxman was not mentioned.

Early the next morning I went to Midnight Millinery, whipped up another ex-wife hat, and hung it in the display window along with a sign: EMBARRASSING SOCIAL EVENT GOT YOU STUMPED? YOUR EX WILL BE THERE AND YOU DON'T KNOW WHAT TO WEAR? MIDNIGHT MILLINERY TO THE RESCUE WITH THE EXCLUSIVE EX-WIFE HAT. YOUR CHOICE OF STYLE IN MANY FASHION-FORWARD COLORS.

In the afternoon the bells on Midnight Millinery's door jangled.

Turner and McKinley strode in.

"My sister could use one of those ex-wife hats," said McKinley. "Her jerk of a husband . . . Ah, forget it. It's a long story, and that's not why we're here."

"Why are you here?" I asked, full of anticipation.

Instead of telling me why they'd darkened my doorway, the two detectives paused for dramatic effect. The pause went on and on and on.

When I finally couldn't stand it anymore, I prompted them. "Come on, guys."

Turner smirked. "We came to inform you that we are well

aware of the instigative role you played in setting up yesterday's arrest incident, and while it was not too terribly risky and actually pretty damned clever, it was also inappropriate. But Detective McKinley and I rose to the occasion, did the right thing, as did Detective Duxman, our lazy, ill-mannered colleague, and I am pleased to inform you that Stan the doorman wilted under pressure and made a full confession and Duxman is in deep shit with top brass."

"Cool. So my theory was correct. Stan was feeding Shelton information he used to blackmail tenants."

"Looks that way. Then Stan got greedy. He wanted a bigger piece of the pie. He and Shelton argued, it got nasty, and Shelton ended up dead."

"What's gonna happen now?"

"Hard to say," said McKinley. "Stan's going away, that's for sure, but for how long, your guess is as good as mine."

I took that as a compliment.

The hot summer finally wound down. Soon after my divorce from Lemmy was finalized, he got the inheritance from his aunt, all thirty-two dollars and sixty-four cents.

Dweena's billboard gained notoriety when irate Soho residents "fed up to here" with gigantic billboards blighting their neighborhood raised a big stink, splattered her billboard and several others with paint bombs and various other projectiles, and made the front page of the tabloids. As a result of all the media attention Dweena got so many requests for personal appearances and modeling work that she asked Lemmy to be her agent.

"Tell me you're joking," I said when she broke the news to me. "You can't stand Lemmy."

"It's like, I'm fully aware that Lemmy's a class A jerk, but I know precisely how much I can't trust him, which is kind of comforting. Besides, I owe him. Without his pale pink satin bra with the wonderful uplift and separation, none of this would have happened."

* * *

Elizabeth, too, felt oddly indebted to Lemmy, when her first art show in decades, the Vacancies series, was a smashing success with the art crowd and critics.

She invited everybody to her gala opening. The Vacancy paintings were great, the bra motif worked well with the neon motel signage, but in my opinion the star of the show was the small portrait of Chuck.

Chuck hated it. "It doesn't look like me." He shoved a handful of cheese sticks into his mouth.

True, the painting was not realistic, but Elizabeth had managed to capture the Chuckness of Chuck. "It's not supposed to," I explained. "Elizabeth has painted the essence of you."

"Very soon now Elizabeth's gonna think of me in a whole different light," he said.

"You're not still on that time travel kick?"

"Just you wait and see."

"Ooh, there's Dweena. Let me go say hi to her. Catch you later, Chuck."

"Earlier," he said.

That night I had a nightmare. Chuck had built a functional time machine and had zoomed off to the past, where he met and fell in love with the young Elizabeth, and together they changed history. Elizabeth never went to jail, never protested the Vietnam war, never gave up art, never lived across the hall from me, and so I never even met Jackhammer, a feeling too sad to express.

But that wasn't all. Changes rippled through time, my entire life was different, even things that happened to me before I knew Chuck. Midnight Millinery didn't exist. I didn't know Johnny.

Jackhammer cold-nosed me out of that nightmare, but it haunted me for days.

In all, I sold only two ex-wife hats. Apparently it wasn't an idea whose time had come, and so I moved on to design my regular fall collection. One day in late September, after a long, hard day of work, as I rolled down the gates on Midnight Millinery, Johnny strolled by.

He hadn't stayed mad about Lemmy's party for long, it simply wasn't his nature. Still, our friendship had been a little strained.

"How're you doing?" I asked.

"Negotiations are moving along," he said. "It looks like *The All New Adventures of Tod Trueman* are a go."

"That's fantastic, Johnny. I'm really happy for you. But I'm curious. How will the writers deal with the destruction of New York City?"

"Easy," said Johnny. "Actually it was Chuck who gave me the idea. Here's how it happened. Tod miraculously survived the blast that leveled the city and killed most of the population. Together with another miraculous survivor, an East Village genius physicist, Tod travels back in time and tweaks things a bit. He makes it so the drug kingpin who destroyed New York in what used to be the last episode gets run over by an out-of-control taxicab before he has a chance to stumble and fall into the detonate button."

"Does the genius physicist happen to be a gorgeous, big-busted blonde?"

"Nope, she's a redhead, in honor of Chuck's fuzzball. But I don't want to talk about *Tod Trueman* anymore. I want to talk about Johnny Verlane. And Brenda Midnight. I want you to know I'm sorry about the fight we had about my orange and yellow shag rug."

"Forget it, Johnny. That was so long ago."

"I went ahead and made that reservation."

Oh my.

Johnny didn't need to say which reservation. I knew this was *the* reservation, the reservation to end all reservations, the reservation at La Reverie. Was I ready? I managed to squeak out, "For when?"

"One week from today. Nine o'clock. So, Brenda, you want to go?"

A minute of dead silence.

Two minutes.

Then, finally, real quick to get it the hell over with, I blurted out, "Yes, I do."

Quirky Mysteries Featuring
Greenwich Village Milliner
Brenda Midnight

by Barbara Jaye Wilson

HATFUL OF HOMICIDE
0380-80356-9/$5.99 US/$7.99 Can
Brenda's birthday is a hatful of surprises, topped off
with a crowning touch . . . of murder.

And Don't Miss

CAPPED OFF
0-380-80355-0/$5.99 US/$7.99 Can

DEATH FLIPS ITS LID
0-380-78822-5/$5.99 US/$7.99 Can

ACCESSORY TO MURDER
0-380-78821-7/$5.50 US/$7.50 Can

DEATH BRIMS OVER
0-380-78820-9/$5.50 US/$7.50 Can

MURDER AND THE MAD HATTER
0-380-80357-7/$5.99 US/$7.99 Can

Tasty mysteries by
Joanne Pence
Featuring culinary queen Angie Amalfi

TO CATCH A COOK
0-06-103085-6/$5.99 US/$7.99 Can
Angie gets mixed up in a deadly stew of family secrets,
missing gems, and murder in another tasty mystery that
blends fine dining and detection.

And Don't Miss

A COOK IN TIME
0-06-104454-7/$5.99 US/$7.99 Can

COOKS OVERBOARD
0-06-104453-9/$5.99 US/$7.99 Can

COOK'S NIGHT OUT
0-06-104396-6/$5.99 US/$7.99 Can

COOKING MOST DEADLY
0-06-104395-8/$5.99 US/$7.99 Can

COOKING UP TROUBLE
0-06-108200-7/$5.99 US/$7.99 Can

SOMETHING'S COOKING
0-06-108096-9/$5.99 US/$7.99 Can

TOO MANY COOKS
0-06-108199-X/$5.99 US/$7.99 Can

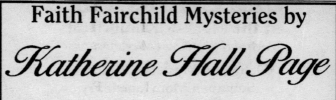

Murder Is on the Menu
at the Hillside Manor Inn
Bed-and-Breakfast Mysteries by
MARY DAHEIM
featuring Judith McMonigle Flynn

DEN OF ANTIQUITY MYSTERIES

by
TAMAR MYERS

LARCENY AND OLD LACE
0-380-78239-1/$5.99 US/$7.99 Can

As owner of the Den of Antiquity, Abigail Timberlake
is accustomed to navigating the cutthroat world of rival
dealers at flea markets and auctions. But she never thought
she'd be putting her expertise in mayhem and detection to
other use—until her aunt was found murdered . . .

GILT BY ASSOCIATION
0-380-78237-5/$6.50 US/$8.50 Can

THE MING AND I
0-380-79255-9/$5.99 US/$7.99 Can

SO FAUX, SO GOOD
0-380-79254-0/$6.50 US/$8.50 Can

BAROQUE AND DESPERATE
0-380-80225-2/$6.50 US/$8.99 Can

ESTATE OF MIND
0-380-80227-9/$6.50 US/$8.99 Can

And coming soon
A PENNY URNED
0-380-81189-8/$6.50 US/$8.50 Can